A Garland Series

Foundations of the Novel

Representative Early

Eighteenth-Century Fiction

A collection of 100 rare titles
reprinted in photo-facsimile in 71 volumes

Foundations of the Novel

compiled and edited by

Michael F. Shugrue
Secretary for English for the M.L.A.

with New Introductions for each volume by

Michael Shugrue, *City College of C.U.N.Y.*
Malcolm J. Bosse, *City College of C.U.N.Y.*
William Graves, *N.Y. Institute of Technology*

The Virgin-Seducer

and

The Batchelor-Keeper

by

John Clarke

The State of Learning in the Empire of Lilliput

Anonymous

A Voyage To Cacklogallinia

by

Captain Samuel Brunt

with a new introduction
for the Garland Edition by
Malcolm J. Bosse

Garland Publishing, Inc., New York & London

The new introduction for the

Garland *Foundations of the Novel* Edition

is Copyright © 1972, by

Garland Publishing, Inc., New York & London

All Rights Reserved

———————

Library of Congress Cataloging in Publication Data

Clarke, John, fl. 1727.
    The virgin-seducer.

    (Foundations of the novel)
    Reprint of The virgin-seducer, and The batchelor-
keeper are reprinted from Atterburyana, a prose
miscellany issued in 1727 by E. Curll; A voyage to
Cacklogallinia, was first published in 1727; and The
state of learning in the empire of Lilliput was first
published in 1728.
    1. English fiction--18th century. I. Clarke,
John, fl. 1727. The batchelor-keeper. 1972.
II. Brunt, Samuel. A voyage to Cacklogallinia. 1972.
III. The state of learning in the empire of Lilliput.
1972. IV. Title. V. Title: The batchelor-keeper.
VI. Title: A voyage to Cacklogallinia. VII. Series.
PZ1.C562Vi 3 [PR1297]   823'.5'08   70-170568
ISBN 0-8240-0561-9

Printed in the United States of America

Introduction

Edmund Curll, a publisher known for bringing out books on timely and sensational topics, issued a prose miscellany in 1729 under the title Atterburyana. *Curll meant to exploit the name of a famous divine, Francis Atterbury, late Bishop of Rochester and a figure of political importance during the reign of Queen Anne. Atterbury was represented in the collection by only two pieces of writing, the remainder being supplied by Curll himself, by a translator of extracts from the letters of Madame de Sévigné, and by a Grub Street writer, John Clarke. Clarke contributed two short novels to the first volume of the miscellany for which he was paid two guineas.*[1]

In the first novel, which goes by the titillating title The Virgin Seducer, *the narrator, Philaretus, debates the pros and cons of seduction with a rake; by winning the debate Philaretus prevents the ruin of a young woman. Then as matchmaker he arranges for the marriage of the couple who "enjoy on Earth an* angelical *Beatitude" (100). In this novel, which is almost devoid of action, the elements of classical rhetoric are markedly evident: antithesis, paradox, periphrasis, hyperbole, and encomium, among other figures. "He gave frequent Proofs of the Pregnancy of his Invention, by caressing in Allusion and courting in Metaphor" (63) is an example of the highly mannered style.*

The second novel, The Batchelor-Keeper, *is also a moral tale which describes the reclamation from*

5

debauchery of a young man who must first be convinced that the woman he loves is in truth a harlot. This is a more vigorous and accomplished narrative, largely because it contains some lively character sketches in the Theophrastian mode made popular in seventeenth-century England by writers like Overbury, Earle, and Hall. Clarke halts his plot now and then for sprightly descriptions in richly figured prose of a hard-working merchant, a foolish young libertine, a cunning doxy, and a petty criminal who beat a girl until "the Effects of his Anger were visible in her Eyes" (131). True of much that Curll published, The Batchelor-Keeper *has its sensational appeal. Philaretus and his young charge spy on the harlot entertaining a guest in her bedroom, which serves as an object lesson for the naïve young man and as a bit of salacious reading for the public.*

An Account of the State of Learning in the Empire of Lilliput, *anonymously written and published in 1728, uses Swift's famous tale to mount a literary attack against Dr. Richard Bentley, royal librarian and master of Trinity College, who was at the center of the "Phalaris controversy." This renowned literary dispute began with Sir William Temple's claim in his* Ancient and Modern Learning *(1692) that ancient writers far surpassed the moderns. In the course of this work Temple praised the literary style of Phalaris, a tyrant of Sicily (c. 570 BC), whose letters were published in 1695 by a young Oxford man, Charles Boyle. In an essay for the second edition of William Wotton's* Reflections on Ancient and Modern Learning *(1697) Bentley asserted that the letters of Phalaris were actually forgeries from the hand of a Greek rhetorician in the Christian era. The*

INTRODUCTION

battle was then joined between Wotton and Bentley on one side and Temple and Boyle on the other. Among Boyle's champions were Francis Atterbury, who wrote a weak defense of Boyle's position, and Jonathan Swift, who used the dispute to create a satire at Bentley's expense in The Battle of the Books *(1704).*

Time has proved that Bentley's Dissertation on the Letters of Phalaris *(1699) is erudite scholarship of superior quality, an early employment of scientific philology to determine historical dates. During his own long lifetime, however, the scholar continued to draw attacks from the Oxford wits.* The State of Learning *is an example of the abusive satire which he inspired. Called Bullum, the Lilliputian emperor's librarian, Bentley is described as a loud, pompous, ignorant buffoon who maliciously withholds books from Gulliver, an obvious allusion to Boyle's claim that Bentley refused him access to a Phalarian manuscript in the St. James Library. Bullum knows nothing of the Lilliputian language (English), creeps under the stick, dances on the rope, and breaks his eggs at both ends, all of which illustrate the author's reliance on Swift.* The State of Learning *is thin if virulent satire, interesting for its relevance to a literary quarrel which embroiled some of the best minds of the age.*

Voyage to Cacklogallinia, *published under the pseudonym Captain Samuel Brunt, is a paradigm of the tendency among eighteenth-century writers to begin a novel in one genre and to end it in another.* Voyage to Cacklogallinia *begins as a travel-adventure story, obviously imitative of Defoe. The narrator goes to sea, reaches Jamaica where his life is saved by a runaway slave, joins a band of pirates in the West Indies, and*

INTRODUCTION

finally is shipwrecked on a deserted shore where, like Robinson Crusoe, he offers up a prayer of thanksgiving: "As we naturally are fond of Life, I return'd Thanks to Providence for my Escape . . ." (28). At this juncture the author shifts from a Defoe-type adventure story, rooted in realistic detail, to a Swiftian voyage in which satire predominates. Samuel Brunt, like Gulliver, visits a marvelous country inhabited by huge birds called Cacklogallinians, who in their politics, religious beliefs, and customs seem to represent the French. Brunt makes a thinly veiled reference to the War of the Spanish Succession, blaming it on the territorial ambitions of the French and the Spanish, the latter called Magpyes. Doubtlessly his commentary on French customs was intended to amuse English readers; of Cacklogallinian family life Brunt observes, "One would think they married to be reveng'd on each other for some former Injuries" (98). Following Book III of Gulliver, *the narrator then introduces projectors, who discuss at length a scheme for "fetching Gold from the Moon" (108). The satire fades as they explain the proposed journey in serious terms of Newtonian gravitational theory, after which the novel assumes the character of an imaginary voyage full of utopian ideas and marvelous adventures. Brunt is taken on the month-long trip in a palanquin drawn by birds; this flight to the moon is illustrated in the crude but charming frontispiece. Arriving on the moon, Brunt funds a utopia inhabited by the Selenites whose cool wisdom reminds the reader of the Houyhnhnms. Then the narrative plunges into a fanciful account of shades, who, a Selenite explains, are "the Souls of the Inhabitants of your World" (143), and who range in height from thirty to a hundred and fifty*

8

INTRODUCTION

feet. Confusing opinions on theology, history, and science then bring the work to an end. The author of Voyage to Cacklogallinia *openly borrows from Defoe and Swift in an attempt to emulate their popularity and in the process adds his own brand of fancy. The result is an interesting patchwork of realistic adventure, satire, and imaginary voyaging.*

Malcolm J. Bosse

NOTE

[1] *Ralph Straus,* The Unspeakable Curll *(New York, 1928), p. 281.*

The Virgin-Seducer

by

John Clarke

Bibliographical note:

This facsimile has been made from a copy in the
Beinecke Library of Yale University
(X178 C92 727A)

The original title was printed in the year 1727 in
Atterburyana, being Miscellanies, by the late Bishop of
Rochester, *pp. 61-100.*

THE

VIRGIN-SEDUCER.

A TRUE

HISTORY

BY

PHILARETUS.

THE

Virgin-Seducer.

 IT was lately my Fortune to take
Lodgings in an Houfe near the
COURT, particularly noted for its
good Entertainment, civil Ufage, moderate Rates, and convenient Situation ; having a large Profpect backwards of
many neighbouring Gardens, and a diftant View
of the Park. At my coming there I received
the Compliments of my Mefs-mates, who were
about fixteen in all; and quickly found, that it
was cuftomary for every New Comer to pay
half a dozen Flasks at Entrance, the reft to
make up a like Number, and the Landlord obliged to provide a fuitable Collation. I made
ufe of this Opportunity to learn my Company,
and eafily perceiv'd 'em to be a Mixture of Perfons of different Stations ; but before I cou'd
adjuft Particulars, my Purfuit of that Defign

was taken off, by remarking some familiar Occurrences which pass'd between a Couple at the Table. The one I understood to be a young Gentleman of a confiderable Estate; who, in his Life-time, had been confin'd to the Country, and, by his Care, had not all that while stept over the *Threshold of Innocence.* He confess'd, he was allowed some rural Diverfions; but never durst venture upon a Debauch. He was *endowed* with good natural Parts, and those very much improved by a *large Portion* of Learning, *attained* by the affiduous Study of several Years : In a Word, he was as compleat, as an ingenious Difpofition and a liberal Education could render him. His Father, the *Guardian* of his *Virtue*, was no fooner laid in his Grave, than out fets my Gentleman for *London*, that imaginary *Paradife*, the *flaming Sword* of his Father's Refolution had fo long kept him out of—— Having knocked off the Shackles of his former Reftraint, he ranges uncontrouled thro' this vaft Wildernefs, eagerly devouring the Variety of *forbidden Fruit*, which fo *temptingly* courted his depraved *Curiofity:* Qualified by a plentiful Fortune, and fpurred by a vitious Inclination, he commences Rake of the firft Rank; encouraged therein by the perfuafive Example of his libertine Companions.

His Oppofite, at the Board, was a young Lady about twenty, the only Iffue of a deceafed Baronet, whofe generous Temper was unequally matched to a fcanty Revenue ; and who, by *levelling his Aim at his Title had overfhot his Income*, and reduced the Extent of his hereditary Acres to a narrow Compafs, fcarce fufficient without a frugal Management to protect his Relict from undeferved Hardfhips, and but
few

few degrees above Neceffity.——But Nature had been as bounteous, as Fortune niggardly to the lovely Fair: Rhetorick would be as fuperfluous in her Defcription, as Art in her Ornament. Her Wit, which was no ways inferior to her Beauty, made her appear as agreeable to a judicious Ear, as the other to a difcerning Eye: Thefe Excellencies embellifhed with correct Breeding and Affability, rendered her an Object worthy of Admiration and Defire.

Of all thofe who put in for the Prize, *Tarquinius* bore the Preference in her Efteem: The Tenders of his Affection were the moft acceptable: Her Eyes, like Oracles, plainly declared, his Love was favourably entertained in her Heart. I could not but fmile to fee how advantageoufly he managed the minuteft Occafion to difcover his Paffion, and turned every Accident into an Opportunity of obliging. Each Word, each Action, were fo many frefh Teftimonies of his Intention to pleafe; while a fweet engaging Air overfpread her charming Face, and her Countenance fhewed fhe approved of his Endeavours. Their Eyes held a long and uninterrupted Parley: When his fwore Sincerity, her's languifhed and anfwered, fhe doubted; but a Side-caft foon gave him to know, that her Hopes overballanced her Fears. I could often perceive him inwardly ftruggling with the Difficulty how to exprefs himfelf fo, that his Thoughts might be plain to her, and an Ænigma to the reft of the Company; and indeed he gave frequent Proofs of the Pregnancy of his Invention, by *careffing in Allufion,* and *courting in Metaphor.* A fudden Slip would fometimes furprize his Vigilance, and overthrow his Caution; and, in fome Meafure, make that obvious, which he

G 2

ftrove

ſtrove to diſguiſe; but no ſooner was he ſenſible of the Inadvertency, than a ready Turn threw
a Veil over the Intrigue, and turned the Appa-
rency into an Ambiguity.

Her Mother, who ſat at the upper End of
the Table, was in the Autumn of her Age; but
her Face and Deportment gave evident Proof,
that *Camaſia* was the *illuſtrious Copy of a glorious Original.* I had ſome Reaſon to believe, ſhe
was neither a Stranger, nor averſe to the Amour;
but that the faſhionable Error of an Indulgence,
which falls little ſhort of Overfondneſs, and the
welcome Intereſt promiſing to accrue from it,
obſtructed the Uſe of that Prudence, the Nicety
of ſuch a Circumſtance required. Tho' her
Virtue was too ſolid to admit Suſpicion, it being founded on Religion, and ſupported by Honour; ſo that the leaſt Imagination of her Daugh-
ter's ſwerving from thoſe ſacred Principles, ſo
ardently and conſtantly inculcated, wou'd no
doubt have proved an unutterable Affliction, and
her real Fall, an inſupportable Misfortune! Yet
was I conſcious, ſhe employed not that Caution
the Affair demanded, by her allowing too exten-
ſive a Freedom; upon a Probability only, that
Tarquinius's Intentions were honourable, without any Aſſurance, they really were ſo. It appeared to me a Matter worth enquiry, whether
he eſteemed the Perfections of her Mind and
Body, an *equivalent Dower for a handſome
Jointure.* This, like a *Touchſtone,* would have
try'd his Heart, and diſcover'd whether his Paſſion were *ſterling* or *baſe.* I was apprehenſive
of the latter, and grew much more ſo by an
impartial Obſervation, which put a Damp to
that Diverſion, the Scene wou'd otherwiſe have
afforded. Supper ended, and our Wine exhauſted,

haufted, we feverally retired to our refpective
Apartments; but my prefent Concern denied me
the Pleafure of a good Night's Reft.

The next Morning, as I was ranging my
little Library, and fettling my felf in my new
Habitation, I was interrupted by a courteous
Summons to the Dining-Room to fhare *Tarquinius*'s Morning's Bounty. I obeyed, and re-
paired to the general Rendezvous. The ufual
Salutations were reciprocally given, and returned throughout the Company; and Coffee,
Tea, and Chocolate promifcuoufly handed about,
that each might choofe as fancy directed. In
this Converfation, according to Cuftom, *News*
led the Van, which *Tarquinius* obliged us with
from that Day's Papers : Variety of political
Comments; and as many uncertain and different
Conclufions, drawn from Defire or Opinion,
followed clofe at the Heels. *Reputation* came
next : Commendation and Praife were fparing-
ly muttered; but Cenfure and Satire flowed in
abundance : Failings were augmented to Crimes;
and *Molehill* Errors to *Mountain* Vices, without any Refpect to Juftice, or Regard to Charity. *Intrigues*, *Fafhions*, and a Multitude of
other Impertinencies brought up the Rear ;
till near three Hours were thrown away
in an unimproveable Chat. *Tarquinius* gives
Order for his Equipage to be at the Door
by three ; but a fudden Change in *Camafia*'s
Countenance, giving him to underftand fhe was
not well pleafed at that : He with the fame
Breath forbids the Performance, while an intel ·
ligible Glance inform'd her, that it was for her
dear Sake he had altered his Intention. The
next Mif-fpender of Time, the Dreffing-Room
call'd the Company away from publick Folly

G 3

to private Vanity: I hafted to my Clofet to bewail my Prodigality in fquandering away fo many precious Minutes: Each of which is of fuch ineftimable Value to every Individual (without Exemption,) that hath a Soul to fave.

Tarquinius had, it feems, in this fhort Acquaintance entertain'd fuch an Opinion of me, that it created an Impatience in him to become intimate. Having dedicated this Day to *Camafia's* Pleafure, he had no Occafion to alter his Drefs; fo that the Interval till Dinner-Time became a Burden to him, which he refolved to eafe himfelf of in my Company; he accordingly comes to my Chamber, and after an handfome Apology, as civilly inform'd me of his Errand. I made him equal Returns of Courtefy; and, from a few introductory Compliments, we foon came to a more agreeable Correfpondence. We gave each other a Narrative of our Lives in Epitome; ran over the Languages, rambled thro' the Arts and Sciences; made a *Tour* to *Divinity*, a *Vifit* to *Philofophy*, and a *Trip* to the *Mathematics*. I was fo extremely pleas'd, that I concluded Providence had fent him, to make amends for the Time I had lately loft. But at laft we touch'd upon *Poetry*; and that naturally led us to talk of *Love*: That Paffion was no fooner mentioned, than he frankly own'd himfelf a Slave to its Power; but withal urg'd in his Defence, that, if any Object was capable of excufing fuch a Folly, the incomparable *Camafia* might juftly be allow'd to atone for his Weaknefs, and fo began to enumerate her Attractions, as a Means to vindicate his Failing, but in fo vehement a Manner, that the violent Motion of his Breaft made

4   it

it plain his Heart was galloping full Speed to her Bosom.

Philaretus. " Sir, (said I) you need not
" make any Defence for being infected with a
" Contagion so epidemical as Love is. I an't
" so severe as to upbraid, or condemn you for
" yielding to a Passion so natural to Mankind,
" and which all, (some Time or other,) under-
" go the Tyranny of. To undertake a Defini-
" tion of it, either philosophically or poetical-
" ly, is nothing to the present Purpose; It dates
" its Original from the Creation, and is, with-
" in a few Hours, as old as the World: For,
" no sooner were the different Sexes fram'd,
" than they felt a reciprocal Tendency to each
" other. And this not only with divine Per-
" mission, but all, for many excellent Ends, by
" *Command* to. *A Man may leave Father and*
" *Mother, and cleave to his Wife,* without a Breach
" of the fifth Commandment. *Mutual Affection*
" *is the best Security of a happy Union* ; which
" makes it necessary that Love should precede
" Matrimony: So that simply of it self, it is
" neither a Trespass upon Morality or Judg-
" ment, but indeed a Preparatory to future Hap-
" piness ; yet the several Circumstances which
" may attend, alter the Case, and Love mif-
" plac'd is opposite to both. *Camasia*, it must
" be allow'd, carries all the Marks of a Con-
" sort, able to render the conjugal State a con-
" tinu'd Scene of substantial Felicity, and *Tar-*
" *quinius* need not blush to acknowledge the
" just Sense he has of her Merit: If therefore
" no unseen, no sullen Impediment intervene,
" to bar your Success, I presume in a little
" Time I may safely pronounce ye are an hap-
" py Couple.

Tarquin

Tarquinius. " *Matrimony* (reply'd Tarquinius)
" is as *unrelishing* to my *Ears* as a *Bolus* to my
" *Taste.* My *Mind* and my *Palate* have an
" equal *Disgust,* and I cannot submit to swal-
" low either, till *Necessity* oblige me. *Why*
" should I tether my self to a narrow *Compass,*
" and for the *Sake* of one full *Meal* feed all
" the rest of my *Days* upon its *Orts?* While
" Pain of parental Chains is so fresh in my
" Memory, it is not to be imagin'd, I should so
" much as dream of nuptial Fetters. I value
" my new got Freedom at a higher Rate, than
" to exchange it even for a golden Slavery; but
" what should I deserve for striking such a Bar-
" gain upon lower Terms? What would the
" World say of me, to *jointure Terra firma* for
" the *transitory Dower* of a *fading Beauty,* make
" a *cornu-copian* Settlement for a *Portion of*
" *Parts,* and sign a *Contract* of annual Pin-
" money for such a Trifle as an *Escutcheon in*
" *Hand?* Perhaps, when satiated with Variety,
" I may think Constancy a Pleasure: Or when
" the Title of my Estate is become a Prisoner
" in a Miser's Chest, I may have Recourse to
" my *dernier Resort,* and fell my self to pur-
" chase its Liberty. —— In fine, marry *Camasia*
" I will not, enjoy *her* I must. She wears such
" Charms, as would warm Age, fire Youth,
" revive the Bedrid, remasculate an Eunuch,
" recall an Hermit from his Cell, a Saint
" from Paradise, and bring down Jove from his
" Throne. Oh! my *Philaretus,* what a tri-
" umphant Victory is it to conquer a Virgin's
" Heart, and bear away the delicious Spoils of
" a Maidenhead? What seraphic Pleasures flow
" from the soft Embrace! The only Bliss on
" Earth, that rivals those of Heaven!

Notice

Notice that Dinner was coming to Table
fufpended my Anfwer, but I refolved to lay
Hold on the firft Opportunity to purfue my
Endeavours, of preventing the fad Effects of fo
vitious a Defign. Providence favour'd my Intention; for, immediately after we had din'd,
Camafia was oblig'd to accompany her Mother
abroad. How unwelcome fuch a Difappointment was to the Lovers is eafier to be apprehended, than defcribed. He was no more able
to hide his Regret, than fhe her Reluctance. As
many of the Company as ftay'd within, fet in
to Play, except *Tarquinius*, who was too much
out of Humour to engage with 'em. Going
out of the Room, and perceiving I was not in-
clin'd to make one, he beckon'd me after him.
" Come, *Philaretus*, faid he, fince I am depri-
" ved of the Happinefs of being with *Cama-*
" *fia*'s Perfon, let me converfe with her in I-
" magination; you'll indulge a Lover in his
" darling Paffion." We immediately retir'd to
his Apartment, and being feated, he began in
the fame Manner he left off before, but ex-
claim'd againft his Fortune, for fo unluckily
croffing his Expectations of the Succefs he had
propofed to meet with, by that Afternoon's
Converfation: But his Paffion foaring an un-
becoming Height, as foon as Civility would permit me, I ftopp'd his Flight in the following
Manner.

Philaretus. " *Tarquinius*, (faid I) the Friend-
" fhip I bear you is fo fincere, that it has given
" Birth to my Concern for you, and put me
" on attempting to extinguifh thofe pernicious
" Flames, which Luft has kindled; and when
" I confider the Worth of the Perfon with
" whom I treat, I have greater Hope of my
" with'd

" wiſh'd Succeſs, than doubt of my kind Re-
" ception.

" Your Forenoon Diſcourſe made me cha-
" grin then, and uneaſy ever ſince. I at once
" both outwardly bluſh'd, and inwardly ſor-
" row'd to hear you ſo ſolemnly reſolve upon
" a Vice, attended with ſo many ill Conſe-
" quences in this Life, and ſo conducive to the
" moſt fatal in the next. You alledge that the
" Pleaſure it affords is a Delight of the firſt
" Magnitude, too ſuperlative to be expreſſed in
" Words, and beyond the Conception of any,
" but the raptur'd Poſſeſſors. Intoxicated into
" a Phrenzy, by a deluded Imagination, you
" plunge into an Abyſs of extravagant Hyper-
" boles, till your frantic Notions make Pane-
" gyric nauſeous, and Encomium ridiculous.
" And what's worſe, theſe Bethlem Tranſports
" often run ſo far beyond the Confines of De-
" cency, that they encroach the Borders of Blaſ-
" phemy.

" To convince you fully of your Error, I'll
" examine all the Particulars that occur to my
" Memory, and rather run the Hazard of tiring
" you with Prolixity, than giving you any Ad-
" vantage by Deficiency.

" When the wanton Eye hath fixed upon an
" Object, a vitious Inclination ſprings in the
" corrupted Mind, and is nouriſh'd by the plea-
" ſing Ideas fram'd in the Imagination. Their
" Contemplations raiſes to ſuch an Height, that
" they ſtir up a Belief in the Heart, that im-
" menſe Felicity will attend Fruition, which en-
" courages the Will, and ſpurs Deſire to an
" eager Purſuit.

" It is no eaſy Matter to correct the Prin-
" ciples of any Perſuaſion, and no leſs diffi-
" cult.

" cult to deal with cupidinian Bigottry. Flat-
" ly to deny your Aſſertion is beginning at the
" wrong End; for to oppoſe an Opinion ſo
" firmly rivetted to every one under your Circum-
" ſtances, is the ready Way to create a Preju-
" dice in you againſt whatever elſe I have to offer:
" I will therefore at preſent admit it, even to
" the Exceſs of your own Apprehenſion, and
" yet doubt not to counterpoize the Weight by.
" conſidering the ſeveral Occurrences that ac-
" company the Deſign in View.

" When Virtue's unguarded, and yields up-
" on Attack, the Victor neither deſerves nor
" deſires the Lawrel; but when ſtrongly for-
" tified with Grace, it reſolves to hold out
" the laſt Extremity. As it deſpiſes the weak
" Attempts of inſinuating Flattery, and all the
" little Arts of obſequious Officiouſneſs; ſo is
" it Proof againſt the moſt vigorous Aſſailant,
" and bids Defiance to the boldeſt Stormer.
" What an Herculean Labour is it carry on the
" Siege? But, to quit the Alluſion, what a
" conſtant Aſſiduity, and continual Fatigue muſt
" he undergo, who ſets himſelf to betray Vir-
" ginity? what Perturbation? what Anxiety?
" what a Legion of Hopes and Fears poſſeſs
" his Mind, both before and after Poſſeſſion?
" what an Abundance of Pains muſt he be at, to
" make her underſtand thoſe Thoughts, he dares
" not tell her for Fear of giving Offence? He
" becomes a Vaſſal to a capricious Humour, and
" makes himſelf a Slave to a Maggot. Her un-
" fixed Fancy is the Rudder, that ſteers him in
" perpetual Traverſes, and her wavering Will
" involves in a Labyrinth. *Proteus*-like, he tranſ-
" forms himſelf into a thouſand Shapes, is Ape
" in Ridicule, and Harlequin in Burleſque.

" Joy

" Joy and Grief alternately elevate and depreſs.
" A Smile toſſes him upon the Summit of Fe-
" licity, but a Frown caſts him into a Depth
" of Miſery. When tickl'd with the Pleaſures
" of flattering Hope, one would believe him
" bit by a Tarantula, but the Gloom of De-
" ſpair throws him into a Lycanthropy. One
" while he begs of Nature to extend his Years to
" *Methuſelah*'s Length. Another while he cur-
" ſes her for not contracting his *Days to leſs*
" *than a Span.* In Converſation he is all up-
" on the Extremes; for he either talks too
" much, or ſays nothing at all. The Æqui-
" nox is left out of his Calendar. He knows
" neither Spring nor Autumn, he lives in a
" Climate of Exceſs, being always ſcorch'd or
" frozen. To Day his Brains are changed into
" Mercury, to Morrow turned into Lead. He
" eſteems Buſineſs a Burden, and Diverſions inſi-
" pid; and ſo conſequently neglects the one and
" deſpiſes the other, but is in Love with Idleneſs,
" and doats on Supinity. Let his Quality and
" Circumſtances be what they will, he is ſo
" profoundly humble, that he voluntarily ſub-
" mits to the Vocation of a Watchman, and
" enters himſelf into their Fraternity, without
" the Reward of Sixpence a Night. He has
" turn'd his Senſes out of Doors; his Eyes are
" ſo fixed upon the ideal Object within him,
" that he takes no Notice of any Thing with-
" out him. You may adventure to aſſault or
" rob him, and not be in Danger of his know-
" ing you again. His Ears are ſeal'd, and his
" Underſtanding benum'd, ſo that he anſwers
" your Queſtions by gueſs, which if ſtarted to
" his Surprize, they are oftener wrong than right,
" and you do him an unpardonable Injury, if
                                        " you

" you force him to exceed a Monofyllable; but
" you extort more, you may quickly difcern
" his Confufion. He talks without his Thought,
" and reads without his Mind. He's alone in a
" Crowd; but you'd believe him in Company,
" if you heard him by himfelf. He is as reft-
" lefs as a big-belly'd Woman, moves from
" Place to Place, and half an Hour's Time
" makes him uneafy any where. In fine, *his*
" *Reafon, like a Limb ftruck with the dead Pal-*
" *fey, retains its Form, but is become ufelefs.*
" The Magic of his Paffion has metamorphos'd
" the Man into a Paradox.— A *rational irrati-*
" *onal Being.* In this Torrent of Viciffitude are
" you now embarqu'd. Your Integrity will
" oblige you to confefs, you already agree with
" fome Part of the Character I have given :
" Your Uneafinefs at this Day's Difappoint-
" ment is a Teftimony of what I affirm; and
" tho' the infant Torment may not be infup-
" portable, yet Maturity will render it intole-
" rable.

Tarquinius. " I muft confefs you have drawn
" a lively Reprefentation of a Mind difordered
" by an impetuous Paffion, that the Difcompo-
" fure in my Breaft, which my prefent Engage-
" ment has created, bears too near a Refem-
" blance to your Defcription : Neverthelefs I
" am encourag'd in my Refolution of proceed-
" ing by two Confiderations. The firft, that I
" think I am pretty well acquainted with my
" own Temper, and capable of ftopping the
" Current of Difturbance, before it carries me
" to Diftraction. And, fecondly, if I fhould
" be miftaken both in the Opinion I have of
" my felf and my Power, fo that I undergo the
" greateft Tortures Perplexity can inflict, I have

" yet more than probable Affurance the joyful
" Harveſt will fufficiently make Amends for
" the preceding Toil. The Prize is ſo inefti-
" mable, that no Purchaſe deſerves the Epithet
" of extravagant. No Price too high, no Dan-
" ger too dreadful, no Hazard too fatal, no
" Labour too painful, to be fcrupled to obtain
" it.

Philaretus. " You'll find your felf deceived
" in depending on either of theſe Concluſions.
" As for the firſt, we meet with but few In-
" ſtances of fuch, as in a ſerene Condition of
" Life, can truly judge how they ſhould de-
" mean themſelves under turbulent Circumſtan-
" ces, and thoſe who in a profperous State, think
" themſelves the beſt fortified, often ſhew the
" greateſt Puſillanimity, when Providence chan-
" ges the Scene, and reduces them to an adverſe
" one. As we are ignorant of our Behaviour
" under a Removal from one Condition to an-
" other, ſo is it a little in our Power to lay
" a due Reſtraint on our iraſcible or concupif-
" cible Affections. 'Tis too difficult for Huma-
" nity to fet a *ne plus ultra* to Paſſion; moral
" Philoſophy has prov'd too weak; a ſtrong
" Faith alone can effect it; a firm Belief of the
" ample Rewards in another World is the beſt
" Support under the Troubles of this. It is this
" alone which is able to preſerve us in the hap-
" py Level of Tranquillity, it not only mode-
" rates our Hopes, expels our Fears, and makes
" even our Calamity ſit eaſy, but produces al-
" ſo in us a generous Diſdain and chriſtian Con-
" tempt amidſt the greateſt Affluence of earthly
" Enjoyments. It debaſes our Pride in an high
" Eſtate, and prevents Deſpondence in a low
" one. 'Tis this only can fix our violate Af-
" fections,

" fections, and check our Defires from be-
" coming exorbitant. But the Faith here men-
" tion'd is an Affiftance arifing from Religion,
" which prefcribes a Life of Virtue as a Means
" to obtain it; and you cannot expect any Aid
" from thence, becaufe that never participates
" in impious Undertakings; and he that ven-
" tures his Bark in a perilous Sea, with hoifed
" Sails, a ftrong Blaft and no Rudder, will be
" Witnefs to a Miracle, if he efcapes Ship-
" wrack, and deferves not fo much Applaufe
" for his Courage, as Contempt for his Folly.

" Your other Apprehenfion is no lefs erro-
" neous than this precarious: For univerfal
" Experience has eftablifh'd it an indifputable
" Maxim, That all fublunary Delights promife
" abundantly more in Expectation, than they
" yield in Fruition. This infallible Truth hath
" met with fuch a general Reception, that the
" wifer Sort readily confent to it, without be-
" ftowing Pains to prove it, who thereby avoid-
" ing the violent Agitations of a boundlefs Am-
" bition, fatisfie themfelves with the immedi-
" ate Difpenfations of Providence, and enjoy
" the fubftantial Happinefs of a bleffed Conten-
" tation. But in all the Variety of particular
" Inftances, that may be made ufe of to expli-
" cate the Veracity of this Affertion, there are
" none fo eafily make it apparent as the Sub-
" ject now before us. Contemplative Wan-
" tonnefs demands more than practical Un-
" cleannefs can fupply. I appeal to the impar-
" tial Sentiments of the grandeft Proficient in
" the School of Lafcivioufnefs, if ever the moft
" falacious Debauch reach'd the Perfection of
" his ideal Letchery. The *tout Amount of our*
" *Luft in Embryo, which while nourifh'd in the*

H 2   " *fruitful*

" *fruitful Womb of an exuberant Fancy, promi-*
" *ses such an Excess of Pleafure, when Action*
" *gives it Birth, dwindles away into a partu-*
" *riunt Montes.* The moft confummate Blifs in
" an unlawful Embrace, is infeparable from an
" Alloy of Regret. A *pannic Fear becomes a*
" *troublefome Companion to us at our earlieft*
" *Approaches to the forbidden Bed; it forces it*
" *felf between the Sheets, and damps the defign'd*
" *Careffes of puiffant Vigor.* It is not to be
" repelled by the experteft Art, but ftubbornly
" refifts the Incantations of meretricious Charms.
" It dictates Danger in the greateft Security,
" and diminifhes one of our Senfes by increa-
" fing two others. It purfues our Steps *like a*
" *Bloodhound,* and tracks us through all the
" Meanders of Obfcenity: But who can de-
" fcribe the Convulfions of a Wretch difcove-
" red in the Act! The fudden Surprize arrefts
" his Intellects, and transforms him into an I-
" deot. Seiz'd by a reproachful Shame, he
" ftands like a Statue, and hath nothing left
" but his Shape to demonftrate his Species. The
" victorious Hero degenerates into a Coward,
" and can patiently bear the Infults of the
" meaneft Abject. The Orator is ftruck fpeech-
" lefs, and has not a Word to plead in his
" Defence; and the Wit is at Lofs for a ready
" Excufe. A *paralytic Trepidation* is the firft
" Symptom of Life, but within a while Anger,
" Rage, and Remorfe, play the Tyrant in his
" Breaft, and put him into the utmoft Confufion.
" Now he *roars like a Lyon lafh'd with his*
" *own Tail,* but in an inftant is *as filent as a*
" *Sheep.* Groans and Sighs divide his Breath.
" Vows, Refolutions, Imprecations, Oaths,
" Curfes, Threats, and Promifes are huddled fo
" clofe

" clofe together, 'tis hard to diftinguifh one from
" t'other. He *becomes defpiccble in his own*
" *Eyes, and believes himfelf fo in theirs that look*
" *at him, tho' they know nothing of the Matter.*
" But above all, admitting he may efcape thefe
" more than probable Accidents, fo frequently
" productive of the moft fatal Inconveniencies;
" yet the felf Conviction attendant upon ftol-
" len Pleafures, retorts fuch corroding Reflec-
" tions in a Mind the leaft Degree fhort of
" Reprobation, that it turns the tranfitory Rap-
" ture into a durable Torture; a Moment's
" Pain of which is by much too grievous, for
" the moft perfect Gratification of our Luft to
" recompenfe. How deficient then will the
" fleeting Trifle prove to ballance the Agonies
" of a Mind for Life, and, without a more than
" ordinary Repentance, the Anguifh of a Soul
" for Eternity?

Tarquinius. " I cannot better fhew the Re-
" fpect I owe your unanfwerable Arguments,
" than by declaring I am convinc'd by them:
" But *Camafia* is fo irrefiftible a Temptation,
" that I have no Power to quit my Refolves.
" In my ferious Intervals I can readily fubfcribe
" to the Excellency of your Judgment: But a
" *Je ne fcay quoy* in the magnetic Object con-
" ftrains my corrupted Will, in Spight of Rea-
" fon, and Defiance of Underftanding. The
" invincible Strength of a tyrannizing Paffion
" hath fubdued all the Faculties of my Soul,
" and brought me under a Neceffity of yielding
" an intire Obedience to her ufurped Authori-
" ty. I have fworn Allegiance, and lifted my
" felf under her Banner, all my Endeavours to
" fhake off her Chains have prov'd ineffectual,

H 3   " tho'

" tho' I am fenfible they confirm me an Enemy
" to Virtue, and a Rebel to Religion.

Philarethus. " This Confeffion equally de-
" monftrates your Ingenuity, and difplays your
" Weaknefs. It is the greateft Madnefs to run
" upon Deftruction with open Eyes ; and the
" moft egregious Folly to act contradictory to
" Knowledge: *Ignorance may palliate an Er-*
" *ror*; but *Wilfulnefs aggravates a Crime*: That
" once renders you liable to human Cenfure,
" and obnoxious to divine Vengeance: *To be*
" *governed by the Dictates of Senfe only is the*
" *Property of Brutes, and to purfue the Sug-*
" *geftions of Inclination the Practice of Repro-*
" *bates*; *but to be guided by the Motives of Rea-*
" *fon is the Attribute of Man, and to repel the*
" *Impulfes of Nature the Perfection of a Chri-*
" *ftian.*

" But to go forward : Upon what do you
" build your Expectation of obtaining your
" End?——— The Freedom of her Carriage
" toward you: The receiving your Addreffes
" with an agreeable Complacency, and her fa-
" vourable Returns to your obliging Services
" are but flender Grounds for a Belief, that her
" Heart correfponds with your Wifhes: She
" being inapprehenfive of your foul Intent in-
" terprets your Devoirs in an honourable Senfe,
" and in that Cafe 'tis no Derogation from her
" Virtue to let you fee fhe is not impregnable.
" *Tarquinius* has Merit enough in Appearance
" worthy *Camafia's* Efteem, and Ladies miftake
" the Rules of Modefty, when they fhroud their
" inward Approbation under a Cloud of out-
" ward Refervednefs. It argues a difingenuous
" Temper, and is the Effect of a fantaftic Pride
" to beget an uneafy Sufpenfe in any one for
" the

" the prefent, whom they defign to make hap-
" py by a Compliance hereafter : Therefore,
" notwithftanding the gracious Behaviour, which
" gives Birth to your Hopes, it ftill remains un-
" certain ; but that, as foon as fhe perceives
" your malevolent Aim, Scorn and Difdain
" may difpoffefs her new-born Regards, and turn
" her warrantable Love into a juftifiable Inve-
" teracy.

" How deeply muft this wound a generous
" Spirit to reflect, that your Guilt has ren-
" der'd you defpicably odious in thofe Eyes in
" which you were ambitious to appear moft a-
" miable? That Face you now behold with
" extatic Delight, you will not then be able to
" look on without a confcious Blufh ; you that
" follicitoufly court her Company, will as in-
" duftrioufly avoid it : Every Glance will up-
" braid your Bafenefs, and add to your frefh
" Confufion : She will proclaim your brutal Of-
" fers throughout her Acquaintance, till the de-
" ferved Reproach brand you with fuch an in-
" famous Blemifh, as will make you at once
" both fear'd and contemn'd by all that have
" the leaft Regard to Honour, or Refpect to
" Virtue.

" But further—Suppofing fhe is not inexo-
" rable ; yet fhe may not be won without Dif-
" ficulty. The Conqueft requires more Time
" and Pains than you are aware on, or indeed
" than it is really worth. There is an innate
" Principle in the Sex, that hinders their fpeedy
" Surrender : *Modefty is not fo eafily put off as*
" *the Garment*, even thofe whofe Meannefs of
" Birth and Education has depriv'd 'em of any
" other Affiftance, have by that Help, join'd
" with a Fear of but one only of the unlucky
" Con-

" Confequences, prov'd fufficient to withftand
" the Force of a libidinous Temptation. But
" in thofe who befides thefe have greater Ad-
" vantages, the true Notions of Honour, and
" a due Senfe of Religion, are certainly not
" to be overcome fo readily. If thefe are once
" rooted in the Heart, they are not fo eafily
" fupplanted. Add to this the many difmal
" Examples of irretrievable Mifery, and the for-
" lorn Condition of the unwary, who have yield-
" ed to lafcivious Allurements, which are no
" fmall Incentives to their cautionary Refi-
" ftance.

" To break thro' all thefe Oppofitions is a
" Task no lefs tedious than intricate, and the
" Methods to accomplifh it are as fervilely bafe
" as the End is notorioufly villainous; he who fets
" about it muft diveft himfelf of Humanity, bid
" adieu to all Laws, moral and divine, and en-
" ter into an Alliance with a Legion of Crimes.
" Hypocrify muft conceal his outragious Luft
" under the Difguife of a vehement Affection,
" and gild his inward Treachery with outward
" Sincerity. A Multitude of Vows and Oaths
" muft be always at Hand to confirm the Truth
" of thofe extravagant Expreffions, his Heart at
" the fame Inftant gives the Lie to. Profu-
" five Promifes with unintended Performances,
" muft be innumerable. Earneft Intreaties and
" moving Perfuafions, muft at once be urgent-
" ly preffed, and well tim'd. Bribing Prefents
" muft give a Proof of his Liberality, and en-
" fnaring Obligations be as prodigally tender'd
" as prudently manag'd. He muft be perfect in
" the Art of Infinuation, and judicially skilful
" in embellifhing Flattery; and yet keep it in
" due Decorum. He muft fhew no Refent-
                                    " ment

" ment at the moſt imperious Behaviour, nor
" haughtily triumph at favourable Treatment;
" but bear Inſults with Patience, and Compla-
" cency with Humility. He muſt be deaf to
" flat Denials, and blind to coy Refuſals; yet
" neither too ſtrenuouſly plead againſt the one,
" nor too boiſterouſly endeavour to fruſtrate the
" other. He muſt debaſe his Senſe by obliging it
" to admire Farce, commend Froth, and ap-
" plaud Impertinence. He muſt paſſively ſub-
" mit to the meaneſt Impoſitions, and induſtri-
" ouſly execute the moſt unreaſonable Com-
" mands. He muſt carefully watch the various
" and ſudden Changes of her Humour, and as
" expeditiouſly ſuit his own to them. He muſt
" be compleat in *young Bookwit's* Art, *able to*
" *know her Mind by her Eye, as well as the*
" *Doctor ſhall her Health by her Pulſe, and to*
" *read Approbation thro' a Glance of Diſdain.*
" He ought to be a Proficient in Love's Aſtro-
" logy, that he may perceive when the propi-
" tious Planet hath gain'd the Aſcendant, and
" diſpenſes its favourable Influences in his Be-
" half. Reſolution and Caution muſt poize each
" other; the former to arm him with Courage
" to make uſe of the critical Minute; and the
" latter to prevent the Danger of miſtaking an
" accidental Circumſtance for a deſign'd Op-
" portunity. In fine, he muſt ſhake Hands with
" Honour, take Leave of Virtue, and renounce
" Religion, to incumber himſelf with a Mul-
" titude of Inconveniencies.—He miſpends his
" Time, conſumes his Eſtate, blaſts his Repu-
" tation, and torments his Mind, till his Days
" become unpleaſant, and his Nights uneaſy.
" He robs himſelf of real Pleaſure by purſuing
" an imaginary one. He macerates his Body
" here,

" here, and damns his Soul hereafter. He courts
" Hell with an Ardor equal to the Paffion he
" bears his Miftrefs; but defpifes Heaven, and
" provokes the God of both.

" But now, Suppofing you arriv'd at the de-
" fir'd Haven, I fear not but a ferious View of
" the ufual Contingencies, will leffen your pre-
" fent Opinion of the Felicity your Imagination
" has fuggefted. A difagreeable Coynefs al-
" ways attends the firft Compliances; and the
" beft Account you can give of the Encounter
" is, that you have made a Conqueft of an *un-*
" *willing willing Victim:* However this may
" heighten the Defire, it certainly abates of the
" immediate Satisfaction. The general Remedy
" for this uneafinefs proceeds from an Hope,
" that Time and Cuftom will remove this Ob-
" ftruction, and render the Pleafure entirely
" compleat. But it moft commonly falls out,
" that (before the Virgin Modefty is fhaken off,
" which gives a Check even to a lafcivious In-
" clination, and hinders that loofe Freedom
" which too probably the Intention had before re-
" folved on) the Man cools, his Mind changes,
" and now he wifhes for more Refervednefs to
" invigorate his declining Appetite; fo that ftill
" the Delight falls infinitely fhort of the Perfec-
" tion, which was expected to be reap'd from it.
" In a little Time a carelefs Indifferency begins
" to affwage the Fury of his Paffion, which
" cultivated in the fertile Soil of an ungrateful
" Breaft, foon increafes to downright loathing.
" All the alluring Methods, and fweet Endear-
" ments of amorous Wantonnefs, do but cloy
" that Appetite they meant to raife: Neither
" perfuafive Arguments, nor the moft evident
" Teftimonies of a doating Fondnefs can pre-
" ferve

" ferve him conftant. The Vows, Oaths, and
" Proteftations, that betray'd her Innocence,
" and inveigled her to Ruin, are now forgot;
" and the pretended Ardency of his violent Af-
" fection is chang'd into a mortal Averfion.
" There is no worldly Gratification that re-
" quires fuch a Share of affiduous Vigilance,
" and laborious Turmoil as this before us;
" none fo ill requites the Pains. The Covetous
" increafes his Store by Induftry and Frugality.
" The Ambitious directs his Aim at Honour,
" or Preferment, and makes Politics or Cou-
" rage the Means to get it; the one no lefs af-
" fects his Brain, than the other endangers his
" Perfon : And tho' it be granted, that the Bo-
" dies and Minds of both muft be emyloy'd in
" their jovial Purfuits; yet are they in a much
" inferior Degree to the Fatigue of a luftful In-
" amorato : But the Difference in the Enjoy-
" ment will appear with vaft Odds on their
" Sides. The bigger the Baggs of the one are
" fwell'd, and the higher in Place or popular
" Efteem the other is advanc'd, the larger is
" their Proportion of Satisfaction, and the lon-
" ger they enjoy their particular Acquifitions the
" happier do they think themfelves. But the
" other by the inconceivable Difquietudes of the
" Methods abovemention'd, having obtain'd his
" End, meets fuch a Difappointment in his Ex-
" pectation, that he quickly repents his Bargain,
" and is not long in Poffeffion before he abo-
" minates his Purchafe.

" Another mifchievous Conclufion may be
" drawn from thefe Premiffes. 'Tis very like-
" ly that Nature has, together with her outward
" Ornaments of attracting Beauty, endow'd her
" with a fruitful Womb, and pregnant Confti-
" tution.

" tution. And, notwithstanding her Timorous-
" ness may render her cautious, and sometimes
" intervene and oppose it self to the luxurious
" Pleasure mutually expected from the wanton
" Embrace, yet is it more than probable, that
" Time may produce the *visible Effects of in-*
" *visible Means*; and as soon as she is confirm-
" ed of the Truth of what she has a while
" doubted, a new Scene opens, but how plea-
" sant a Prospect it will discover you may judge
" anon. Imagine her then in this Condition,
" and your self paying her a Visit, transported
" at the Thoughts of seeing her after a Lo-
" ver's Age of constrain'd Absence, with an
" obliging Present in your Hand, your Mind
" replenish'd with good Humor, and not the
" least ominous Suspicion of any unlucky Ac-
" cident that may intrude it self, to prevent the
" Bliss of the eagerly expected Delight you pro-
" mise your self from this Adventure.

" Please your self with a Design of surprizing
" her, and at your first Approach you may be-
" hold Grief so powerfully struggling with her
" natural Beauty, that 'tis hard to determine
" which will be Victor. Amaz'd at the Sight,
" and inapprehensive of the Cause, a Multitude
" of confused Reflections jostle for Room in
" your Breast. Impatient in Suspense, you fly with
" open Arms to embrace the lovely Mourner,
" and earnestly demand the Reason of her deep
" Concern. A dismal Sigh supplies the Place
" of a courteous Welcome, and a Flood of
" Tears is all the Answer her Sorrow will al-
" low her to give. In a while she tells the me-
" lancholy Tale, and turns a *Niobe* for an
" Hour after. When the briny Torrent that
" stopp'd the Passage of her Voice by the Help
" of
3

" of repeated Groans, has made Room for
" Speech, she breaks her Silence in penitential
" Lamentations, indigested, intermix'd with up-
" braiding Reprehensions of her own Folly,
" and your Vileness. Now Memory plays the
" Tyrant in you both, forcing you to rumi-
" nate on all the self Reasonings, the yielding
" to an head-strong Passion which occasion'd you
" to stifle her, recollecting the deluding Artifices
" you made use of to procure her Ruin, and
" obstruct her virtuous Resolves. The Price of
" many paternal Acres must be deposited, to
" defray the Charges of Exoneration, and a
" tottering Reputation cannot be supported with-
" out extravagant Bribes to secure Secrecy.
" Another Parcel must be allotted to rear, edu-
" cate, and make a future Provision for the
" illegitimate Off-spring. The Father must be-
" stow his Benevolence on the Issue he's asham-
" ed to own, and the Child wear an undeser-
" ved Blemish, too deeply stampt by his incon-
" siderate Parents for Time to efface, till the
" whole Line be extinct. This is the least E-
" vil can ensue, and 'tis no small Mercy to
" withstand the Suggestions of Rage, Vexation,
" and Despair, which in these Cases prescribe
" an *Amblothridion*, to destroy the Embryo ; or
" dictate a more superlative Impiety, by adding
" to the capital Crime already committed, that
" most execrable Sin of murdering the Infant,
" as an infallible Preservative against future Ex-
" pence, and spreading Disgrace. After every
" Thing necessary on this Occasion, is, with a
" great deal of Precaution and Trouble, agreed
" upon, her easy Credulity prompting her to re-
" ly on the solemn Promises you have made
" her, of your best and faithfullest Services un-

I   " der

" der the unhappy Juncture, and a Continuance
" of your fincere Love to her may, perhaps,
" in fome Meafure, moderate her Concern, and
" mitigate the Tortures of her Soul; yet there
" ftill remains fuch muddy Dreggs of anxious
" Doubts and prophetic Tears, as render her
" better qualified for a mournful Ceremony,
" than amorous *Tendreffes*; befides, frequent
" Pukings, and breeding Qualms are but *unre-*
" *lifhed Ragoufts* at *venereal Banquets*. What a
" gloomy Cloud hath eclipfed your bright Ex-
" pectations of this Day's Delight! No fooner
" parted, but your refolving Thoughts bring to
" your View all the untoward Occurences, and
" infufe frefh Subjects for a melancholy Con-
" templation! What a pondrous Weight have
" you laid upon your own Shoulders, that muft
" carry the double Burden of your own Afflic-
" tion and her Mifery? All her future Infamy
" and Misfortune will lie as heavy on you, as
" the Reflection of your own Ignominy, which
" you will ever bear about you, as long as there
" remains the leaft Spark of Generofity, and
" common Honefty unextinguifh'd. But, more
" than this, the Load of her Guilt, as well as
" your own, will crufh your very Soul, whilft
" any Part of common Confcience continues
" unfear'd; fo that, to quit your felf of thefe
" agonizing Torments, you muft refolutely
" plunge into the fatal Gulph of Reprobation,
" there to lay, unlefs drawn from thence by the
" almoft miraculous Interpofition of an an-
" gry, as well as merciful God, till Death re-
" move you to irrevocable Damnation. To
" plead the Pliancy of human Nature, the Force
" of a refiftlefs Temptation, or the Vehemency
" of a Paffion, will but little avail: The firft
" might

" might as eafily have been correated as the fe-
" cond withftood, and no Chriftian can be de-
" ftitute of fufficient Means for both, the Mif-
" application only of the third is the Crime ;
" for let the Affection be never fo violent, 'tis
" as juftifiable, provided the End be perfectly
" honeft, and concurrent with the Laws of
" God, and the Cuftom of the Country, where-
" in you live ; but it is adorning Luft with an
" undeferv'd Title to name it Love. The Ca-
" taftrophe makes it evident, for it is an irre-
" concileable Contradiction, and demonftrative
" Inconfiftency for a pure and fincere Love to
" any Perfon, to endeavour its total Undoing
" in this World, and, as much as in it lies, its
" eternal Deftruction in the next.

   " Laftly, to the reft of thefe direful Affoci-
" ates, that are to accompany you in the be-
" wilder'd Paths of Beftiality, add an outragi-
" ous Jealoufy. Ask your felf, if you can be-
" hold another look wifhfully on her without
" harbouring an ill Thought toward him, or can
" you fee her caft a favourable Glance at any
" but your felf, without the ftabbing Pangs of
" a furly Rage? Can you in the leaft diftruft her
" and fit contendedly quiet, without a Defire
" of being convinc'd of your Error, or confir-
" med of the Truth? Can you fee her careffed
" with an Ardor equal to your own, without
" the defperate Refolution of an implacable Re-
" venge?---But can you tamely look on, whilft
" her inviting Behaviour, and the intelligible
" Language of her Eyes, invite another to her
" Arms and Bed, and not be thunderftruck at
" the amazing Vifion ? How many undefign'd
" Paffages, tho' utterly groundlefs, will for the
" prefent, put you upon a Rack? The Optics

                                                                " thro'

" thro' which Jealoufy takes its Obfervation,
" have that magnifying Quality of fwelling *a*
" *Pifmire* to the Size of an *Elephant*, and ma-
" king Appearances look like Realities. *Proba-*
" *bility, like a Confumption, leifurely impairs*
" *the Vitals, but Proof, like a Bullet, gives Death*
" *with the Blow.* Words are wanting to ex-
" prefs the Torments of a Mind poffeffed with
" Jealoufy. It imbitters all the Comforts of
" Life, and renders its unhappy Slave incapa-
" ble of the leaft Enjoyment, amidft the high-
" eft Excefs of Fortune's Bounty. It eclip-
" fes the brighteft Pleafure, and benights the
" moft refplendent Rays of dazzling Profperity.
" It baffles the Aim of fportive Recreations,
" and fruftrates the Defigns of facetious Diver-
" fions: For, while a Smile plays upon the
" Lips, the Heart droops under a pungent Sor-
" row, it abates Mirth, but heightens Mifery.
" In fine, it overwhelms Reafon, and drowns
" Underftanding ; it makes a Man either ftu-
" pidly penfive, or rafhly furious ; the one is
" troublefome, the other pernicious. To be
" always chagrin and uneafy in Mind, is the
" Perfection of Wretchednefs, and a Refolu-
" tion to remove the Caufe by violent Means
" muft inevitably produce terrible Effects. The
" Heart's Blood of a Rival is an improper Opi-
" ate, to compofe the agitated Spirits of a dif-
" truftful Breaft. Boldly to look Death in the
" Face may, in many Cafes, betoken a noble
" Soul, and chriftian Courage ; but to ftorm
" Hell, demonftrates an accurfed Prefumption,
" and wicked Fool-hardinefs. To fall in the
" Conteft, is to fink from a momentary Mifchief
" to an eternal Mifery ; and all the Advantage
" of Victory is, very probably, but the Addi-
" tion

" tion of a few wretched Days to an uncom-
" fortable Life, which muſt quickly end in
" a deſervedly ignominious Death: The beſt
" that can be hop'd from ſuch a Dilemma is,
" that the ſincere Contrition, and Repentance
" of the whole Remainder of Time, may prove
" ſuccefsful to expiate the horrid Guilt of a ſu-
" perlatively impious Act: But 'tis much to be
" fear'd the Heinouſneſs of complicated Crimes
" may, inſtead thereof, infuſe a fatal Deſponden-
" cy; the Efficacy of the former muſt be whol-
" ly owing to an Infinity of Mercy; and the
" Conſequence of the latter is to be everlaſting-
" ly undone.

" The Landskip I have here ſet to your View
" is but a Draught in Miniature, of what you
" muſt of Neceſſity meet withal, in the Profe-
" cution of a lawleſs Amour. Every Step in
" the Paths of this Vice is followed with immi-
" nent Danger, at leaſt with ſuch incommodi-
" ous Circumſtances, as pall the promiſed Sa-
" tisfaction, however inviting they may ſeem
" to a purblind Senſuality, which is delighted
" with the beauteous Appearance, but diſcovers
" not the devouring Boggs and prickly Thorns,
" that lie hid under the verdant Surface, and is
" too near ſighted to behold the frightful Pro-
" ſpect of thoſe Chambers of Death to which
" they lead.

" The real Value and ſincere Concern I have
" for you, but more eſpecially my tender Re-
" gards for your immortal Soul, have made
" me deal thus freely with you."

It was with no ſmall Pleaſure I beheld a relenting Air in *Tarquinius*'s Countenance, while
I was diſcuſſing theſe ſerious Truths. I gladly
perceiv'd by his Looks, the Impreſſion I had

I 3

made

made on his Heart, and could not be more impatient to hear his Reply, than he to return the following Anfwer.

Tarquinius. " What a thick Film had an head-
" ftrong Paffion fpread over my darken'd Eyes?
" How did it hinder my Perception of remote E-
" vents? How did my unheeded Dimnefs over-
" fhadow the illuftrious Rays of Reafon, and ob-
" ftruct the refulgent Beams of preventing Grace?
" But your folid and pious Arguments have,
" like a fovereign Opthalmic, reftor'd me from
" a fatal Blindnefs to a perfect Sight. You have
" not only expell'd my falfe Notions by an im-
" partial Reprefentation of the Invalidity of the
" expected Joy, and thereby confuted the Error
" of my Apprehenfion; but by your lively De-
" fcriptions and judicious Obfervations, form'd
" in my Mind a fettled Belief, that the fulleft
" Fruition of my ideal Wifhes wou'd be over-
" poiz'd by the fmalleft of thofe Evils, fo un-
" avoidable in the Attainment of 'em. This
" alone might be fufficient to put a Check on
" any one, who is not intirely divefted of Ra-
" tionality: But what lefs than an hellifh Pre-
" fumption can look beyond the Grave, and with
" the Eye of Faith behold the *numberlefs Tor-*
" *ments of Tophet,* and yet dare to perfift in thofe
" Courfes, which will render him liable to no fmall
" Share in them, and that not for the fhort Space
" of an uncertain Life, but the immenfe Dura-
" tion of an unmeafur'd Eternity? This Thought
" has feized me with awful Dread, and quench-
" ed the heated Fury of my deftructive Flames.
" You have given me fuch an evident Teftimo-
" ny of your faithful Friendfhip, that I fhou'd
" be the moft unworthy of it in the World, did
" I not make a due Acknowledgment. But to-
" wards

" wards finifhing of the good Work you have
" begun, there is ftill wanting your farther Aid
" in preventing my Relapfe; for I now more
" heartily fear *Camafia's* Return, than I before
" lamented her Abfence. The downy Wings
" of my juft fledg'd Remorfe are too feeble to
" bear me up amidft the Tempeft of her Charms ;
" to you I fue for Shelter or Support; be you
" the Guardian Angel of my Soul, and by your
" fage Advice inftruct your infant Convert how
" to tread in the narrow Paths of Virtue; teach
" me to fhun her Ruin and my own. Your
" prudent Dictates, back'd with the divine Affi-
" ftance, may work the glorious End. What-
" ever you enjoyn, fhall be received with an
" unfeign'd Thankfulnefs, and perform'd with
" a punctual Obedience.

Philaretus. " It is the greateft Prudence to
" refift a Temptation at the firft Offer, for then
" is it eafieft to be vanquifh'd; to parley with
" it, is to give it a greater Power; faint Deni-
" als are the Forerunners of Confent, but pe-
" remptory Anfwers baffle fecond Attempts ;
" tho' this Advice comes too late in your Cafe,
" you have loft the Opportunity of fubduing
" the injurious Strength of a libidinous Inclina-
" tion, and have no other Means left, than an
" immediate Flight from it: This I would ad-
" vife you to at leaft, till Time and Confide-
" ration enable you to rally your heartlefs Forces.
" A fmall Refpite, and an affiduous Applica-
" tion, may infpire new Courage; and if you
" earneftly implore the omnipotent Majefty of
" Heaven, it will gracioufly fupply you with
" fuch a numerous Hoft of powerful Succours,
" as will make you invincible to the moft furi-
" ous Affaults of Satan, and fecure you from

" all

" all the crafty Stratagems and subtile Wiles of
" the Devil.

To this he readily agreed, and ordered his
Coach to be got ready; whilst himself dispensed
with the usual Formalities of Dressing, and his
Valet huddled on all the Appurtenances of his
Equipment. He could not have made more Haste
to an Assignation with the fair Enamorels of
his Soul, than he now does to avoid his adored
Camasia. He engaged me to go with him, and
bad his Coachman drive to his Uncle's at *Ken-*
sington; where we quickly arrived, and were received by the Gentleman of the House, with a
more real Friendship in his Face, than affected
Ceremony in his Behaviour. I had only time
to share the decent Bounty of a chearful Hospi-
tality, and observe the harmonious Regularity of
a well disciplined Family, the Effect of the prudent Management, and pious Care of its worthy Master. I was very glad I was to leave
him in such excellent Company, where Virtue
and Goodnels were instilled both by Precept and
Example. *Tarquinius* quickly informed his venerable Relation, that, with his Leave, he intended to stretch his Visit to a Moon's Age:
His Uncle rejoiced at the News, affectionately
embraced his Nephew, and desired him to limit
the space of his Abode, by no other Bounds
than the Welcome he should find, which he affured him should be always increasing toward
him, as long as he continued there. He had
made himself a Stranger to this Gentleman ever
since his Father's Decease, for fear of having
his Ears boar'd with those austere Reprehensions,
his youthful Extravagances had justly merited: But
that Counsel, he before dreaded, he now flies to,
as the Means of establishing him in his designed
Reformation.   The

The Sun had already pafs'd the Horizon of our Hemifphere, and the impatient Night was haſtily drawing her ſable Curtains to ſhut out the little Remainder of Light was left, when I was deſirous to take my Leave; but neither would permit me, till I had given my Word, I would be there again the next Day, and to make it the eaſier to me, I was to have the Uſe of *Tarquinius*'s Coach for that Purpoſe; as alſo for any other Occaſion I might have for it, during his Stay at *Kenſington*. *Camaſia* was at home before me; and unexpectedly miſſing him, whom her *Soul loved*, divided herſelf between an Uneaſineſs at his Abſence, and the Hopes of his quick Return. The Inſtant the Coach ſtopt at the Door ſhe flew to the Window, her Eyes ſparkling with Joy, and her lovely Cheeks ſhining with the natural Dye of a Carnation Bluſh made her look more than ordinarily beautiful; whilſt her Lips were adorned with a graceful Smile, as it were, on Purpoſe at once to demand a Salute, and expreſs a Welcome: But when ſhe ſaw only me alight, and the empty Carriage hurry toward the Stables; the Diſappointment of her Expectation ſo altered her Countenance, that ſhe appeared a much properer Object for a Phyſician's Skill, than a Painter's Art. Supper came to Table juſt after I had entered the Room, but neither *Camaſia* nor my ſelf could eat any thing: Yet our Reaſons were very different; I could not, becauſe I had had a ſufficient Repaſt ſo lately; ſhe, becauſe the Idol of her Heart was abſent, whoſe Company alone could have given a Gaiety to her Spirits, and a Reliſh to every Bit ſhe eat. It drawing towards Bed-time, ſeveral began to make enquiry after *Tarquinius* : For a good while I returned no Anſwer,

fwer, tho' I could perceive *Camafia's* Ears were
wide open with an impatient Defire of being
informed every Time the Queftion was put;
and as often were her Eyes fixed upon my
Lips, as imagining them the only authentic Oracles that could declare the myfterious Secret,
and fatisfy her Doubts. Many Conjeﬤures were
made concerning him. Some believed he was
detained by *Bacchus*, at whofe Feftivals the
Hours infenfibly glide away; and few of his
Devotees allow it a reafonable Time to depart
his Sacrifices, as long as they are able to pay
him the Homage of another Glafs; others, that
Cloe's Arms were fo faft about his Neck, he
could not eafily difengage himfelf from 'em,
and that he might be in Bed, tho' he were not
at home. Two or three fuppofed him either
curfing or careffing Fortune, and that he was
endeavouring to thwart his ill Luck, or vi-
goroufly purfuing his good Succefs. I knowing the particular Charaﬤers of thefe fafhionable Cenfurers, from thence concluded I might
fafely judge their different Opinions fprang more
from the Motives of their own Hearts than any
thing elfe; and yet I fhould not make that Tref-
pafs upon Charity which they had done. By a
blunt Manner of replying, I gave them to underftand what my Sentiments were, which produced as great a Variety in their Faces, as there
was before in their Thoughts. The Modefter
of them redened with a confcious Blufh: The
infenfibly foolifh fuppofed, that an aukward Grin
would turn it into Ridicule; and the ftubborn
natured Animals added an angry Frown to their
morofe Looks, in order to frighten me from
future Reprimands. At laft I told them, that
Tarquinius, being a little indifpofed, was gone to
a Re-

a Relation's of his out of Town for the Air; from whence he would hardly return in lefs than a Month. I confefs I did not forefee, that what I had faid was likely to yield frefh Subject for Calumny ; when, it feems, every Word was *a Propos* to the partial Conceptions of an antiquated Satyrift among the Herd, who clamoroufly extoll'd the Profundity of his own Judgment, which was able to fathom the deep Meaning concealed in my Account of him : I turned my Ear to him with a thirfty Attention, but wifhed he had made ufe of a fpeaking Trumpet; for the Palate of his Mouth being in Part mifplaced, his Voice defcended to the nethermoft Part of his Belly, and left us nothing but a rebounding Eccho to underftand him by : It was with fome Difficulty I apprehended his Conclufions to be, that he imagined *Tarquinius* had, by the *fhorteft Way*, and without the Trouble of fearching the Depths of Nature, fully proved the Truth of Dr. *Garth's* Maxim in the *Difpenfary :*

" That the fame Nerves are fafhion'd to fuftain
" The greateft Pleafure, and the greateft Pain :

And that what I had reported of him was but a meer Excufe for his Abfence, during the Time requifite to repair the Damages fuch an Experiment had occafioned. It filled me at once with Surprize and Grief, to hear the grey-headed Letcher audacioufly boaft, and impudently glory in his paft Impiety, by acknowledging his prefent Cenfures were founded upon the Rules of his own former Practice ; aftonifhed at the Excefs of his Folly and Height of his Wickednefs, I could not readily compofe my felf to
make

make him a suitable Return: But whilst I was framing a Reprehension, that might express both my Resentment and Pity, another of the Company declared himself of the same Opinion; and modestly affirm'd, that his Concurrence therewith proceeded from a Reflection of the many like Pretences, which had reached his own Knowledge. " My Conjectures (said he) " are neither the Products of a splenetic Constitu- " tion, nor the Dictates of an ill-natur'd Tem- " per; but the Station, in which the greatest Part " of my Life has been employed, has afforded " me an Opportunity of being an Eye-witness " to abundance of such Instances in Men of all " Degrees. I have indeed known some, who " have proclaimed their own Shame before-hand " among all their Acquaintance, as if their " wretched Condition were rather an Honour " than a Misfortune, and have triumphantly " marched into the Powdering-Tub, with a Re- " tinue of their Associates of the same Frater- " nity. Others have had the good Luck, after " some space of Confinement, to appear again " in Public, without Suspicion; and they might " have preserved their Reputation, if their own " Simplicity had not exposed it, by foolishly " publishing that Truth they had before taken " such Pains to conceal; nay some, I am sen- " sible, have been so affectedly vain, as to think " it a Discredit not to be in those fashionable " Circumstances, and have therefore, from these " ridiculous Principles, imposed on the Belief " of their Companions, by averring themselves " to be so; when, in Reality, they had good " Reason to esteem it a Comfort they had not " met with their Desert: But as for the Um- " brage you have made use of to shroud *Tar-*

3   " *quinius*'s

" *quinius*'s Retirement, it is a thread-bare De-
" ceit left off by all the modern Debauchees,
" that have the leaft Defign to hide their Dif-
" grace; fome City Dolts excepted, who won't
" be put out of their old Road; or for want
" of Converfation, have not been better in-
" formed: Such ufe it ftill on thefe Occafions,
" but the more refined of 'em, who are tutored
" at this End of the Town, are grown wifer,
" and feek for another Cover, unlefs the Va-
" cation favour the Cozenage, and then a Coun-
" try Progrefs, among their Chapmen, falves up
" the Matter: The Pretence of avoiding for a
" while the Clamours of importunate Cre-
" ditors, or their unmerciful Attendants, hath
" oftentimes proved a more eligible Evafion,
" they choofing rather to bear the Scandal of
" Infolvency, than the Difgrace of a loathed
" Diftemper; and the prefent general Deficien-
" cy fets a Glofs upon the Excufe. Therefore,
" to ftop the Afperfion, which is likely to fpread,
" and be conftrued to his Difadvantage by your
" Report, *Tarquinius* will do well to convince
" the World by fome public Evidence, to avoid
" the Prejudice of private Jealoufy.

" Innocence (reply'd I) ftands in no need of
" Vindication; yet I give you my Word you
" judge falfely, and I expect that to be a fufficient
" Teftimony; but a little Time may give you
" a more ample Proof. Here the Company
broke up, every one entertaining that Belief,
which Fancy fuggefted, without any deep Concern, whether they determined right or wrong:
— But *Camafia*, who had too great a fhare in this
Bufinefs to remain indifferent, carried to her
Bed fuch a multitude of difturbing Thoughts,
as rendered the Attempts of Sleep unable to

make the leaft Conqueft o'er her Eyes; neither
could fhe fo fmother her Sighs and Sobs, but
that her Mother, who was her Bedfellow, par-
ticipated of her Uneafinefs, and was thereby alfo obliged to pafs the tedious Night without the
Pleafure of a gentle Slumber.

The next Day, immediately after Dinner, I
haftened to perform my Promife to *Tarquinius,*
who had already told his worthy Uncle the Occafion of his being there, and by what Means
Providence had made me the happy Inftrument
of preventing the deplorable Confequences of
his beftial Defigns. The Joy that this bleffed
Alteration raifed in the Breaft of his pious Relation, made the good old Gentleman receive
me with a more than ordinary Kindnefs; and
tho' our Acquaintance was of fo fmall a ftanding, we, from that inftant, link'd ourfelves to
each other by the Bonds of an inviolable Friendfhip. Our mutual Engagements ended, we entered upon the Affairs of *Tarquinius,* who gave
us an entire Satisfaction, by his hearty and fincere expreffing an abhorrent Deteftation of his
late Errors; but added further, that, altho' he
had perfectly banifhed all Thoughts of purfuing
the Vice, yet his Affection for *Camafia* was not
in the leaft abated. Her exquifite Beauty and
divine Accomplifhments had rendered his Heart
Proof againft all the Arguments her Difparity of
Fortune could fuggeft to oppofe his poffeffing
fo much Excellence. Paffion and Prudence
had held a long Conteft within him: The one
fpurred him to an ardent Defire of Enjoyment,
and the other pleaded the Unfuitablenefs of the
Match; and how incongruous to Reafon and
Cuftom it would be to marry upon fuch un-
equal Terms: This Confideration had put him
upon

upon endeavouring to gratify the former, without acting contradictory to the latter; but being now happily convinced, that the Danger he was running into was so infinitely greater, than that he intended to avoid. He had prevail'd with himself to quit the unadvised Undertaking, yet he hoped the lesser Folly might be complied with; as a plausible Excuse for which he alledged, that the Violence of his Love did in no wise exceed the Merit of the Person, his whole Ambition was centered in; and to confirm the Truth of his Assertion, he willingly appealed to my Judgment, whether he had in any particular glossed her Character with the Varnish of a Lover's Flattery. I readily acknowledged, that I could not, without Injustice, deny; but that *Camasia* was a Lady every way answered his Description, and truly deserved all that could be said in her Commendation. The Unhappiness so often met with in those Matches, where Interest hath been chiefly consider'd, without the more material Circumstances so essential towards making the nuptial State happy for Life, influenced the indulgent Uncle to acquiesce in his Nephew's Choice: He, at the same time intimating, that as high Perfections united with an equal Fortune might have been found, which would have given his Consent a freer Passage; for tho' he wisely foresaw the many ill Consequences, which usually follow the obstructing the headstrong Desires of inconsiderate Youth, either by striving to turn the Current of their Affections, or by the imperious Power of an awful Authority commanding it to direct its Course to the Point assign'd, however diametrically opposite it might be to the Inclination of the necessitously obe-

dient;

dient; yet could he not freely agree to the dif-
advantageous Bargain, *Tarquinius* had rashly re-
solved on, wherein there was not the least Proportion to give Encouragement to his Approbation: But as his Experience, in remote Cases,
gave him a View of the Hazards might accrue
from Compulsion, and made him timorous of
putting his Nephew's future Discomfort or
Miscarriage to the Venture; so his wonted
Goodness, conspicuous on all offered Occasions, at length prompted him to a kind Compliance; and well knowing that Speed in Performance doubles a Favour, he generously re-
solv'd to treat with *Camasia*'s Mother the next
Day. To conclude the particular Agreements,
and other the minute Circumstances of the Marriage being foreign to my present Purpose, I shall
only inform you, that, in a few Weeks, I had
the Satisfaction to witness Heaven had blessed
my Endeavours with Success, by seeing *Tarquinius*'s and *Camasia*'s Hands joined in the sacred Ceremony; and that the Uncle's Joy,
which was but little short of the Felicity of the
glad Couple, incited his bounteous Disposition
to make up the Deficiency of *Camasia*'s Fortune for the present, and to settle his whole
Estate upon *Tarquinius* and his Heirs after his
Decease. The immense Happiness, in which
they afterwards lived, proved sufficient to silence
those contumelious Tongues, which take a ma-
licious Pride in casting an Odium on that honourable and useful State of Matrimony; and
made it evident, that it was not only possible,
but easy to enjoy on Earth an *angelical Beatitude.*

THE

The Batchelor-Keeper

by

John Clarke

THE
BATCHELOR-KEEPER.

Numb. II.

By *PHILARETUS*.

THE

Batchelor-Keeper.

 HE Pleaſantneſs of a Summer's Ev'ning invited me into the Fields, and my Love of Solitude made me chuſe the moſt lonely Walks. As my Mind was ſeriouſly engag'd in a deep Meditation, I was haſtily ſurpriz'd with a familiar Salute from a Gentleman, I could not preſently call by Name, tho' we had been intimately acquainted many Years, and our daily Correſpondence not long ſince interrupted; yet the Suddenneſs of the Accident, the Unlikelyhood of meeting him there, and the great Alteration of a few Months had made in his Face and Mien, gave ſuch a Check to my Memory, that I could not immediately recollect him : But I remain'd not long in this Labyrinth before his Information, joyn'd with an hearty Embrace, fforded my Remembrance the Clue, that readily
ly

ly conducted me to the Knowledge of him. My Joy to fee him was not greater than my Wonder at his Metamorphofis. The Freedom of his Air, and the Cheerfulnefs of his Countenance were overwhelm'd with a Cloud of Melancholy. My Friendfhip, more than Curiofity, made me inquifitive to know the Caufe of that Sorrow, to which this apparent Change was owing. The deep fetch'd Sighs which follow'd my Requefts, pierc'd my very Heart ; and the Show'rs of Tears that trickl'd from his aged Eyes, melted me into a Sympathy ; but thefe difmal Fore-runners at length made Way for the following Relation.

" You know, *Philaretus* (faid he) with what " indefatigable Induftry, Labour and Pains, I " have acquir'd a decent Competency, and what " Methods of Frugality and Carefulnefs I have " taken to preferve it. You are fenfible of the " Hopes I had, which fweeten'd all my Toil, " and made ev'n the Fatigue of Bufinefs fit " eafy on me, but they are all blafted now, and " the fad Difappointment makes me lament my " infignificant Affiduity. You, *Philaretus*, are " happy, who feel not the Weight of a Child's " Mifcarriage, and are not capable of a Parent's " Grief.----My Son, my only Son, my once " (nay, to my Shame, my ftill) beloved Son, " is pofting on to Ruin. His Mother's pur- " blind Fondnefs conniving at his juvenile Fol- " lies, and, lavifhly fupplying his wanton Pro- " digality, has excited his vitious Inclination to " afcend gradually from the Slips of Youth to " the Summit of Debauchery. Scarce a Day " paffing that my Ears a'n't alarm'd with fome " unlucky News of his Extravagance. For " fome Time I held my Liberality under a ftrict
" Rein,

" Rein, and his Mother's too late Repentance
" for her former Weaknefs, fix'd her in a Re-
" folution to withftand his wheedling Intrea-
" ties: But thefe Cautions prov'd fo fruitlefs,
" that, inftead of ftopping his Career, they
" were a Spur to his Infolence, and turn'd his
" artful Civility into downright ill Language,
" and haughty Behaviour; and what with undu-
" tiful Speeches, and clam'rous Threats, he has
" fo wrought upon her tender Fears, that fhe
" was oblig'd to continue her private and large
" Supplies by Way of Prevention. I then laid
" afide thefe abortive Means, and would have
" purchas'd his Duty at the Price of my Boun-
" ty, patiently expecting his Gratitude would be
" proportion'd to my Excefs of Favour. I had
" indeed fomewhat more of his Company, but
" generally bought it at a dear Rate. I propos'd
" to him an unexceptionable Match, and made
" him fuch Promifes on his Marriage, as wou'd
" have given moft Fathers Reafon to cenfure
" my Prudence; or, in cafe he had any Objec-
" tion to this Offer, I affur'd him of my free
" Confent to his own Choice. His Silence a
" while kept me in a painful Sufpenfe, and my
" ill grounded Conjectures laid the Caufe on
" his Modefty, which I fought to embolden by
" repeated Proteftations of performing the En-
" gagements my fatherly Affection had brought
" me under: My Condefcenfion gave him the
" Imprudence to anfwer my Indulgence with a
" flafhy and lewd Satire upon Matrimony, and
" it was no fmall Trouble to me to perceive
" by his wild Harangue, that his Difguft pro-
" ceeded from an atheiftical Libertinifin, and
" not from the Motives of a virtuous Conti-
" nence. In fine, to compleat himfelf in all
the

" the neceſſary Qualifications of a modern
" Rake, he long ſince enter'd himſelf in For-
" tune's Academy, to learn the profound My-
" ſteries of Gaming, and is ſo well vers'd in e-
" very Particular of it, from Bowling with his
" Grace to playing at Putt with a Cobler, that
" the Groom-Porter has deputed him to decide
" all the nice Queſtions belonging to Play. He
" coggs a Die, and ſlips a Card with the Dex-
" terity of a Juggler, and can diſtinguiſh a Bite
" from a Bubble in the twinkling of an Eye.
" To this he has added the glorious Art of abo-
" minable Swearing, and often gives Proofs of
" his Skill in ſuch Volleys of new coin'd Oaths,
" and emphatic Imprecations, that the Ignorant
" wonder, and the Wiſe tremble to hear him;
" there's not a Peer nor a Porter can outdo
" him: Nor is he leſs expert in the Punctilios
" of drinking; he baulks not his Glaſs till he
" drops from his Seat, and then he ſtares with a
" Grace, and ſtaggers with an Air; he ſtammers
" in Tune, hiccups the Time, and belches the
" Chorus. If he foots it home, his Head gets
" the Start of his Heels, and keeps its Diſtance
" all the Way a Yard before them; and there's
" not a Night in the Week but he's liable to
" an Indictment for robbing the Scavenger. He's
" a Gentleman of a very uneven Temper, ſome-
" times he's as fierce as a Tiger, at a ſmart Re-
" partee; at other Times as gentle as a Lamb
" at the grandeſt Affront. He fights like an
" Hero, and ſtabs the Villain in every Part of
" his Body if abſent; but ſubmits to be lugg'd
" by the Noſe, and will ſtand a caning if his
" Adverſary be preſent. He's very good at bilk-
" ing Coaches, which he often practiſes for
" Diverſion, and an hearty drubbing finiſhes the
" Teſt.

" Teft. There's hardly a Magiftrate in the Ci-
" ty, from the Chain to the Lanthorn, but has
" tranfgreffed the Law out of refpect to me, in
" permitting his Outrages to pafs unpunifh'd,
" and ordering him to be conducted to my Ha-
" bitation, when he has juftly deferv'd to be fent
" elfewhere with a Guard and a Mittimus; fo
" that when I walk the Streets, I am forc'd to
" wear one Hand in my Pocket, and the o-
" ther on my Hat, that I may be ready to return
" the different Salutations in a proper Man-
" ner. But he has feldom the Luck to efcape
" fo well on the other Side the Gates; it is ge-
" nerally his Fortune to be detain'd there, as an
" Hoftage, till Satisfaction is made for the Mif-
" chief has been done in fome glorious Frolick,
" or notable Rencounter, and about Nine the
" next Morning a Letter is privately conveyed
" to his Mother, with as many Lies in the Be-
" ginning as are neceffary to patch up a falfe
" and melancholy Story; in the middle as much
" Hypocrify as is fufficient to procure her Be-
" lief and Pity; and at the End the Sum total
" requir'd for Recompence and Ranfom; which
" in Compliance with her Correfpondent's Ad-
" vice, fhe punctually pays at Sight. And, as
" foon as he is let loofe, he makes home, his
" only Care being to avoid my feeing him come
" in, fo up he fteals to his Chamber, and moft
" expeditioufly gets himfelf new vampt, and then
" comes down again in fuch a Manner, as be-
" fpeaks him rather willing than afraid to be
" heard, and he is fure to hunt in every Room,
" doubling and redoubling, like a Whelp that
" has loft the Scent, till he has thrown himfelf
" in my View, that I may fuppofe him juft ar-
" riv'd *a Levee*; and tho' every one in the
" Houfe

" Houfe is, by my Wife's Directions, a Con-
" federate in the Deceit; yet Fame, either out
" of good or ill Will, feldom keeps his Ro-
" gueries long from my Knowledge. His
" Cloaths are of the neweft Cut. He wears a
" Sagamore's Revenue at once on his Back,
" and peeps thro' the Price of a Lordfhip. His
" Phyfician, Surgeon, and Apothecary have a fet-
" tled Salary; yet he finds them fo much Bufi-
" nefs, they grow fick of their Bargain. He's
" fat and lean by Turns; when three Months
" Epicurifm has fwell'd him to the Size of a
" Porpus, a Month's fpitting reduces him to a
" Skeleton. To finifh the exquifite Accom-
" plifhments of a Man in Fafhion, he hath late-
" ly pitch'd upon a mercenary Strumpet to ha-
" ften his Undoing. He has taken and furnifh'd
" her an Houfe fit for a Countefs. She fleeps
" upon Down, is cloath'd in Tiffue, ferv'd up-
" on Plate, and ftirs not abroad without her
" Chair.—What, *Philcretus*, muft be the End
" of all this? The Gallows, or a Prifon, will
" infallibly be his Doom. The Reflection of
" his prefent Condition makes my Life a Bur-
" den, and the Thoughts of his future Deftruc-
" tion render the Apprehenfion of Death moft
" terrible."

Here a new Flood of Tears drown'd his Speech,
and gave me an Opportunity of condoling his
Misfortune. The Drops from my Eyes demonftrated the Softnefs of my Heart, and afforded
him juft Reafon to believe I bore a Part in his
Affliction. I confider'd that the tend'reft Compaffion without other Affiftance was but Lip-
labour, and rather aggravated Sorrow, than re-
liev'd it: Wherefore, joyning to that the cor-
dial Promifes of my beft Endeavours to reclaim
the

the young Tranfgreffor, the Hopes of my Succefs fomewhat moderated his Grief. We employ'd the Remainder of our Time in contriving
Methods to effect my Defigns; and after many
difapprov'd Projections, we, at laft, came to a
very promifing Conclufion.

My former Familiarity with the Father occafion'd my having been frequently at his Houfe;
and confequently I cou'd not be unknown to
the Son, who always expreffed fo much good
Manners, as to pay me the Deference due to
one whom his Father honour'd with a more than
ordinary Efteem.

It may not be improper to inform you, that
my Friend Mr. *Richbottom* was a wealthy Tur-
ky Merchant, who defpifed the finifter and precarious Methods of ftockjobbing and wagering, and
all other the fraudulent Means (which fometimes are fo pernicious to the Authors, and thofe
concern'd with them in particular, and infallibly tend to the Prejudice of Traffic in general:
An epidemical Diftemper the Commerce of this
Nation hath a long Time groan'd under, notwithftanding the wholefome Phyfic the Legifla-
ture have provided to cure the Malady) contented himfelf with the honeft Rules of Trade,
which he purfu'd with fo ftrict a Probity, that
the faireft Opportunity, or greateft Advantage
cou'd not make him deviate from them; he
bought at the beft Hand, and fold at eafy Rates;
thereby experiencing the Benefit of quick Returns. As his punctual Payments gain'd him
Repute from his Creditors, fo did his patient For-
bearance Applaufe from his Debtors. His Practice prov'd it more elegible to fupport than ruin
an honeft Infolvent. He paid his Cuftoms with
Cheerfulnefs and Exactnefs, and was as inno-

cent of the Guilt, as free from the Punifhment
attendant on Concealment. He was in all refpects one of thofe very few that ever think of
the Freeman's Oath after they have taken it,
and cou'd not difpenfe with Perjury notwithftanding the Motive of univerfal Example.
He did not believe Induftry a Crime, nor Frugality a Vice, yet kept both within fuch due
Bounds, that he deferv'd neither the Character
of a Muckworm, or Mifer: He was neither an
Enemy nor a Slave to Diverfions, but knew
how to enjoy and not abufe them. He wou'd
fometimes raife his Spirits with a Glafs, but never drown them. He liv'd in a Mean between
the Prodigal and the Niggard, and could fhew
himfelf gen'rous without being lavifh. His Houfe
was provided with every Thing neceffary and
decent, without the gaudy Flourifhes of fuperfluous Trifles. His Table was covered with
the beft Subftantials, not the coftlieft Delicacies;
and his daily Supplies were fuch as plainly fhewed he defired neither Want nor Wafte. He was
not fo bafely miftruftful as to be always prying
into his Books and Cafh; nor fo negligently
carelefs, as not fometimes to infpect both. He
was always cautious of meddling with publick
Matters, not for Want of Judgment, but to
avoid Popularity. He had a due Regard to the
Grandeur of the City, but no Defire to fhare
in the tranfitory Dignities belonging to it; his
vigorous maintaining his Rights never ran coun-
ter to the Court's Intereft; but if ever they in-
terfer'd, he rejoic'd at the Expedient that preferved both. No Party could claim him for their
own. Providence rewarded his Pains with a
vaft Increafe; yet was he not more eminent for
his Wealth, than his Goodnefs; nor happier in
his

his Poffeffions than his Contentment.

The Comforts he enjoy'd in a Wife were no finall Addition to his Happinefs. She was one of the younger Iffues of a Coronet, whofe Portion confifted of more intrinfic Virtue than Sterling Specie; but, being a Stranger in the cuftomary Ambition of a vain-glorious Appearance, fhe confin'd her Expectations to the Limits of a decent Moderation, and thereby prov'd a better Fortune than many others with a larger Dowry. She was train'd up in a Court Education, retaining the graceful Carriage of a Woman of Quality, without any Tincture of the Pride and Vanity that is generally infufed by it. She chang'd her Station without altering her Principles, and the aukward Formalities of her new Affociates no more corrupted her native Noblenefs, than the Levity of the old ones had tainted her Solidity. She became an Ornament to the City, and her bright Example fo influenced the unpolifh'd Beholders, that they quickly turn'd their wonted Stiffnefs into unaffected Gentility, which introduced a Reformation among her Acquaintance, in Spite of Nature, and Defiance of Cuftom. She kept an admirable Medium in her Behaviour, demonftrating an inviolable Modefty without a precife Refervednefs, and could be vivacioufly facetious, without any Symptom of Coquetry. She knew as well how to be filent, as when 'twas convenient to fpeak; and tho' fhe employ'd more Time in Books of Devotion, than on Pieces of Poetry, and was much better read in the Precepts of Religion, than the Flights of Romances; yet her agreeable Converfation gave evident Tokens of her Wit, but not the leaft Sign of her being a Bigot. The Failings of her Sex were Subjects that afforded her no Diverfi-

on;

on; she, contrary to modern Practice, took more Pains to stifle the Report of a Miscarriage, than others to proclaim it. Her honest Love to her Husband made the Duties of a Wife not only easy but pleasant; and tho' *Sarah* like, she rever'd him as her Lord, and paid a perfect Obedience to his unlimited Will, yet her prudent Conduct so wrought upon her excellent Temper, that she became his Partner in Authority. She was neither arrogant nor servile, but always esteem'd it more commendable to prevail by persuasive Reason than domineering Compulsion. Her Counsel often guided his Actions, and Success generally attended the Harmony of their Judgments. He experienc'd her faithful Breast to be a safe Repository for his Secrets, and cou'd confidently trust his most important Affairs in that sacred Asylum. In all Occurrences he observ'd an equal Fidelity, so that they both were as void of Fear as free from Reserve to each other. Her obliging Complaisance added to his Happiness, and her indulgent Treatment alleviated the Misfortune of an adverse Turn. She was as delightfully pleasant in her Youth, as venerably grave in her Age; yet neither wanton in the one, nor peevish in the other. In a Word, the whole Course of their Lives gave a Proof, that Piety and Discretion were the most necessary Qualifications to render this Life happy, tho' too soon, alas! are they convinc'd, that there is no Stability in Enjoyments here; the Remembrance of all their past Beatitude being suspended by their present Affliction.

But to return.—According to Appointment, I went to my Friend's House, which discovered one of the most melancholy Scenes I had a long while met with. After we had waited
above

above an Hour beyond the ufual Time of dining, our young Gentleman came in without
any Apology for his Rudenefs, in giving a
whole Family the Pain of Attendance: And,
as foon as we had din'd, he was *fans ceremo-
nie* making his Exit, when his Father rather in-
treated, than commanded him to ftay; and tho'
he did not refufe to comply, yet he could not
conceal his Reluctance.----Set over a Bottle of
Burgundy, we began to talk of Things indifferent, and foreign to the main Bufinefs; but his
Father came quickly to the Point, repeating a-
gain what he told me before, and putting a
Reftraint upon his natural Tendernefs, he acted
a real Paffion to the Life.

" My Patience, *Philaretus*, (faid he) is now
" worn out, and I am refolv'd to bear no lon-
" ger with him. In vain have I tried all the
" moft probable Ways to prevent his Deftruc-
" tion, and I will not rack my Brains for new
" Inventions. His refty Heart will neither be
" conquer'd by Violence, nor won by Gentle-
" nefs. I will not be beggar'd while I live,
" nor leave the Fruits of my Labours to be
" fquander'd away upon Debauchery after my
" Death; but for the future fhall indulge the
" Demands of my own Fancy, without con-
" fulting the Price of the Purchafe. I'll make
" an Alms-houfe my Heir, and a Parifh my Ex-
" ecutor. He has his Eftate in his Pocket: I'll
" not give him another Doit, were it to procure
" him a Reprieve. I have empty'd his Mo-
" ther's Exchequer, fo that what fhe before
" granted by Conftraint, fhe muft now deny
" thro' Neceffity. He fhall not harbour here:
" I'll fhut him out of my Mind and Houfe at
" once. What he has, his Harlot and he will

" quickly

" quickly confume; but the Highway is a fub-
" ftantial Banker, and always pays Bills upon
" Sight. If an unlucky Hue and Cry trip up
" his Heels, and throw him into *Newgate*, he
" will not lodge there long, before he'll be
" conducted to the glorious Tripos; from
" whence, after a whining Tone, and a fhort
" Speech, he heroically leaves this World, and
" fwings into the next, having his Name im-
" mortaliz'd by his Fellow Mifcreants, for
" the meritorious Villany of dying hard."

Here I perceiv'd Nature had almoft got the
upper Hand of Art; but as he never ftood in
more Need of Courage, fo he never fooner re-
gain'd it. The Force of a firm Refolution refifted the Attacks of Humanity; yet I could not
without Wonder obferve, that the Countenance
of the harden'd Profligate was fteel'd with a
furly Refentment, without the leaft Appearance
of a penitent Compunction.

" It is (anfwer'd I) a common Misfortune,
" that the Generality of Youth are poffeffed
" with a perverfe Incredulity, that they will not
" take the moft folid Truth upon Truft from
" their Elders, without the Conviction of a dear
" bought Experience, but rather entertain a Pre-
" judice againft all Advice, and are thereby
" prompted to conclude, that a Perfuafion from
" the Follies and Vices their Years are liable to
" hath more ill Nature than Reafon in it, and
" that it is an unjuft Severity to debar them
" from enjoying thofe Pleafures they fee before
" them. The virtuous Reftrictions of Parents
" are look'd on as infupportable Hardfhips,
" and imagin'd to proceed only from an un-
" reafonable Defire, that their Children fhould
" in the Spring of their Days conform them-
" felves

" felves to thofe Aufterities, which their Age-
" has obliged them to comply with, not thro'
" Choice but Neceffity. Converfation with o-
" thers of the fame Principles confirms the em-
" braced Opinion, and Example encourages
" their corrupt Inclinations to an obftinate Dif-
" obedience. Having by thefe Means, tho' per-
" haps with fome Strugglings at firft, broke
" thro' the Bounds of their Duty, they arrive by
" Degrees to an Excefs of Impiety; for Cuf-
" tom naturally begets Habit, and a Perfeve-
" rance in Wickednefs an irreclaimable Obdu-
" racy. Hence chiefly are we furnifhed with fo
.** many difmal Inftances of lamentable Cata-
" ftrophes, which always bring up the Rear of
" a vicious Courfe. Many have too late lamen-
" ted their Neglect of that pious Counfel they
" defpifed when given: But the happy few,
" who pay an obfervant Allegiance to pa-
" ternal Admonition, or, with the Gofpel
" Prodigal, return betimes from their diffolute
" Excurfions, feel the bleffed Effects of it in
" the happy Confequences.
" I hope, that either Report has been too bu-
" fy with the young Gentleman's Failings, or,
" that your own Averfion to Vice, and ardent
" Zeal for his Welfare, make you mifconftrue
" fome of his youthful Levities into more than
" flight Mifcarriages. Your Anger, however
" warrantable it may feem at prefent, I fhall ra-
" ther feek to abate by proper Means, than turn
" into Fury by the Oppofition of Perfuafion:
" And, fince you have difcarded him for appre-
" hended Faults, I fhall, with a true Regard to
" both, endeavour a Reconciliation: But if my
" narroweft Infpection, and moft diligent En-
" quiry, will not allow me to undeceive you,
" I

" I intend not to part with him, till he's quali-
" fied for your Favour by a true Repentance,
" and thorough Reformation."

This positive Resolve was much more terrible to the Son than his Father's rigid Treatment, and it was no hard Task to read the Perplexity of his Mind in the Variety of his Looks.
The Restraint he expected from me appear'd as
dreadful as to be immur'd, and, had not his pro-
jected Brain supplied him with Hopes, by contriving a Way for his Escape, he could never
have so much as bore the Thoughts on't.

It was not long before I took my Leave, and
by the Help of an Hack, my new Charge and
I got quickly to my Lodging: But, as the Coach
turned the Corner of the Street where I lived,
he seem'd very much surpriz'd, and his Amazement increased all the rest of the Way, till we
stopp'd at the Door directed to. I led him to
the Apartment *Tarquinius* had lately quitted; and,
without any Return to the Civilities I paid him,
he hastens to the Window, standing there for a
while, as if he had been fixed to the Place. I
spoke to him several Times, but his Confusion
had stopp'd his Ears. He would now and then
take a disorder'd Turn about the Room, but
soon retir'd to his Post again. Tho' it was e-
vident something particular drew him to the
Sash so constantly; yet could I not, by the stric-
test Observation, discern what it was that had
that attractive Faculty. In one of his Intervals
I took Occasion to ask him how he lik'd the
Lodgings? when pulling out his Watch, he answer'd me 'twas past six. My Landlord coming up to salute his new Guest, paid Abundance
of Compliments, without Notice taken of any
of 'em; the over Ceremoniousness of the one,
and

and the Unconcernedneſs of the other, afforded
a Scene I could not forbear ſmiling at. He had
all this while (*inter alia*) been plotting a De-
vice for his Enlargement, and made the ſpecious
Pretence of earneſt Buſineſs the Means to affect
it, binding many Promiſes, with as many Oaths,
to aſſure me of his ſpeedy Return. I alledged
the Engagement I had laid upon my ſelf hinder-
ed my Conſent; but, if his Affairs were ſo very preſſing, I would bear him Company; that
I found was what he neither expected nor deſired, and his weak Evaſions made it plain, that
he could eaſier diſpenſe with Omiſſion, than admit me a Witneſs. My Refuſal gave him the
Spleen till Bedtime, maugre all my Efforts to
divert his Humour.

The firſt Week I made but a ſmall Progreſs:
For, his Thoughts being fill'd with Variety of
Reflections, and ruffled by different Paſſions, his
Spirits were in a continual Flutter. He was
ſometimes all Flaſh, another while perfectly ſtu-
pid, one Minute chagrin, the next outragious.
Shame, Anger, Hope, Fear, and a Multitude of
&c.'s kept their Revels in his Breaſt, ſo that
it was no eaſy Matter to govern his unſteady
Will, and ſtop its running into Extreams. As
Occaſion required, I ſometimes reproved, ſometimes encouraged him, being altogether as cautious of chilling his Warmth, as encreaſing his
Flame. When I exclaimed againſt his Enormi-
ties, he audaciouſly juſtiſied his Actions. If I
touch'd upon his Extravagance, he averr'd, Avarice was much more unpardonable, the firſt being a Generoſity of Soul, the ſecond a baſe and
grovelling Sordidneſs; and that retrenching the
one was adhering to the other in equal Proportion,
denying the Poſſibility of a Mean between either.

2　　　　　To

To what I called profuse Gaming, he gave the Title of genteel Diverfion; where he had (he faid) as fair a Chance to improve, as impair his Fortune: And therefore it did not deferve the Cenfure I had beftowed upon it. Unneceffary Oaths he counted as trifling Sins, but allowed 'em the grand *Embellifhments of Difcourfe, and the moft glorious Ornaments of modern Eloquence.* The fcandalous Practice of midnight Exploits he put in the Lifts of youthful Frolics, which tend only to the Advancement of Mirth, and declared that the Statutes ought to be burnt which coupled a Punifhment to them. He affirm'd exceffive drinking merited a Place in the Catalogue of heroic Exercifes, and that to pafs a Glafs, argu'd no lefs Cowardice than to put up an Affront. To baulk a Bumper to his Miftrefs's Health, he deemed as difhonourable as to refufe fighting for her. He heard me relate his Father's Threats of Difinheritance with as little Concern as *Æfop*'s Ideot, who cared for nothing, and was no more fhock'd at the Denouncements of future Vengeance, than *David*'s Fool the Atheift. When I tax'd him with the Folly of keeping a *perfidious Dalilah*; he deny'd the Fact, but, infatuated with the meretricious Artifices of his charming *Maggy*, launched out into all the Extravagancies of an hyperbolical Defcription. He painted her as the *Nonpareil* of the whole Tribe. — " She has " (faid he) a moft exquifite Beauty, curious " Shape, quick Wit, and fweet Temper. Her " Carriage is pleafantly free, but never nau- " feoufly loofe, keeping Boldnefs and Coynefs at " a due Diftance, fo that the one may not cloy, " nor the other ftarve the Appetite. She is at " all Times ready to oblige, and as eafy to be " pleafed.

" pleafed. She is loving to Excefs, and con-
" ftant to a Miracle. Her endearing Careffes
" fhew all the Tokens of an hearty Sincerity,
" without the leaft Mixture of a crafty Diffi-
" mulation, and fhe is doatingly fond, but not
" fubtilly fawning. She deferves the *Indies*,
" but is content with Trifles, and defires to be
" decent, but affects not to be gaudy. She ut-
" ters her Farewel with an Excefs of Sorrow;
" but falutes my Arrival with a tranfitory Joy.
" She droops in my lamented Abfence, under a
" languid Penfivenefs, which finds no Intermif-
" fion till my wifh'd Return brings the reviving
" Reftorative. She as cheerfully as induftri-
" oufly ftudies a Conformity with my prefent
" Humour; and therefore neither by a lafcivious
" Wantonnefs excites me againft my Will; nor
" by an icy Coldnefs damps the Warmth of
" my Inclinations. Force made a Conqueft over
" her Perfon, but not her Heart; and the infulting
" Ravifher, who plunder'd her Innocence, was
" ftab'd with her Hate: He bore away the
" Booty of her Virginity, but left the more va-
" luable Trophies of her Affection to adorn
" my Triumphs. In fhort, the known Lofs of
" her Virtue is the only Stain fhe wears; but
" that Defect is fupplied by her being Miftrefs
" of every other commendable Quality the Sex
" can boaft of. However odious Scandal may
" make her in the Eyes of thofe Pretenders
" to Honour and Confcience, who are, in Re-
" ality, beholden to a frigid Conftitution, ill
" Nature, or Pride, for the Prefervation of their
" Chaftity, and value themfelves for this fingle
" Grace, when they are deftitute of all the reft;
" as alfo of thofe, whofe obfcene Thoughts
" and

" and secret Wishes are no less criminal than
" the Act it self, which their outward Hypo-
" crisy conceals under the Covert of a formal
" Modesty, and demure Air; and likewise of
" the numberless Multitudes of private Sinners,
" who pass in the World for publick Saints,
" only because their Caution, or Luck, has con-
" fin'd their Crimes to the Corner they were
" committed in, and so owe their undeserved
" Repute to them alone; yet is she worthy to
" be exempted from all those opprobrious Epi-
" thets, so justly applicable to notorious Strum-
" pets. And tho' it may be allowed many
" Women can upbraid her Conduct and For-
" tune, in being so exposed; yet it is as true
" as severe, that there are but few who can
" condemn her, without the Repulse of a self
" Conviction in Will or Deed. I heartily con-
" dole the Uneasiness she has long undergone
" for my sake; for she has lived like a Recluse
" ever since my being here. Her Bed and her
" Closet have been the only Confidants of her
" mournful Lamentations; for tho' she lives in
" the opposite House, yet has not all my Vigi-
" lance been rewarded with the Glympse of
" her."

I eagerly snatched at the Discovery, which
at once informed me of what I so earnestly desired to know, and was likely to prove in a
great Measure instrumental to the effecting my
Designs; but it was yet too early to put them
in Practice.

Coming one Morning into his Chamber, before he was stirring, he received me more re-
spectfully than he had hitherto done, and I joyfully discerned an unusual Sedateness in his
Mind.

Mind. His Reafon began to gain Ground, and his Underftanding to recover its true Tafte. Morality was now no longer naufeous, nor Advice infipid. He could hear with Patience, and anfwer with Prudence; *As the Brute wither'd, the Man flourifh'd, and the Libertine gave way to the Chriftian.* He entertained new Sentiments of his Vanities. His Father's Frowns, and a future Vengeance had their proper Influence; by the one he believ'd the Calamities of this Life, by the other the Miferies of the next. His *Maggy's* Allurements held him fafter than all the reft of his Vices put toghether: The barb'd Temptation ftuck in his Breaft, and it required more Policy than Violence to difentangle him. The falfe Opinion he entertained of her was the greateft Bar to his Converfion; which, there was no Likelihood of removing, unlefs the Cheat could be laid open. I prevailed on him to make trial of her Sincerity; and he was the eafier induced to it by an Affurance, the Experiment would redound to my Difadvantage, and invalidate my ftrongeft Arguments: He forthwith arofe, and, as agreed on, wrote the following Letter.

My Dear Maggy,

I Think it very fevere an exceffive Love fhould meet with any Interruption: But a Father's Power over-rules a Choice, which fhould otherwife give you a Proof, that the moft important Bufinefs fhould not keep me from you. The unwelcome Occafion will detain me a Fortnight longer; during wnich tedious fpace, I fhall feel the Pains of your Impatience in my own

Agonies. It will be the higheſt Happineſs when my Tongue, inſtead of my Pen, can aſſure you that

I am, Deareſt,

Moſt faithfully Yours.

T. RICHBOTTOM.

The Billet was carefully conveyed to the Doxy, who not long after appeared at her Window, attired in a neat looſe Morning-Dreſs, put on with an artful Negligence. A blue Damask-Gown cover'd moſt Parts of her Body; but was purpoſely left ſo open before, that it neither hid her Breaſts, nor a good Part of the fine lac'd Shift ſhe had on. *Italy*, *Spain*, and *Portugal* contributed their Products to lend her a quotidian Face; and ſhe as skillfully diſpoſed her Colours in the framing a counterfeit Beauty, as a Painter could his on the Canvaſs, to bring a Lady to a good liking of her own Complexion. The Gaiety of her Mien ſhew'd not the leaſt Symptom of a melancholy Mind. When ſhe had wantonly look'd out a while, ſhe thruſt an End of one of the Curtains thro' the open Saſh, which waved in the Street like a *Flag on the Topmaſt of an Admiral.* It ſeemed indeed like an Accident; but the Conſequence confirm'd it a *Signal.* Anxious Expectation made her reſtleſs, and for ſeveral Times ſhe frisked backward and forward, like a Kitten after a Feather. ——But at length a certain Animal came in View; who, no ſooner ſpy'd the Token, than he flew to the Door, his rolling Eyes being buſy on the Scout, to learn if he were

taken

taken Notice of. Being quickly admitted we observed their Meeting to confist of so many mutual Embraces and Kisses, as testify'd him neither a Stranger nor unwelcome. These ardent Caresses continued an unreasonable Time, till I was as much tired, as my Pupil tortured at the Sight. They seated themselves close together; and *Ezekiel* the Foot-Boy, *Jane* and *Lucy* the Maid Servants, entered the Room with a familiar Obeysance to receive their several Instructions. The Fop drew out a Purse from his Fob; but Madam *Magdalene* claiming a Right to the Disposal of its Contents snatched it from him; and gave what was sufficient to provide the intended Treat, reserving a Parcel in her Hand, which a few inveigling Smiles excused the Return of. Miss taking the Hint from some intelligible Leers nimbly skips from her Gallant, who as hastily pursues her to the *cubicular Elysium*, where the Cloud of a Partition obstructed our farther View: But Jealousy, and his own former Practice, enabled young *Richbottom* to give a very narrow Guess into all the Transactions of their Retirement, which lasted some Hours. About five the libidinous Pair returned from Love's Altars; but in such a Dishabillee, as made it no Difficulty to imagine what sort of Devotions they had been paying. The Cully with his Coat unbutton'd, his Stockings ungarter'd, and a Night-cap on his Head: The Punk with her Gown wrapt about her; which, opening by Chance, as she stept along, left nothing but a rumpled Smock to shroud her infectious Carcass: Her Patches were lost, her Varnish sullied, her Headclothes loose, and her Hair about her Ears; all which made her Figure more loathsome than tempting: In this

Pickle

Pickle they placed themſelves at a Table ſpread
with a luxurious Regale, wherewith they were
to reimburſe Nature her Expences, whoſe Treaſure had been exhauſted by their late Profuſion.
A ſmutty Jeſt paſſed inſtead of a Grace, and they
fell to without any other Ceremony than ſome
wanton Geſtures. Obſcene Healths were alternately toaſted; and, as they laugh'd, the Wenches
ſneer'd, and the Boy grinn'd. ---- (Such Free-
doms muſt be diſpenſed with : For an awful
Reverence is not to be expected from ſordid
Minds; which, being privy to the Failures of
their Superiors, ſet a Value upon themſelves
for their Secrecy.) Refreſhed with their Viands,
and fluſhed with their Wine, they waſted the
Remainder of the Day in frolicſome Sports and
wanton Dalliances, till the duſky Twilight,
which favoured the Sparks going out, put a Fi-
nis to the filthy Farce.

How mortifying a Proſpect this muſt be to
young *Richbottom*, may be eaſily gueſſed by
thoſe who have been in the ſame Circumſtances. I was not diſpleaſed with his Reſentment,
which I carefully improved with ſuitable Ag-
gravations; and left him in ſuch a Diſpoſition
of Mind, as allowed me ſome Hopes, the Occurrences of this Day would largely. contribute
to my Wiſhes : --- But a few Hours gave an unexpected turn, and blaſted my blooming Glad-
neſs; for, by the next Day, his Anger abated,
and his partial Fancy ſo miſguided his Judgment, that he rather excuſed than blamed her:
The evident Conviction of her Falſhood he accounted for by a favourable Interpretation; and
tho' he could not give his Eyes the Lie, yet he
blinded his Senſe, and impoſed upon his Reaſon by
pleading in her Defence; urging, that her Yeſter-
day's

day's Digreſſion might proceed from the Neceſſity of a former Correſpondence, and the binding Obligations annext to it, tho' contrary to a
free Choice or real Inclination ; and that her
Complaiſance was conſtrained, and her Ardor
counterfeit. His erroneous Notions infuſed a
Faith in him, that the firſt Opportunity he had
to tax her with her Inconſtancy, ſhe would confeſs the Truth, lament the Cauſe, and atone for
the Crime with a Deluge of Tears. I reproved
his credulous Folly, and pitied his Deluſion,
not doubting but a Succeſſion of freſh Proofs
would confirm the old.

As ſoon as he was up, we placed ourſelves
as we had done the Day before ; and in leſs
Time than would have tired the Patience of a
longing Woman, we obſerved truſty *Ezekiel*
enter the Houſe, who was immediately followed
by a Couple of elderly Ladies, not deſpicably
mean in their Habit ; but ſo particularly attired,
that their Appearance was diſagreeably remarkable. Sixteen and ſixty were induſtriouſly blend-
ed together ; but thro' a natural Antipathy, they
would not be incorporated. Lean Cheeks and
wrinkled Foreheads receive no Advantage from
diminutive *French* Heads, which covering only
the Crown, expoſe to view more Hair than
Face. A Maſk of white and red no more ſup-
plies the Want of Teeth, than a flaunting Breaſt-
knot adorns the wither'd Skin of a tan-leather'd
Neck. It is to be ſuppoſed, they rather con-
ſulted their Purſes than the Seaſon, when the
one had a velvet Scarf over a crimſon Sattin
Gown, and the other a cloth Cloak, and in the
Height of Summer. *Lucy* introduced them to
her Miſtreſs, who received them with Extaſy,
and had Rapture in Return, which laſted till the

Brandy-

Brandy-Bottle interrupted. After two or three hearty Glaſſes apiece, they began a clamorous Chat, followed by an obſtreperous Laughter, ſo that they alarmed the Neighbourhood a good Way round. But *Nantz* getting Poſſeſſion of their Noddles, *Jane* helped the two Aunts into the Coach, and *Lucy* led her Miſtreſs to her Chamber. Recovered a little by a Nap, ſhe equipt her ſelf, and went abroad, and we heard no more of her till paſt Twelve that Night, when the Street was all in an Uproar, occaſion'd by a Coachman quarrelling with her Ladyſhip about his Fare; he laſh'd her with Bear-garden, ſhe maul'd him with Billingſgate; he would have out-curſed her, but ſhe damn'd faſteſt. From Words they fell to Blows, he kick'd, ſhe ſcratch'd, ſhe threatened him with an Action and a Priſon, he her with a Warrant, and a ducking Stool; Dog, Bitch, Whore, and Rogue. were often exchanged between them; he ſtorm'd, ſhe rav'd, he ſtutter'd, ſhe hiccupt; he ſpit in her Face, and ſhe ſpewed in his; but the Watch came at laſt and parted the Fray.

For two Days ſhe buried her ſelf in Obſcurity, but whether Shame or Indiſpoſition kept her from appearing, I cannot determine. The third ſhe came to Light again, when we ſaw her in the Afternoon ſtepping into a Chair, compleatly ſet out in her beſt Array; we could not by any Means find what Intrigue was now in Hand, which put Mr. *Richbottom* in a melancholy Mood. The Spur is often as uſeful as the Curb; and Diverſions are not only ſometimes allowable but neceſſary. The preſent Depreſſion of his Spirits required a Re-elevation, I therefore popoſed going with him to the Play, to which he conſented with a dull Indifference.

We

We got into the Pit the Beginning of the third
Mufic; and, as we were taking a tranfient Sur-
vey of the Audience, we efpy'd *Maggy* in the
Stage-Box deeply engaged with a Gentleman,
whofe Garb befpoke him a *Mars*, but his Countenance declared him an *Adonis*; a Compact of
Contradictions, a martial Outfide, and a femi-
nine Soul. Her Familiarity betokened either an
intimate Acquaintance, or a brazen Affurance,
and fhe was too intent on her Affair to lend
her Eyes a caft towards us. My rafh Youngfter
would fain have confronted her, but I prevented
him, and undifcover'd withdrew to another Seat,
where we could fee them with Eafe, and yet
not be eafily feen ourfelves. The feveral Paffages during the Play were fuch, as increafed
his Difguft, and fir'd his Refentment. We drove
directly home, but heard no Tidings of our
Ephefian Matron till ten the next Morning;
when, being at the old Stand, we faw her come
in: She ran up Stairs; her Maids after her, to
whom, with wringing Hands, fhe told a moft
deplorable Tale: Her Headclothes were torn
to Tatters; off fhe flung them in a Fury, and
fome of her Hair followed. Her Gown and
Petticoat were in fuch a wretched Condition,
that fhe looked as if fhe had been rolled in a
Kennel, and afterwards wafhed in Claret; and
there was no Part of her Rigging but what had
received fome Damage. *Lucy* fawningly be-
wailed the Difafter; but *Jenny*, unable to curb
an unlucky Smile, kifs'd her Ladifhip's Hand
fomewhat harder than fhe defired. Lamenting
and fcolding divided a Breath. She howled like
a Widow before Company, and over-acted all
the Parts of a frantic Paffion: She made a Foot-
ball of her Tea-Table, and trampled its Appur-

2   tenances

tenances to Atoms. She viewed herself in her Looking-Glass, and revengefully dashed it to Pieces for impartially reprefenting her hideous Phiz. ——

Evils commonly go by Pairs; before her late Misfortune, and the Addition her own Folly had made to it were well over, and a little forgot she falls under another. Scarce had she shifted her Cloaths, and got the Room to Rights, when one, that Mr. *Richbottom* knew, came to the Door, and demanded a speedy Admittance by a thundering Knock. Fear jostled out Sorrow, and she dreaded nothing more than him who it really was. The Man you must know was by Nature a Mongril, the illegitimate Spawn of an Efcutcheon and a Kitchen Wench; who, as he came into the World by Chance, was maintained in it by Fortune, and being neglected in his Youth, was good for nothing in his Manhood. Idlenefs had gained an abfolute Dominion over him, and enervated his active Faculties. He esteemed himfelf as much above, as he was really unfit for Bufinefs; and tho' he fcorned to work, yet he would not starve. His Perfon was very paffable, bearing a good Face, and clean Limbs. From a truanting Scholar he became a Tavern-Drawer, where Affability and Neatnefs got him Encouragement, and his Vails purchafed him Raiment. He was as compleat a Pimp, as a Celler-man, and knew as well how to rank an Intrigue, as range a Vault: A rotten Carcafs and stummed Wine were forted together for his niggardly Cuftomers; but found Flefh and all neat were referved for his beft Benefactors. A Set of new Faces yielded him a new Suit, and he picked a Diamond-Ring out of a Maidenhead. He kept

a Lift

a Lift would vie Numbers with the Mufter-
Rolls of a Regiment, and was as expert in the
Knowledge of their Quarters, as a thorough-
paced Corporal. He took Tythe in Kind from
his favourite Sheets, but the reft paid their Poun-
dage in Specie: When the tedious Time of his
Apprenticefhip was expir'd he wrote himfelf
Man; and tho' he had not a Stock to make
himfelf a Mafter, yet could he not fubmit to
continue a Servant. He quitted his Trade to
follow a Calling; and became a *Broker upon
Love's Exchange*, where he had *Commiffions from
Traders* of all Degrees, and free Accefs where-
ever he came. He might be covered before a
Garter, fhake Hands with a Judge, take the
Wall of a City Chain, and joftle a Common-
Council-Man without any Offence. A young
enter'd Bubble adored him, and a ftaunch Sportf-
man would embrace him; a Knight of the Shire
paid him Refpect, and a Country Gentleman
did him Reverence. He kept the long Robe at
a Diftance, and had the Caffock at his Back.
Young Heirs, Apprentices, and marry'd Men,
paid double; one Moiety for Procuration, and
the other for Secrecy. Every male Correfpondent was his Banker, and he went fnacks with
the Women. The Multitude of Dribblets wife-
ly manag'd would have grown to Wealth; but
he had the Proverb on his Side; for his daily
Expences declared him one of thofe who could
not be accufed of taking care for the Morrow;
fo that, notwithftanding his frequent Supplies,
he remained as miferably indigent, as defervedly
defpicable. What he got from many he confumed
on one: They lived upon each other by Turns;
and being void of Forecaft, they feafted one
Day, and fafted another. Sometimes their
Dreffes

Dreſſes rivalled Quality, another while they
were levelled with the Black Guard. The Tally-
man and Pawn-broker divided the beſt Part of
their Subſtance: What they took up at 60 l. *per
Cent.* above common Price, they pledged at
30 l. *per Cent.* Extortion to pay for. A good
Booty procured a Redemption; but a ſmall
Stop put 'em under the Ticket. A lucky Hit
prevented his Thought; but Neceſſity awakened
his Invention. He was eaſy with his Clients in
Plenty; but Poverty made the Rogue unmerciful. He had a great many of both Sexes in his
Power, whoſe Imprudence had given him the
Diſpoſal of their Fates, and brought 'em under
an Obligation of furniſhing his Wants. A kept
Miſtreſs, that had proved unfaithful, tho' by his
own Inſtigation, durſt not deny his Demands.
Amongſt theſe he often took his Rounds, and
would not return empty: The Failure of one
made the next fare the worſe. He would threaten
a Diſcovery to frighten 'em into a Compliance,
but was alway wiſer than to make it; foreſee-
ing, that would not only ſpoil his Buſineſs, by
bringing a Scandal on the Profeſſion, but would
alſo put the caſt-off Wenches out of a Capacity for the future; and therefore he choſe rather
to exerciſe his Authority on their Perſons by a
Baſtinado, than run the Hazard of a double De-
triment. He had the Impudence to ask high,
but the Meanneſs to accept a Trifle; he would
boldly inſiſt on a Guinea, and as tacitly ſneak
off with a Shilling. One of theſe Extremities
was, it ſeems, the Occaſion of his preſent Viſit
to *Maggy*; who, knowing his Errand, would
willingly have ſaved her Bones by Apologies
and Promiſes; but his Affairs were too urgent
to diſpenſe with a Denial: He knew Mr. *Rich-
bottum*'s

bottom's bountiful Allowance yielded a good
Fleece, and all her Arguments were too weak
to bear down his. In fine, he made her feel,
as well as hear his Refentment, and he left her
Body in as much Pain as her Mind: She wore
the Marks of his Tyranny all over her; and *the
Effects of his Anger were vifible in her Eyes.*

Her being really unfit to be feen kept her
out of our Sight fo long, that we gave over our
conftant Attendance, and diverted ourfelves
abroad fome Days together; till coming home
one Evening very dark, but not very late, we
perceived a Couple before us ftriking up an
amorous Bargain; but we could eafier hear their
Difcourfe, than difcern their Perfons. Mr. *Richbottom* whifper'd me, it was his *Maggy*'s Voice,
and perfuaded me to accompany him in the
Purfuit of this Adventure. We followed 'em
at a proper Diftance to an Hedge-Tavern, and
had the Fortune to be fhewn into a Room next
'em. I gave him the Liberty of making the
beft Improvement he could of this Accident;
and Convenience ufual in fuch Places let him
into the Sight of a lewder Scene than he had
ever been Actor in. Her Mate was the Beau's
Footman I not long ago mentioned; and the
Rewards of her Favour to him were only his
Promifes of preferving his Mafter's Efteem for
her, and ufing his good Offices to continue the
Correfpondence. He could not learn from her
Manner of Behaviour, that fhe made any Diftinction between a Livery and Embroidery, but
that fhe expreffed as much Love to the Lacquey,
as fhe did to the Mafter; and was as obliging in
an eleemofinary Embrace, as in the Enjoyment
of himfelf, on whom was her chief Dependance.
He found, that this Meeting had been before
agreed

agreed on, and heard 'em make another Appointment.

This laſt Confirmation gave the finiſhing Stroke to his Conviction, and turn'd his paſſionate Love into a downright Loathing. He witneſſed the beaſtly Action with an umoved Temper, and ſedately teſtified a ſettled Hate. Her Ingratitude and Baſeneſs conſpired to eſtabliſh his Averſion, and Memory aſſiſted to compleat it, by bringing to his View many paſt Paſſages; and, tho' they had carried ſuſpicious Symptoms, yet her cajoling Art had hood-wink'd his Senſes, and ſtifled his Jealouſy in Embryo. How probable ſoever her Laſpes appeared by the Evidence of corroborating Circumſtances, the Want of full Proof was her double Advantage, in giving her Cunning an Opportunity to juſtifie her pretended Innocence, and upbraid his tim'rous Surmiſes. Upon the firſt Intimation of his Doubts ſhe would craftily fathom the Depth of his Penetration, and with inſinuating Stratagems learn, whether he built his Accuſations upon the firm Foundation of a poſitive Aſſurance, or only the ſandy Bottom of chimerical Conjectures, labouring under the Pain of Anxiety, till his unwary Tongue had declared his Thoughts without Reſerve. When ſhe joyfully found the Extent of his Miſtruſt to fall ſhort of the Truth, and not reach the Fact, ſhe rouſes her Rage, puts on a haughty Air, and covers her Guilt by triumphing over his Weakneſs. Anon the unfortunate Creature weeps moſt bitterly, as if her Grief were inconſoleable; but if her Policy exceeded not her Sorrow, ſhe might eaſily paſs by the Injury with dry Eyes. His moſt earneſt Entreaties, patient Perſuaſions, and ſubmiſſive Acknowledgments, join'd with reiterated Promiſes

of

of a generous Confidence in her for the future, avail not toward a Reconciliation, till his Purſe or a Preſent ſue out a Pardon, which quickly reduces the good natur'd Thing to her wonted Kindneſs, and turns her from a Tyrant to a Sycophant. Theſe, and other Reflections, together with what himſelf had beheld in this Fortnight's Probation, wrought a perfect Cure on him. He was now ſenſible, that all her ſeeming Kindneſs was mere Hypocriſy, and that ſhe had no more Honour than Virtue, nor Affection than Grace. Her Diſguiſes became tranſparent, and he could read the Deformities of her filthy Soul thro' the deceitful Veil, and perceive the Treachery of her Heart, tho' ſhrouded with bewitching Looks. Her Inſults have loſt their Terror, and her Allurements their Charms; he can ſmile at the one, and deſpiſe the other. In a Word, he look'd upon her as a Compound of Luſt and Perfidy, whoſe Careſſes were artful, and *Tranſports a Trade*, and his Cheeks wore the Badges of a relenting Shame for being ſo long impoſed upon by one all over Counterfeit, and whoſe Mind was no more real than her Face.

I deſign'd to let a few Days paſs before I would mention his Return to his Father, that I might obſerve if he continued in the ſame remorſeful Frame of Mind, and to give him ſuch Advice, as might confirm his Penitence: But his own eager Deſires outran my Intentions; for with all the Tokens of an hearty Contrition he entreated me to intercede with his juſtly provoked Parents to forgive his paſt and hated Faults, and that he would hope for their Favour upon no other Terms than the Merits of his future Obedience; and, that he might have no Occaſion to truſt himſelf in her enticing

Company, after he had quitted my Protection, he concluded it proper first to get what should be thought convenient out of the House, as the Plate, Jewels, and some Part of the Furniture, and dispose of them as I should direct, designing to leave her some Necessaries for her Use; for tho' she deserved not any Thing from his Hands; yet, for his own Reputation, he would not quite strip her. To set the better Face on this Contrivance, he proposed to give a Judgment, under Pretence of Debt, to any one I should chuse. I approved of the Method, and we went immediately to a fit Person, as faithful as able to perform it. The Instrument was soon prepar'd, sign'd, seal'd, and deliver'd, and as speedily enter'd up, and was to be executed the next Day at an appointed-hour. It was agreed he should be there before-hand, he being willing to hear what a forged Account she would give of herself, and the Excuses she would make for her late Transactions, and prevent the concealing of any Thing that was to be taken away. All the Particulars relating to the Affair were punctually managed, and a lasting Separation followed: But I must not omit the Dialogue which past between them, it being very material to the only Aim I have.

I must inform you, that, when the Time limited in his Letter before mentioned was expired, we perceived a new Turn in the House, every one in it was prepared for his coming, all Things were put in exact Order, and the Servants busy in their several Stations. Expectation appeared in their Looks, and *Madam* set out her self in the attractive Air of a languishing Countenance, and clean Dress. A little more white than usual, suited her Face to
the

the Part she was to act. Mr. *Richbottom*, armed against her Wiles, took a Turn, and went to her with a Deceit equal to her own, and after the dissembling Raptures of both were over, she accosted him as follows.

Maggy. " If I should tell you how over-
" joyed I am to see you, it would be more
" than you deserve, who tho' you know what
" a Torment your Absence is, could stay so
" long from me. I have fretted and fasted my
" self to nothing. Those that are ignorant of
" the Matter, tell me, I am going into a Con-
" sumption. I have been a Stranger to a com-
" fortable Minute, or a Night's Sleep, since I
" saw you. I'm so alter'd, I don't look like
" the same Person I was.---I cannot bear this
" Life.---Neither Father nor Business ought to
" make you neglect me, but you are glad of
" any Pretence. 'Tis an unfortunate Thing to
" love so ungrateful a Man to the Excess that
" I do; yet you won't believe me, if you did,
" you would not serve me thus. You often say
" kind Things indeed, but your Actions don't
" agree with your Words. You are sensible
" soft Expressions please me, and therefore vent
" them for your own sake, that I may be in
" an Humour to pleasure you in every Thing :
" But when you are gone, you hardly think of
" me, till your Fancy prompts you to come
" again. I sometimes imagine what you say is
" real, but you give me so many Occasions to
" believe the contrary, that I as often call my
" self Fool for my Credulity. You cannot
" think what I suffered till I heard from you.
" A thousand Fears possessed me.---One while
" I was apprehensive you were sick, and thought
" it very hard I could not see you. Alas ! (said I

" to

" to my felf) he has no Body at home to nurfe
" him with that Care and Tendernefs I would.
" Then the many Accidents that happen, made
" me fearful another while, that you were
" dead; but I refolved to follow you as foon
" as I fhould hear it. Then the Inconftancy of
" you Men gave me a Conceit you had chofen
" a new Favourite, and I underwent all the
" racking Tortures of Jealoufy. Thefe and many
" more Diftractions were my only Companions.
" I told you at firft what an uneafy Creature I
" fhould be when once I fet my Heart on you,
" and fure you might have found fome Way
" or other to have fhortened my Pain. Had
" you not one Hour to fpare? No Contrivance
" in you! Had I been in your Place, I would
" have invented fome Way or other to have
" regained your Quiet. No Neceffity you can
" urge is fufficient to excufe you. You are not
" a Boy, tho' you are content to be made one.
" I wonder when you intend to take the Privi-
" lege of your Years, and free your felf from
" your Father's Fetters. Sure it is reafonable
" now you fhould be Mafter of your own
" Time and Fortune, and not cringe for every
" Penny, and afk Leave for an Holiday?
" But your Sheepifhnefs, forfooth, has not the
" Courage to encounter that imaginary Giant,
" called Duty. When you are to go abroad with
" him, you fhould tell him you are engaged to meet
" Company, and muft not difappoint them. If he
" orders you Bufinefs, you muft excufe your felf
" from doing it, by pretending greater of your
" own. If he would have you ftay at home,
" be fure to go abroad. Grumble at his fhort
" Allowance; and, if he refufes to add to it,
" get to his Cafh, and be your own Carver.
" He

" He is but a Tenant for Life, and it is but
" making ufe of your own a little fooner than
" foolifh Cuftom allows. Was you pin'd in
" your Chair? or tied with a Thread to the
" Bed-poft, that you could neither come nor
" fend for above a Week together? But why
" do I ask that Queftion? the very Letter it
" felf fhews it was your want of Will.---On-
" ly two or three Lines—fhort and fweet.---You
" thought you muft fay fomething, but did not
" care how little. It difpleafed me almoft as
" much as it fatisfied me, and, tho' it drove
" away my firft Perplexities, it gave me new
" Difturbances.---I wifh I knew what you have
" been doing all this while, it may be purfuing
" Matrimony, and courting that delightful *Blow-*
" *zabella* your wife Father has pointed out for
" you; if fo, tell me, that I may wean my felf
" from you before that unhappy Day; for I re-
" folve to have no more to fay to you, when
" it comes to that. You perfuade me, he has
" left you to your own Choice; if fhe be the
" Perfon, take her.---I acknowledge my own
" Folly in entertaining other Thoughts."

Her ready Tears knew their Cue, and ftopp'd
her Tongue to utter their own prevailing Eloquence: But the Language of either fo little affected him now, that he had much ado to cover
his Compofure with a Mask of Concern. His Eyes
were no lefs intent than his Ears, and he obferved all the fideward fleering Glances that attended her colloguing Periods. He was not very forward in replying, neither did fhe grant
him any more Time than while fhe could dab
up the few Drops fhe had let fall, and pocket
her Snivel, before fhe thus began again.

N 3 *Maggy.*

Maggy. "Sure, I'm the moſt unhappy Wretch
" that breathes; I have not only been tormented
" for want of you, but have had an hundred
" other Vexations at home. You know what
" a ſmall Pittance you left me, but I might
" live on the Air for you: I have been plagu'd
" with Tax-Books, and twenty ſmall Duns,
" which I could not pay, but I hope you in-
" tend to diſcharge them now, and not let me
" be teaz'd in this Manner. I am contented
" with what no Body would, and yet you grudge
" me mere Neceſſaries. You think every Thing
" too much for me, and yet pretend to love
" me. I dare not tell you what has happen'd,
" becauſe your miſtruſtful Head is apt to make
" wrong Conſtructions of Miſchances. Poor
" *Lucy* is out of her Wits, and won't come
" in your Sight. The heedleſs Thing cleaning
" the dining Room, left open the Saſh, and
" the Wind being very high, blew down my
" Picture that hung over the Tea-Table, and
" has broke every Thing that was upon it
" to Pieces; G—d knows, I rally'd her ſound-
" ly for it in my Paſſion;--But 'tis over now.
" She offered to pay for her Folly; but I think
" that too hard. She has cry'd her ſelf ſick;
" be good natur'd for once, and ſay nothing
" of it.---*Tommy*, the Squirrel has gnawed both
" the Toes of my beſt Shoes, ſo that I can't
" dreſs me till I get another Pair; but take your
" own Time, I an't in haſte. I'd never wear
" my Cloaths, if it were not your Deſire I
" ſhould. You ſay you love to ſee me fine,
" and that makes me put them on ſometimes:
" But truly mine have ſeen their beſt Days, and
" are known every where. I begin to be out
" of Love with them: But if you'll give me
                                    " another

" another Suit, thofe fhall be new dy'd and
" made up, and they'll ferve well enough for
" common Dreffing. You promifed me fuch
" a Brocade as my Lady *M*——— has; I like
" it becaufe you do, and expect you fhould be
" as good as your Word, to make me amends
" for all that I have endured for you. Nay,
" *Bruty*, don't finile; that fha'n't do Mun;—or
" are you plotting to fend it me unawares, as
" you did the Silver Tankard in a Basket of
" Walnuts;—well, do if you will, 'tis very
" pleafant to be agreeably furpriz'd. But I have
" more ill News to tell you, rummaging my
" Clofet, I fet the Bandbox, wherein was my
" new Mechlin Head upon a Chair, and that
" plaguy little Devil *Cupid* muzzled open the
" Lid, got it out, and in an Inftant tore it to
" Bits; I paid the Rogue heartily, and, had he not
" been your Darling, I'd have hang'd him for't.
" Another Day hearing fome Body knock at
" the Door, I thought it had been you, and,
" running in Hafte from my dreffing Table,
" the Sleeve of my Gown catch'd Hold of the
" Looking-glafs, flung it down, and broke it.
" All thefe unlucky Mifhaps made me mad,
" not fo much for the Damage, as the Appre-
" henfion my ill-boding Mind fram'd of the
" prophetic Omens. New Fears about you
" were ever before me; but now that I fee
" you well, I am fatisfied, if I'm to be the Ob-
" ject of their evil Portents. I can meet the
" worft Fate with Pleafure, if you are exemp-
" ted. Why does my dear Soul fhake his Head,
" and look as if he gave no Credit to what I
" faid?

Richbottom. " Dear *Maggy*, you confound me;
" your prefent apparent Sincerity fo contradicts
                                        " the

" the Information I have had of you, that I know
" not what to think. The Relation ſtruck me
" with Amazement, and it exceeds my Belief,
" that ſo much Vileneſs ſhould be gilded with
" ſo becoming a Sweetneſs. I came with a
" Reſolution to upbraid you, and take my fi-
" nal Leave: But your artleſs Behaviour ſo
" clearly demonſtrates your Innocence, that it
" would be the higheſt Injuſtice not to believe
" you. I was told, that ſoon after you receiv-
" ed my Letter, a Gentleman was ſeen to
" come to you, and ſtay'd here all Day, which
" gave Grounds for Malice to ſuſpect the
" worſt, and that Account was aggravated with
" ſpiteful Comments ; but your candid Decla-
" ration will ſet me right, and confirm me in
" the Notion I have already entertain'd of ſome
" underhand Dealing betwixt us.

Maggy. " This is ſome Body that ill-natur'd
" Fellow your Father has employ'd to make
" a Difference between us; an Engine of his.
" If you are to be catch'd by that Trick, fare-
" well all my future Joy, and welcome the worſt
" of Miſery. You'll be perpetually alarm'd in
" this Manner, if you don't put a Stop to't at
" once. But I forſee your natural Jealouſy,
" which you pretend proceeds from the Vio-
" lence of your Affection, will one Day be
" impoſed on to my undeſerved Ruin. If your
" Love was real, you would never have ſuch
" mean Thoughts of me, as to imagine, that
" I could counterfeit my Paſſion towards you,
" or prove falſe to the only Man on Earth I
" doat on. I ſhan't deny the Truth—there was
" a Gentleman here, and one whom, were it
" not for your ſake, I could be very happy
" with. He dearly lov'd me many Years ago,
" and

" and would fain have married me, but I cou'd
" not like him. He went out of *England* to
" cure the Wounds of my Difdain, and is but
" juft returned. He found me out, and came
" to fee me; and, tho' he has heard the Mif-
" fortunes that have befall'n me, continues in
" the fame Mind ftill. You could have had no
" Reafon to apprehend any harm from him, if
" you had been here; and you do him a great
" deal of Injury to doubt his Honefty: He has
" a truer Value for me; but I defired him to
" defift from any fuch Defign, and he promifed
" me he would never more attempt it; and
" refolves to be gone again in a little Time.
" —Muft I be branded for this? You are cruel
" to accufe me; I have no other Fault, than
" that of loving you too well: You may blame
" me for it indeed; but I never expect you'll
" be convinced, till you find the fatal Effect of
" your Unkindnefs, and then it will be too
" late for me to reap the Joys of your Acknow-
" ledgment.

Richbottom. " Nay, now you diftract me:
" I both believe, and forgive you; but I muft
" blame one Mifcarriage, and am heartily vex'd,
" you made me and yourfelf fo public, by
" coming home at Midnight difguifed in Drink,
" and fo clamoroufly contending with a faucy
" Coachman: Your Indifcretion is in every
" one's Mouth; and ill Nature is not want-
" ing to augment it with ridiculous Circum-
" ftances.

Maggy. " Ay! I would you had been here,
" if you had not ftuck the Dog, I'd ne-
" ver have feen your Face again. You muft
" know, that, in the Morning, my two Widow

" Aunts

" Aunts were here; I gave 'em a Dram or
" two, and they would force me to drink a
" Cup with 'em. My weak Head was over-
" turned with it; and after a little Sleep, maud-
" lin as I was, I went to Mrs. *Swill-belch* our
" trufty Hoftefs. The honeft Man and good
" Woman were heartily glad to fee me, and
" made me welcome with a little Sneaker of
" Punch, and an Hot-Pot : We drank your
" Health, and talk'd of you till it was late : Then
" I took Coach home, and the Fellow, who was
" more fenfible of my failing, than I was my
" felf, took the Advantage, and offered to be
" rude; but I refifted the Rafcal; and he, in
" Revenge, exacted upon me more than was
" his due; and that with what had pafs'd before
" fo provoked me, that being a little elevated, I
" loft the Ufe of my Reafon, and am very for-
" ry upon your Account for what happened;
" but indeed, Deary, I'll do fo no more.

Richbottom. But, pray *Maggy*, how came you
at the Play with a Colonel, and to ftay out all
Night?

Maggy. " Good lack-a-day! Do you know
" that too! ——I find I have been narrowly
" watch'd; but I'm glad of it, that you may be
" fatisfy'd I don't tell you a Lie. I'll tell you
" how 'twas. I had fat moping fo long at
" home, that even the poor Wenches below in
" Pity perfuaded me to divert myfelf a little a-
" broad : I took their Advice, and went to my Sif-
" ter *Freelove*'s ; and while I was there who fhould
" happen to come in but Mr. *Greenwit*, who
" it feems courts her, and brought the Colonel
" along with him. She treated 'em with Tea;
" and at laft, they agreed to go to the Play.
" The

" The Colonel asked me; but I refufed. Lord!
" He was a naufeous homely Thing. My Sifter
" would make me bear her Company; and
" finding it in vain to deny 'em, I went: But
" I'm fure I was fo dull all the while, they
" wondered what was the Matter with me.
" The Colonel was very civil, and try'd all he
" could to give my Humour a Turn; but my
" Melancholy conftrued his Courtefy into Im-
" pertinence. My Thoughts were fo much
" another way, that I declare I don't remem-
" ber a Word of the Play. When 'twas done,
" we all returned to my Sifter's; I would have
" gone home, but they would not let me; and
" Mr. *Greenwit* provided an handfome Supper,
" which kept us very late; but I continuing as
" I was, firft one teaz'd me, then another, to
" know what I ailed; and tho' I fpoil'd Com-
" pany, they would not part with me; fo my
" Sifter engaged me to ftay with her all Night.
" Now I warrant this Accident has been made
" black enough to you, and fill'd your Head
" with fine Imaginations. If I muft neither
" ftir abroad, nor fpeak to any body, but you'll
" prefently judge harfhly of me, you'll make
" your own Life very unhappy, and mine no
" lefs miferable.

Richbottom. " There was nothing in this but
" what may be allow'd of, tho' it was other-
" wife reprefented to me: But as to your being
" the other Night at a Tavern with a Footman,
" how will you excufe that? Deny it I'm fure
" you cannot!

Maggy. " L—d! you're a ftrange Man. Well!
" I'll tell you all, if you'll give me Leave;
" —But you have no Patience. --- I never faw
" any

I

" any body of your Temper in my Life.—D'ye
" think there was any harm in meeting a Rela-
" tion? He is a-a-a Half-Brother of mine; I
" never intended you should have known any
" thing of him, because he wears a Livery. But
" 'tis his own Fault, he might have done better
" if he wou'd: My Father provided very well
" for him; but his own Folly and good Nature
" have reduced him to what he is. He serves
" a Country Gentleman, and does the Business
" of a Steward there. He is in very great Fa-
" vour with his Master, and will quickly be in
" a better Station : He came to Town last
" Week, and sent me a Letter. He wanted to
" see me, but would not come to my House
" for fear of disgracing me. I took his Mo-
" desty very kindly, and appointed to meet him
" that Night, as I thought, unknown to any
" Body; but I find I am mistaken: Perhaps, I
" may never see him again, so that need not
" trouble you. Have you done now : I pro-
" mise you I'll never do any thing to disoblige
" you: Let me have your Company, I desire
" no ones else ; I'll do all I can to please you.
" Come, my dearest Life, lets forget all that's
" past, and be more Friends than ever. This
" Kiss and you know what shall cancel all
" Animosities, and renew our lasting Loves.

My young Man was put to his Neck Verse,
when my Friend and *R* —'s, at the Head of a
Crew of Mirmidons, came to his Assistance,
seiz'd him, and ransacked the House. They gave
him Leave to detect the Falsity of her evasive
Account, whereby she was sensible he knew
the whole Truth of her Proceedings; and then
hurried him away leaving her in a Confusion

not

not eaſy to be apprehended, and much harder
to be deſcribed.

I lodg'd the Moveables in ſafe Hands, diſ-
charged the ſeveral Agents, and regained my
Convert. My next Day's Buſineſs was to carry the happy Tidings to the deſponding Parents,
whoſe hovering Doubts oppoſed their ready Belief : But my ſolemn Affirmation of the welcome Truth, in a while, met with Credit, and
revived their drooping Hopes. I requeſted an
Interview, and an indulgent Reception; both
were promiſed. His firſt Approaches were attended with profound Submiſſion; proſtrating
himſelf at their Feet, he moſt preſſingly implo-
red their gracious Pardon. His penitential Flood
was ſeconded by a Shower, their Joys had gather'd. Their compaſſionate Hearts directed their
willing Hands at once to raiſe him from the
humble Floor, and bleſs him with an affectio-
nate Embrace, which gave him an Earneſt of
their ſucceeding Forgiveneſs. The Sight was as
delightfully pleaſant, as movingly tragical. The
Son abjured his Crimes, and the Parents buried
'em in Oblivion. In a Word, his after Life
made amends for his former, and turn'd their
direful Misfortune into a real Comfort. His
Duty was his Delight, and to pleaſe his Parents
his greateſt Pleaſure. He conform'd himſelf
wholly to their Wills, and cheerfully ſubmitted
to their Directions. His filial Obedience was
rewarded with a fatherly Benediction; and he
reaped the double Felicity of their Joy, and his
own Tranquillity. He marry'd, not only with
their Conſent, but by their Appointment; and
experienced, that the Promiſes of a kind Father
were inviolably ſacred. His Wife tranſcended

in

in Virtue, and abounded with Love : *She be-*
came like a fruitful Vine upon the Walls of his
House, and his Children like flourishing Olive
Branches surrounded his glad Father's Table. He
proved as good an Husband, as he was a Son,
and nothing was wanting to compleat a Family's Happiness.

The State of Learning
in the
Empire of Lilliput

Anonymous

Bibliographical note:

This facsimile has been made from a copy in the
Beinecke Library of Yale University
(IK B838 727)

An ACCOUNT of the

State of Learning

IN THE

Empire of *Lilliput*.

Together with

The HISTORY and CHARACTER of *BULLUM* the Emperor's Library-Keeper.

Faithfully *Tranfcribed out of*
Captain LEMUEL GULLIVER's
General Defcription of the Empire of Lilliput, *mention'd in the* 69th *Page of the Firft Volume of his Travels.*

LONDON:
Printed for J. ROBERTS in *Warwick-Lane.*
M DCC XXVIII.

An ACCOUNT of the
State of Learning
IN THE
Empire of *Lilliput*.

Price Six-Pence.

An Account of the

State of Learning

IN THE

Empire of *Lilliput*.

 S I always had a
ftrong Inclination
to Reading, from
the Time I firft
went to *Emanuel-*
College in *Cambridge*, and had
gone through the moft valuable
ancient

ancient Writers; during my ftay in *Lilliput*, I was very inquifitive about the ftate of Learning in that Nation, and received the following Information upon that Subject.

In former Ages, the Government of the Ifland *Blefufcu* was, in many refpects, like what we call a Commonwealth, and for a long time flourifhed both in Arms and Learning, whilft the *Lilliputians* were a barbarous People; at this Time many excellent Books were wrote in Oratory, Poetry, Hiftory, and Philofophy, but the *Blefufcudians* having at length loft their Liberties and Form of Government,

ment, which was changed into
an Empire, Learning decay'd a-
mongft them very faft ; the
fafter by reafon of hot Difputes which arofe concerning
the proper manner of Dreffing
and Eating Eggs ; and in thefe
the whole Studies of all the
Learned Men of that Age were
confumed.

THE firft Emperor of *Blefufcu*, that he might ingratiate
himfelf with his People, whom
he had enflaved, undertook an
Expedition againft the Ifland of
Lilliput ; which being then governed by feveral petty Kings,
ignorant of the Arts of War,
was, by Degrees, fubdued to the
Em-

Empire of *Blefufcu.* During
this Intercourfe between the two
Nations, the *Blefufcudian* Language was very much changed,
by the mixture of the *Lilliputian* ; and thofe Authors who
wrote in the old Language were
neglected, and underftood by
very few.

IN procefs of Time the *Lilliputians* grew weary of Subjection, flung off the Foreign
Yoke, fet up an Emperor of
their own with great Succefs,
and ever fince have been a di-
ftinct Empire from that of
Blefufcu.

As

As they were an Ingenious People, and bleſſed with a Race of good Emperors, they ſoon excelled their Neighbours in Learning and Arms; they got together all the old *Blefuſcudian* Books, their Emperor founded a *Gomflaſtru*, or Seminary, with different Schools, to inſtruct their Youth in the old *Blefuſ-cudian* Language and Learning; and from thence choſe their *Nardacs*, *Glumglums*, and *Hurgos*, and the Emperors had them-ſelves a large Collection of theſe Books in a Library belong-ing to the Palace.

Thus the *Lilliputians* flou-riſhed in Politeneſs and Litera-

B   ture,

ture, for some Ages ; till at
length, by the Plenty of a long
Peace, they also grew Corrupt,
gave themselves up to Idleness,
Luxury, and Intriguing, and
fell into Controversies about
breaking their Eggs ; the old
Blefuscudian Books were laid
aside, and nothing regarded but
Eggs and Politicks. The *Gom-*
flastru indeed continued, each
School had its *Mulro*, or Governour and Scholars ; but the
taste of the Age being changed,
they only turned over the old
Authors to amuse themselves,
and enjoy'd the moderate Revenues bequeathed to them by former Emperors. The present
Emperor indeed had endeavour'd
to

to bring them into Efteem again, he encreafed their Poffeffions, and gave a Noble Prefent of Books to the *Gomflaftru*; but having a debauched inconftant People to rule over, and being kept in continual Alarms of Wars by his Neighbours, he had not leifure to perfect his good Intentions.

I was at this Time in his Favour, and when He heard that I had been inquifitive about thefe Affairs, He very gracioufly defired me to look into his Library, and fent Orders to the Keeper of it to ufe me with great Refpect, and to prefent me with Five Hun-

dred

dred Books, fuch as I fhould choofe.

ACCORDINGLY, upon a Day appointed, I went to the Library, which I took a view of in the fame manner as I had done of the reft of the Palace, by lying down and looking in at the Window : The Building was ruinous, the Infide dufty, the Books many in Number, but fcattered about in great Diforder ; the Library-Keeper, whofe Name is BULLUM, was alone ftalking amidft the Rubbifh. As foon as he faw my Face at the Window, he made his beft Bow, and began his Speech to me, which, as I was afterwards informed, he had

taken

taken a great deal of Pains about, knowing me, to be in the Emperor's good Graces. Moft part of what he fpoke was ünintelligible to me, by a ridiculous Mixture of the old *Blefufcudian* Language : And what I did underftand was fulfome Flattery, and Complements that nothing mortal could deferve.

THIS was very dull Entertainment to a Man of my Modefty, and thereupon finding his Speech would be long, and that he was forced to ftrain his Voice to make me hear at that diftance ; I thought it would be a kindnefs to us both

to

to put a ſtop to him, which
I did, returning him Thanks,
in few Words, for his great
Opinion of me, and deſired to
ſee him the next Day, that I
might chooſe out the Five Hundred Books which the Emperor
had given me,

Bullum, as I heard after-
wards, was in great Wrath,
and loaded me with many opprobrious Names, for refuſing
to hear his Speech out, and
daring to treat a Man of his
Learning with ſo little reſpect.
However, he ſtifled his Reſentment a little for the preſent,
and came to me at the Time
appointed.

I D E-

I DESIRED him to ſhew
me a Catalogue of the Books,
and to give me ſome Account
of what they treated of, that
I might be able to make a
Choice. He replied, That he
had not troubled himſelf to
bring a written Catalogue, but
that he had one in his Memory,
and immediately he repeated to
me the Titles of a vaſt Number of old *Blefuſcudian* Books,
and run on with a great flu-
ency of Speech, till he was out
of Breath.

IT was a Pain to me to forbear Laughing, to hear BULLUM
ſputter out ſo much Jargon ;
at

at laſt I told him, That I was
not in the leaſt wiſer for what
he had ſaid, becauſe I underſtood not a Syllable of the Language he ſpoke. At that, as
he ſtood on the Table before
me, he put out his Under-Lip,
and ſtaring me full in the Face,
ſaid, with a great deal of Contempt, *Not underſtand* Blefuſcudian ! *What do you underſtand?*

I WAS a little Diſcompoſed
at this Treatment ; but not
knowing then what Intereſt he
had at Court, I reſolved to uſe
him Civilly ; and replied, That
I underſtood eight or nine Languages, if there was any Merit
in that ; but that none of the
Books

Books i n his Library would be of any Ufe to me, that were not written in *Lilliputian*. *Lil-liputian!* fays he, *I cannot re-peat the Titles of many of them, but I will fend you Five Hun-dred in a few Days* : And thus he left me.

I was very impatient to re-ceive this curious Prefent ; but BULLUM broke his Word ; for about this Time my Intereft at Court began to decline. I could not prevail upon him to deliver the Books to me : At laft, after much Importunity, he came to me himfelf, atten-ded by a Servant, with only Five Books.

C   I WAS

I WAS ſurprized at this, and
aſked if the reſt were upon the
Road : He anſwer'd, That ſince
he had ſeen me laſt, he had
ſpent ſome Days in carefully
peruſing the Emperor's Orders;
that he had diſcovered the
Word *Hundred* to be an In-
terpolation ; and that the true
Reading was *Five* Books, which,
in Obedience to the Emperor,
he had brought me.

I HAD indeed been put off
ſo long, that I ſuſpected I
ſhould have had none, and
therefore agreed to have the
Five Books, deſigning to have
made my Complaint afterwards,
but

but B ULLUM had another
Trick to play me. It was the
Cuftom, he faid, for all Strangers to make him a Com-
plement in Writing, which he
defired me to comply with, and
then he would deliver the Books
to me. He had brought the
Form, which I was to tranfcribe
and fign with my own Name.
The Words were thefe :

    " Be it known to all Men,
" That B ULLUM the Great
" Library-Keeper to the Empe-
" ror of *Lilliput*, and *Mulro*
" in the *Gomflaftru*, is a Man
" of vaft Erudition and Learn-
" ing; all Parts of the World
" ring with his Praifes; and
        C 2   " whilft

" whilſt **I** was honoured with
" his Acquaintance, he uſed me
" with ſingular Humanity.

Quinbus Fleſtrin.

O u t of an earneſt Deſire
to get Poſſeſſion of the Books,
I ſubmitted even to this Demand
of B u l l u m, who then ordering
them to be flung down before
me, turned nimbly upon his
Heel and left me. He had
picked out for me the Five
worſt Books in the Library,
according to his Judgment; but
when I came to peruſe them
with a Microſcope, (the biggeſt
being a Folio about half an Inch
long) I found they were very
Curious

Curious in their kind, but treating of Subjects that B U L L U M was not converfant in. There was,

1. A Collection of Poetry.

2. An Effay on Humility; neceffary for all *Lilliputians*, who are very much inclined to think well of themfelves, and meanly of others.

3. A Differtation upon *Tramecfans* and *Slamecfans*, or High-heel'd and Low-heel'd Shoes.

4. A Bundle of Controverfies concerning the primitive way of breaking Eggs.

5. The *Blundecral*, or *Alcoran*.

THESE

THESE Books I brought fafe with me to *England*, and defign either to publifh them, or elfe to prefent them to the Univerfity which I had once the Honour to be a Member of.

BUT to return to BULLUM. I was amazed at his Behaviour towards me, efpecially confidering I was a *Nardac*, to which Title he generally paid a profound Refpect. This made me defirous of getting an Account of his Hiftory and Character, which, having fomething extraordinary in them, I fhall lay before my Reader.

BUL,

BULLUM is a tall raw-bon'd
Man, I believe near six Inches
and an half high; from his In-
fancy he apply'd himself, with
great Induſtry, to the old *Blefuſcudian* Language, in which he
made ſuch a Progreſs, that he
almoſt forgot his native *Lilliputian*; and at this Time he can
neither write nor ſpeak two
Sentences, without a Mixture of
old *Blefuſcudian* : Theſe Qualifications, joined to an undaun-
ted forward Spirit, and a few
good Friends, prevail'd with the
Emperor's Grandfather to make
him Keeper of his Library, and
a *Mulro* in the *Gomflaſtru* ; tho'
moſt Men thought him fitter to
be

be one of the Royal Guards.
These Places soon helped him
to Riches, and upon the Strength
of them he soon began to de-
spise every Body, and to be de-
spised by every Body. This engaged him in many Quarrels,
which he managed in a very odd
manner ; whenever he thought
himself affronted, he immediately
flung a great Book at his Adversary, and, if he could, fell'd
him to the Earth ; but if his
Adversary stood his Ground and
flung another Book at him,
which was sometimes done with
great Violence, then he complain'd to the Grand Justiciary,
that these Affronts were designed
to the Emperor, and that he was
singled

fingled out only as being the
Emperor's Servant. By this
Trick he got that Great Officer
to favour him, which made his
Enemies Cautious, and him In-
folent.

BULLUM attended the Court
fome Years, but could not get
into an higher Poft; for though
he conftantly wore the Heels of
his Shoes High or Low, as the
Fafhion was, yet having a long
Back and a ftiff Neck, he never
could, with any dexterity, creep
under the Stick, which the Emperor or the Chief Minifter held.
As to his dancing on the Rope,
I fhall fpeak of it prefently;
but the greateft Skill at that

D   Art

Art will not procure a Man a
Place at Court, without fome
Agility at the Stick.

BULLUM, vexed at thefe
Difappointments, withdrew from
Court, and only appeared there
upon extraordinary Occafions, at
other Times he retired to his
Poft of *Mulro* in the *Gomflatu*,
there he led a gloomy folitary
Life, heaped up Wealth, and
pored upon the old *Blefufcudian* Books. It might have been
expected, that from fo long an
Acquaintance with thofe admirable Writers, he fhould have
grown more Polite and Humane;
but his Manner was never to
regard the Sence or Subject of
the

the Author, but only the Shape of the Letters, in which he arrived to fuch Perfection, that, as I have been affured, he could tell, very near, in what Year of the *Blefufcudian* Commonwealth any Book was written ; and to this, and to reftoring the old Characters that were effaced, all his Labour was confined.

Upon thefe Points he had wrote feveral Books, fome in the *Blefufcudian,* and fome in the mixed Language ; and whenever he had finifhed a Book, he prefented it to fome Great Man at Court, with a Panegyrical Oration ; fo contrived that
it

it would fit any Man in a great
Post ; and the higheft Bidder
had it.

Whilst I was in *Lilliput*,
he propofed to publifh a new
Blundecral of *Alcoran* ; and, that
he might do fomething uncommon, he began at the End, and
defigned to have wrote backwards ; but the *Lilliputians*,
fome liking the old *Blundecral*,
others not caring for any, gave
him no encouragement ; and
therefore he defifted from that
Project.

As this Nation was very
much divided about breaking
their Eggs, which they generally

rally eat in Publick once a Day, or at leaft once in Seven Days, I defired to know how B u L- L u M behaved himfelf in this Particular ; and was told, That he was thought to have an Averfion to Eggs, for he was never feen to eat any in Publick, but once or twice in a Year, when his Poft obliged him to it : At thofe Times he gave Orders to have them ferved up to him ready Dreffed, and the Shells and Whites being care- fully taken off, he gulped up the Yolks in a very indecent manner, and immediately drank a Bumper of ftrong Liquor after them, to wafh the Tafte out

of

of his Mouth, and promote the
Digeſtion of them.

WHEN any one repreſented
to him the ill Example of this
Practice, his Anſwer was, That
his Modeſty would not let him
devour Eggs in Publick, when
he had ſo many Eyes upon
him ; That he was not yet determined at which End he ought
to break them ; That the Shells
and Whites were inſipid, and only
fit for Children : But for the
Eggs themſelves, he was ſo far
from hating them, that he had
a Diſh at his own Table every
Day. But whether this was
Truth, or if they were at
his Table, whether he eat of
them

them or not, I could never learn.

BULLUM was always of an haughty Mind, and, in his own School, took a great deal of Pleasure in mimicking the Actions of the Emperor. Thus, he got a little Stick and used to divert himself in seeing his Scholars leap over, and creep under it, as he held it between his Hands. Those who performed best, were rewarded, sometimes, with a pompous Title in the old *Blefuscudian* Language, signifying, MOST LEARNED, MOST FAMOUS, MOST ACCOMPLISHED YOUTH, or the like : Sometimes with little

little Sugar-Plums ; and sometimes only with the Promise of
them.

In dancing on the Ropes
he took great delight himself ;
and this was the only Bodily
Exercise he used. Those who
had been Eye-witnesses, informed me, that he could cut a
Caper very high, but that he
did it in a clumsy manner,
and with little delight to the
Spectators, who were in continual apprehensions of his falling, which sometimes he did
very dangerously.

It was observed, that he
danced best in his own House,
but

but that he never danced before the *Gomflaftru* with Succefs. When he firft came to
his Place of *Mulro*, he did
nothing but Dance and cut
Capers on the Ropes, for a
Year together : As this was
a new Sport in that Part of
the Ifland, he got a great deal
of Money by it ; but ftriving
to leap higher than ordinary,
he fell off from the Rope,
broke his Head, and difordered
his Brain fo much, that moft
People thought it would inca-
pacitate him for his Poft of
Mulro : However, at length,
he pretty well recovered; he
himfelf fays, he is as well,
or better, than he was before

E   his

his Fall : But his Enemies think his Brain is ftill affected by it.

SOME Years after, the prefent Emperor, in a Progrefs through his Dominions, came to the *Gomflaftru* ; and BULLUM, without being afked, was refolved to divert His Majefty with his Performance on the Strait-Rope ; up he mounts, and Capers bravely, for fome time ; at laft, endeavouring to fhew the utmoft of his Skill, in the midft of an high Caper, he reached out his Right-Hand too far, which gave him a terrible Fall.

MOST

MOST People imputed it to his Over-reaching himſelf; but he laid the Fault partly upon the Robes he was obliged to wear before the Emperour, which, as he ſaid, entangled his Feet; and partly upon the malicioufneſs of a Bye-ſtander, whom he accuſed of pulling the Rope aſide, as he was in the midſt of his Caper: However that was, poor BULLUM broke his Leg, and was carried to his own Houſe, where he continued Lame above Two Years, not being able to ſhew himſelf in Publick all that Time; and it was thought he would never have recovered, if the

E 2   Em-

Emperor at laſt, had not taken
pity on him, and ſent one of
his own Surgeons to him, who
cured him immediately.

AFTER all theſe Misfor-
tunes BULLUM could not for-
ſake his beloved Diverſion, but
as ſoon as he was recovered,
he forgot all that was paſt,
and danced again in his own
School every Day; where, by
his frequent Falls he ſo bruiſed
himſelf, that it was believed
they would come to a Mor-
tification : Beſides, he dances
ſo long upon the ſame Rope,
that through Age and Rotten-
neſs, and his great Weight, it
muſt break at laſt ; and the
Em-

Emperor would fcarce lend him
a Surgeon a fecond Time; which
indeed would be in vain, for
he can never leave off the
Sport, though he performs worfe
and worfe every Day; fo that,
in all probability, he will break
his Neck for a Conclufion.

F I N I S.

A Voyage To Cacklogallinia

by

Captain Samuel Brunt

Bibliographical note:

This facsimile has been made from a copy in the Beinecke Library of Yale University

A

VOYAGE

TO

Cacklogallinia:

With a Defcription of the

RELIGION, POLICY, CUSTOMS and MANNERS, of that COUNTRY.

By Captain SAMUEL BRUNT.

LONDON:

Printed by J. WATSON in *Black-Fryers*, and
fold by the Bookfellers of *London* and *Weft-
minfter.* 1727.

[Price Sticht, Two Shillings and Sixpence.]

A

VOYAGE

TO

Cacklogallinia, &c.

NOTHING is more com-
mon than a Traveller's
beginning the Account
of his Voyages with one
of his own Family; in
which, if he can't boaſt
Antiquity, he is ſure to
make it up with the Probity of his Anceſtors. As it can no way intereſt my
Reader, I ſhall decline following a Method, which I can't but think ridiculous,
as unneceſſary. I ſhall only ſay, that
by the Death of my Father and Mother,
which happen'd while I was an Infant,
I fell to the Care of my Grandfather by

B   my

my Mother, who was a Citizen of some
Note in *Briſtol*, and at the Age of Thir-
teen ſent me to Sea Prentice to a Maſter
of a Merchant-man.

My two firſt Voyages were to *Jamaica*,
in which nothing remarkable happen'd.
Our third Voyage was to *Guinea* and
Jamaica; we ſlaved, and arrived happily at that Iſland; but it being Time of
War, and our Men fearing they ſhould
be preſs'd (for we were mann'd a-peak)
Twelve, and myſelf, went on Shore a
little to the Eaſtward of *Port Morante*,
deſigning to foot it to *Port Royal*. We
had taken no Arms, ſuſpecting no Danger; but I ſoon found we wanted Precaution: For we were, in leſs than an
Hour after our Landing, encompaſs'd by
about Forty Run-away Negroes, well
arm'd, who, without a Word ſpeaking,
pour'd in upon us a Volley of Shot, which
laid Eight of our Company dead, and
wounded the reſt. I was ſhot thro' the
right Arm.

After this Diſcharge, they ran upon
us with their Axes, and (tho' we cried
for Mercy) cruelly butcher'd my remain-
ing four Companions.

I had ſhared their Fate, had not he
who ſeemed to Head the Party, inter-
poſed between me and the ſatal Axe
already

already lifted for my Deſtruction. He ſeized the deſigned Executioner by the Arm, and ſaid, *No kill te Boy, me ſcavez him; me no have him make deady.* I knew not to what I ſhould attribute this Humanity, and was not leſs ſurprized than pleas'd at my Eſcape.

They ſtruck off the Heads of my Companions, which they carried with 'em to the Mountains, putting me in the Center of the Company.

I march'd very penſively, lamenting the Murder of my Ship-mates, and often wiſh'd the Negro who ſaved me had been leſs charitable; for I began to doubt I was reſerved for future Tortures, and to be made a Spectacle to their Wives and Children; when my Protector coming up to me, ſaid, *No be ſadd*, Sam, *you no ſcavez me?* I look'd earneſtly at the Fellow, and remember'd he was a Slave of a Planter's, a diſtant Relation of mine, who had been a long while ſettled in the Iſland: He had twice before run from his Maſter, and while I was at the Plantation my firſt Voyage, he was brought in, and his Feet ordered to be cut off to the Inſtep (a common Puniſhment inflicted on run-away Slaves) by my Interceſſion this was remitted, and he eſcaped with a Whipping.

I aſk'd

I ask'd if his Name was not *Cuffey*, Mr. *Tenant*'s Negro? *My Name* Cuffey, said he, *me no* * Baccararo *Negro now*; *me Freeman*. *You no let cutty my Foot, so me no let cutty your Head; no be sadd, you have* bumby grande † yam yam.

He endeavour'd to comfort me under my Afflictions in this barbarous Dialect; but I was so possess'd with the Notion of my being reserv'd to be murdered, that I received but little Consolation.

We marched very slowly, both on account of the Heat, and of the Plunder they had got from some Plantations; for every one had his Load of Kidds, Turkies, and other Provisions.

About Three in the Afternoon, we reach'd a Village of run-away Negroes, and we were received by the Inhabitants with all possible Demonstrations of Joy. The Women sung, danc'd, and clapp'd their Hands, and the Men brought *Mobby* (a sort of Drink) and Rum, to welcome the return'd Party. One of the Negro Men ask'd *Cuffey*, why he did not bring my Head, instead of bringing me alive? He gave his Reason, at which he seem'd satisfied, but said it was dan-

* Baccararo, *the Name Negroes give the Whites*.
† Yam yam, *in Negroes Dialect, signifies Victuals*.

gerous

gerous to let a *Baccararo* know their
Retreat; that he would tell Captain
Thomas, and he muſt expeᶜt his Orders
concerning me.

Cuffey ſaid he would go to give Captain *Thomas* an Account of what had
happen'd in this *Sortie*, and would carry
me with him. As they ſpoke in the Negroes *Engliſh*, I underſtood them per-
feᶜtly well. My Friend then went to
Captain *Thomas*, who was the Chief of
all the run-away Blacks, and took me
with him. This Chief of theirs was
about Seventy Five Years old, a hale,
ſtrong, well-proportion'd Man, about
Six Foot Three Inches high; the Wooll
of his Head and his Beard were white
with Age, he ſat upon a little Platform
rais'd about a Foot from the Ground, accompanied by Eight or Ten near his own
Age, ſmoaking Segars, which are Tobacco
Leaves roll'd up hollow.

Cuffey, at his Entrance, threw himſelf
on his Face, and clapp'd his Hands over
his Head; then riſing, he, with a viſible Awe in his Countenance, drew nearer, and addreſs'd the Captain in the
Cholomantæan Language, in which he
gave an Account, as I ſuppoſe, of his
Expedition; for when he had done
ſpeaking, my Comrades Heads were
brought

brought in, and thrown at the Captain's Feet, who returned but a short Anſwer to *Cuffey*, tho' he preſented him with a Segar, made him ſit down, and drank to him in a Calabaſh of Rum.

After this Ceremony, Captain *Thomas* addreſs'd himſelf to me in perfect good *Engliſh*. *Young Man*, ſaid he, *I would have you baniſh all Fear; you are not fallen into the Hands of barbarous Chriſtians, whoſe Practice and Profeſſion are as diſtant as the Country they came from, is from this Iſland, which they have uſurp'd from the original Natives.* Capt. Cuffey's *returning the Service you once did him, by ſaving your Life, which we ſhall not, after the Example of your Country, take in cold Blood, may give you a Specimen of our Morals. We believe in, and fear a God, and whatever you may conclude from the Slaughter of your Companions, yet we are far from thirſting after the Blood of the Whites; and it's Neceſſity alone which obliges us to what bears the Face of Cruelty. Nothing is ſo dear to Man as Liberty, and we have no way of avoiding Slavery, of which our Bodies wear the inhuman Marks, but by a War, in which, if we give no Quarter, the* Engliſh *muſt blame themſelves; ſince even, with a ſhew of Juſtice, they put to the moſt cruel Deaths thoſe among us, who*
have

have the Misfortune to fall into their Hands ; and make that a Crime in us (the Desire of Liberty, I mean) which they look upon as the distinguishing Mark of a great Soul. Your Wound shall be dress'd ; you shall want nothing necessary we have ; and we will see you safe to some Plantation the first Opportunity. All the Return we expect, is, that you will not discover to the Whites our Place of Retreat : I don't exact from you an Oath to keep the Secret ; for who will violate his Word, will not be bound down, by calling God for a Witness. If you betray us, he will punish you ; and the Fear of your being a Villain shall not engage me to put it out of your Power to hurt us, by taking the Life of one to whom any of us has promis'd Security. Go and repose your self, Captain Cuffey *will shew you his House.*

I made an Answer full of Acknowledgments, and *Cuffey* carried me home, where my Hurt, which was a Flesh Wound, was dress'd: He saw me laid on a Matrass, and left me. About Eight, a Negro Wench brought me some Kid very well drest, and leaving me, bid me good Night. Notwithstanding my Hurt, I slept tolerably well, being heartily fatigued with the Day's Walk.

Next Morning, *Cuffey* faw my Wound
dreft by a Negro fent for from another
Village, who had been Slave to a Surgeon feveral Years, and was very expert
in his Bufinefs. The Village where I was
contained about Two and Fifty Houfes,
made of wild Canes and Cabbage Trees;
it was the Refidence of Captain *Thomas*.
Here were all forts of Handicrafts, as,
Joyners, Smiths, Gunfmiths, Taylors, &c.
for in *Jamaica* the Whites teach their
Slaves the Arts they feverally exercife.
The Houfes were furnifhed with all Neceffaries, which they had plundered from
the Plantations; and they had great
Quantities of Corn and Dunghill Fowl.

Captain *Thomas* fometimes fent for
me, and endeavour'd, by his Kindnefs,
to make my Stay among 'em as little
irkfome as poffible. He often entertain'd
me with the Cruelty of the *Englifh* to
their Slaves, and the Injuftice of de-
priving Men of that Liberty they were
born to.

In about a Fortnight, my Wound was
thoroughly cured, and I begg'd of Captain *Thomas* to let me be directed to the
next Plantation. He promis'd I fhou'd,
as foon as he could do it with Safety.
I waited with Patience, for I did not
think it juft he fhould, for my fake, hazard

zard his own, and the Lives of his Followers.

About a Week after this Promife, I reminded him of it, and he told me, that a Party from a Neighbour Village being out, he cou'd not fend me away: For fhou'd thofe Men mifcarry, he might be fufpected of having, by my Means, betray'd 'em to make his own Peace with the Whites; for (faid he) the Treachery our People have obferved among thofe of your Colour, has made 'em extreamly fufpicious. I was obliged to feem contented with his Reafon, and waite the Return of this Party, which in about ten Days after, came back, laden with Provifions, Kitchen Furniture and Bedding; but the moft acceptable part of their Booty, was Two fmall Caggs of Powder, of Eight Pound Weight each, and near Two Hundred of Lead. They alfo brought with 'em the Heads of the Overfeer, and the Diftiller belonging to *Littleton*'s Plantation, both white Men, whom they met feparately in the Woods.

Captain *Thomas* now promis'd me, that the next Day I fhould be guided to *Plantane-Garden-River-Plantation*, which was no fmall Satisfaction to me. I left the Captain at Eleven o' Clock who gave Orders for the entertaining the Party, **and**

and the fpending the Day in Merriment.
About Three, when they were in the
midft of their Jollity, one of the Scouts
brought Word, that he had difcovered a
Party of white Men, who were coming
up the Mountain. The Captain immediately ordered all the Women and Children to a more remote Village, and fent
for the ableft Men from thence, while he
prepared to give the Enemy a warm Reception. Every Man took a Fufil, a Piftol, and an Axe: Ambufcades were laid
in all the Avenues to the Village; he
exhorted his Men to behave themfelves
bravely, there being no way to fave their
Lives, but by expofing them for the common Safety. He told 'em, they had many Advantages; for the Whites did not
fo well, as they, know all the Paffages to
the Mountain; and that they could not,
at moft, march in the wideft, above
Two a-breaft; that the Way was rugged,
troublefome to climb, and expos'd them
to their Fire, while they lay hid in their
Ambufcades he had appointed 'em. *But
(*faid he*) were we to meet 'em upon even
Terms, yet our Circumftances ought to infpire Refolution in the moft fearful: For,
were any among us of fo poor a Spirit, to
prefer Slavery to Death, Experience fhews
us, all Hopes of Life, even on fuch vile
Terms,*

Terms, are entirely vain. It is then cer-
tainly more eligible to die bravely in De-
fence of our Liberty, than to end our Lives
in lingring and exquifite Torments by the
Hands of an Executioner. For my Part,
I am refolved never to fall alive into the
Hands of the Whites, and I think every
one in the fame Circumftances ought to take
the fame Refolution.

After this Exhortation, and the De-
parture of thofe laid in Ambufh, he order'd me to go with the Women, Children, and *Cuffey*, whom he had fent to
head the Men he had commanded from
the other Village. I had not been gone
a Quarter of an Hour, in which time I
was hardly got Half a Mile, before I
heard a very warm Firing. We went
ftill higher up the Mountain, thro' a very difficult Paffage; the Village we were
order'd tò, was about half a League from
that we left, than which it was much
larger, and more populous; for here were
at leaft One Hundred and Twenty Houfes, and as many able Men, with about
four times the Number of Women and
Children.

The Alarm had been given them by
an Exprefs from Captain *Thomas*, and we
met about half way, near Fifty Negroes
arm'd in the manner already mentioned.
They

They were headed by an old Woman, whom they look'd upon a Prophetefs. *Cuffey* recommended me to her Protecti- on, took upon him the Command of the Men, and return'd, after asking this Bel- dame's Blefling, which fhe gave him with Affurance of repelling the Whites.

The Fire all this while was very brisk, and the old Woman faid to me, that fhe faw thofe in Ambufh run away from the Whites, tho' fhe lay with her Face on the Ground. *No matter,* continued fhe, *let the Cowards perifh, the Whites will burn* Cormaco (the Village I came from) *that's all. They come again another Day, then poor Negroes all loft.*

The Shot continued near two Hours, but not with near that Brisknefs it be- gan; and the old Woman rifing, bid me fee the Smoke of *Cormaco. Captain Thomas,* faid fhe, *fend away the white Man.*

I ftaid by my Protectrefs, whom I durft not quit, tho' I did not like her Company. About half an Hour after the Shot began, and continued for near that Space pretty brisk, and then ceas'd. Soon after, we faw a Negro difpatch'd by Captain *Thomas,* who told us the Whites had burnt *Cormaco,* but were gone away, and that Captain *Thomas*
was

was coming. He appeared not long after with *Cuffey*, and about Forty other Negroes. I learn'd from him, that the *English*, by Fault of their Scouts, had seized the Places where he defign'd his Ambufhes, kill'd Part of the Men he had fent, and purfued the reft to the Village, where they defended themfelves, till the Whites had broke thro' the back Part of fome Houfes, and fet Fire to the whole Village; that he then retired with his Men up the Mountains, the Whites following him; but he having the Start, while they were bufied in burning and plundering, he wheel'd round, and came upon their Backs, and from the Woods and Bufhes poured in his Shot; his Men being all well cover'd, the Whites did them no Harm, and thought proper to retire with the Lofs of Six Men, and many wounded, for there were Thirty and a Captain. We have loft, faid he, Twenty Two Men, and our Village is burnt. Soon after, we were join'd by about Forty more Negroes, and we all went to the Village I was order'd to, which they called *Barbafcouta*.

The next Morning, a Council was call'd, which breaking up, four Negroes, who had not behaved well in this laft
Action,

Action, were brought bound, and laid in the largeſt Street upon their Backs; all the Women and Children piſs'd upon them; after which, Captain *Thomas* told 'em, That the Example they had given, had it been follow'd, muſt have ended in the Deſtruction of 'em all; and tho' their Crime was pardon'd, and their Lives given 'em, yet they muſt not hereafter think of being Freemen, ſince they did not deſerve that Liberty which they were not zealous in defending; neither cou'd they, after the Diſgrace they had ſuffer'd, and which they deſervedly had brought on themſelves, hope ever to be admitted into the Company of brave Men, were they exempted from the Slavery to which their Puſillanimity had condemn'd 'em. After this they were ſold to the beſt Bidder. I remember, he who was ſold at the greateſt Price, brought no more than Two Dozen of Fowls and a Kid, to be paid the next publick Feſtival. The Scout who had not given timely Advice of the Enemy's Approach, was next brought out and beheaded; and Three, who run away at the firſt Attack, were hang'd. Out-Centinels were placed, and all the Men lay that Night on their Arms, for *Qwanaboa*, their Propheteſs, foretold another Attack, which ſhe apprehended wou'd

prove

prove their Ruine, if not prevented by uncommon Vigilance and Bravery.

Four Days pafs'd, and none of the Enemy appearing, they began to recover their Spirits, and grew lefs cautious; their moft advanced Scouts were recall'd, and they imagin'd the *Englifh* had no Knowledge of this Village. The Fifth at Night, when they were in perfect Tranquillity, the *Englifh*, who had, by a diftant and difficult way, climb'd the Mountains, and got above the Village, about Twelve at Night, came down upon 'em, and were in the Streets before the Negroes had any Inkling of their being fo near. They enter'd the Village with Thirty or Forty Men, and about half that Number intercepted all the Ways. Here began a cruel Slaughter, for none they could light on were fpared, but Women and Children, who were all taken. Capt. *Thomas* fought, and died like a Hero; my grateful *Cuffey*, join'd by about a Dozen more, made all poffible Refiftance; but finding their utmoft Efforts ufelefs, taking me with them, with Menaces, if I did not go freely, they clamber'd over fome Rocks, and skulking thro' the thick of the Woods, reach'd a Morafs on the top of the Mountain, where we lay hid Three Days. The Fourth, prefs'd by Hunger,

Hunger, Six of 'em ventur'd out to get
Plantanes, but they never return'd; for
which Reason, the Fifth Day we went
in Search of Food.   At Night we got into a Plantane Walk, from whence, after
having fill'd our Bellies, and loaded our
Backs, with the ripe Fruit, we retired to
the Woods.

Next Day, *Cuffey* went out by himself,
and, at his Return, told us, he had observ'd a large Canoe with Sails and Paddles, at the Sea Side, which belong'd he
believ'd to some Fishing Negroes.   He
propos'd the siezing, loading it with Plantanes, and going to the *Spanish* Coast,
which he was sure he could make shift to
find, having been there with the *Buccaniers*.
This was unanimously agreed to by the
rest.   I desired to be left behind, but their
Fear wou'd not let 'em consent to my
Stay. At Night we went again to the
Plantane Walk, where I hop'd to make
my Escape; but one of 'em always held
me by the Arm, suspecting I would give
'em the slip.   Being loaded, we follow'd
Cuffey to the Canoe, where we found a
Negro asleep, whom they bound, and
having taken what Plantanes they
thought fit, and found two large Runlets
of Water in the Canoe, with Fishing-
nets and other Tackle, they set Sail about
Eleven

Eleven o' Clock with a fine Hand Breeze, which carried us before Day to the laſt End of the Iſland.

The next Day about Even, we ſaw *Hiſpaniola*, and landed at Four o' Clock the Day following in a Creek, where we filled our Runlets with freſh Water, and going up into the Country, we catched a Number of Land Crabbs, which we dreſs'd and eat.

We lay two Days in this Creek, and in the Night of the ſecond, coaſted along the Iſland unperceived ; but as we croſs'd the Streights between Cape *Maeſe* and Cape *Nicholas*, which divides the Iſlands of *Hiſpaniola* and *Cuba*, we were ſeen and chaſed by a Sloop, which very ſoon came up with us, and proved a Free-booter, whoſe Crew was of all Nations and Colours. They offer'd the Seven Negroes their Liberty, and each Half a Share of an able Seaman, which they readily accepted. To me they would have given a whole Share, but I refuſing to join 'em, they reſolved to ſet me on Shore with the firſt Conveniency, tho' ſome were for throwing me over-board.

We were Eight Days without ſeeing a Sail, but the Ninth, about Break of Day, the Man at the Top-maſt Head, deſcried one on our Leeward Bow. The

C   Pyrates

Pyrates immediately prepared for an Engagement; we clapp'd our Helm a-wea-
ther, eas'd out our Main-fheet, and gave
Chafe. She proved a tall Ship, and did
not feem to make Sail to avoid us;
which was the Reafon we brought to,
and a Confultation was held, whether
it was fafe or not to venture upon her?
It was refolved in the Affirmative. In
Confequence of this, we bore away for
her, and when we were in lefs than Gun
Shot, we perceived fhe was very deep,
Spanifh built, and mounted Thirty Guns
by the Number of Ports, tho' we were
furprized they were all clofe, and not
a Man appeared on her Decks.

The Refolution was taken, to board
on the Quarter, which they did; but
feeing no body appear, they feared fome
Stratagem. However, fome of the Crew
ran into the Steerage and Great Cabbin; but feeing nobody, they went between Decks, and, upon Examination,
found her a Ship abandon'd, and that
fhe had Six Foot Water in the Hold.
They took out of the Great Cabbin Two
Chefts of Pieces of Eight, with fome
Hammocks and Cloaths from between
Decks, and fo left her.

The next Day, we fpied another Sail,
which gave us Chafe; We lay bye, till
we

we faw fhe was an Overmatch for us; for by the Canvafs fhe fpread, we concluded her no lefs than a Man of War of Fifty Guns. We clapp'd upon a Wind, and made all the Sail, and lay as clofe as we poffibly could, but it blowing a frefh Gale, we found fhe gain'd upon us. This obliged our Men to throw over the Treafure which they had found the Day before, and had been the Caufe of no fmall Joy. Finding fhe ftill gained upon us, we threw over our Eight Guns, which together with the Wind's flackening, was the Means of our Efcape; for now we vifibly wrong'd the Ship, and in lefs than Six Hours, loft her.

The Lofs of the Money was a confiderable Affliction to the Crew, but that of their Guns was fo great a one, it had well near fet them all together by the Ears. Some condemn'd the Captain for ordering them to be thrown over, others juftifying what he had done, as the only Means of their Efcape. At length, good Words, and a Bowl of Punch the Captain made for each Mefs, laid this Storm for a while; but that which at firft pacify'd thefe turbulent Spirits, was what blew them up again : For when they were all drunk, the Boatfwain faid the Captain was a Coward, and took a Mer-

chant-

chant-man for a Man of War: That his
Fear had magnified the Object, and deprived them of the Means of either taking others, or defending themselves. This
he faid in the Captain's Hearing, who,
without returning any Anfwer, took a
Piftol from his Girdle, and fhot him dead;
and then feizing another Mutineer, he ordered him a Hundred Lafhes at the Gang-
way, which were very honeftly paid him.

After this, he called all Hands upon
Deck, and told them he fhould not be
fit to command fo many brave Fellows,
would he fuffer any to infult him : That
if any on board thought he was a braver
Man than himfelf, he was ready to fhew
him his Error, either with his Fufil, Piftol, or Cutlafs: That fince they had
done him the Honour to chufe him Captain, he would carry Command, which
all brave and experienced Men knew
neceffary, and none but Cowards would
murmur at. That, as to the Boatfwain,
he had deferved his Death, fince one
Mutineer was enough to breed Confufion in the Veffel, which muft end in
the Deftruction of them all. *What*, continued he, *I have already faid, I repeat,
If any Man has a Mind to exchange a
Ball with me, I am ready for him ; but
while I am Captain, I will be Captain,*
                                    and

*and let the boldeft of ye difobey my Com-
mands.* This refolute Procedure quafh'd
the Mutineers, and he ever after kept a
ftrict Command, and was efteemed a
gallant Man.

Two Days after this, we fell in with a
Spanifh Garde de Cofta, and Two Sloops;
they boarded, and with very little Refiftance, took the Ship, tho' fhe had Four-
fcore Hands on board, and our Sloop but
Ninety. She was mounted with Twenty
Guns, but her great Shot did us but little
Damage. The two Sloops were *Englifh,*
going to the Bay of *Campechy* with Provifions, which we wanted very much.
They were taken but the Day before by
the *Spaniards,* and tho' they endeavoured
to get off, when they faw we had carried
the Frigate, yet our Sloop wrong'd 'em
fo much, that we foon came up with,
and took them. There were Twelve
Englifhmen on board the Prize, Four of
which took on with us.

Our Captain now quitted his Sloop,
went on board the Ship, which he called
the *Bafilisk,* and left the Three Sloops to
the *Spaniards.* The Eight *Englifh,* who
refufed to take on with him, he kept on
board, promifing to fet them on fhore
on the Eaft End of *Jamaica* in few Days,
but refufed them one of the Sloops,

C 3 which

which they defired; I fuppofe, fearing, at their Arrival, fome Man of War might be fent in Search of him, or, may be, hoping to bring them over, for, it's certain he had no Defign to land them as he promis'd.

Our Ship's Crew was now extreamly jocund, for they had Provifions for at leaft Three Months, with what they took out of the *Englifh* Sloops, and, in Money, they found upwards of an Hundred and Sixty Thoufand Pieces of Eight, and Two Thoufand Gold Quadruples. We loft but Three Men in boarding, fo that our Crew, with the Four *Englifh* who join'd 'em, confifted of Ninety and One Man.

For Three Weeks after we met with no Adventure; wherefore the Captain refolved to cruize off the *Havana*, and many of our Water-casks being emptied, and we not far from the River of *Chagre*, we made for, and came to an Anchor at the Mouth of that River, and fent our Boats afhore with the Casks.

After we had water'd, we fteer'd for the *Havana*, and between *Portobello* and *Carthagena*, we fpied a Sail; as fhe clapp'd upon a Wind, as foon as fhe defcry'd us, and we went upon One Maft, we foon met, but were as willing to fhake her off, as we had been to fpeak to her.

her. She proved a Forty Gun *French* Ship, which handled us without the leaft Ceremony. We began the Fight by a Broad-fide, as we were under her Stern, which raked her fore and aft, and muft, doubtlefs, as fhe was full of Men, do great Execution. She return'd the Compliment; and tho' we loft but few Men, yet they miferably cut our Rigging. Our Captain found his Bufinefs was to board, or her Weight of Metal would foon fend us to the Bottom. We enter'd the greater Number of our Men, who were fo warmly received, that but few came off; and as fhe was preparing to board us in her Turn, if we had not, by a lucky Shot, brought her Main-top-maft by the board, by which Accident we got off, fhe had certainly carried us. Upon this we got our Fore-Tack to the Cathead, hoifted our Top-fails a-trip, and went away all Sails drawing. In few Hours we loft Sight of her, and then upon the Mufter, we found that fhe had kill'd us Two and Forty of our Men, and wounded Fifteen, which was a very fenfible Lofs, and made the Captain alter his Courfe, and think of lying off *Campechy*, in hopes of geting more Men.

He order'd all the well Men upon Deck, and propos'd it to 'em: They all

agreed

agreed it was the beſt Courſe they cou'd
take, and many of them adviſed to quit
the Ship, for the firſt good Sloop which
ſhould fall in their Way. The Captain
anſwered, it was Time enough to think
of that when they had met with one for
their Turn.

They now fell to knotting and ſplicing
the Rigging, when the Day began to be
overcaſt, and threaten dirty Weather:
The Thunder growl'd at a diſtance, and
it began to blow hard ; a ſmart Thun-
der-ſhower was ſucceeded by a Flaſh of
Lightning, which ſhiver'd our Main-maſt
down to the Step. A dreadful Peal of
Thunder follow'd ; the Sea began to run
high, the Wind minutely encreas'd, and
dark Clouds intercepted the Day ; ſo that
we had little more Light, than what the
terrifying Flaſhes of Lightning afforded
us. Our Captain, who was an able Seaman, at the firſt Signal of an approaching
Storm, handed his Top-ſails, took a
Reef in his Foreſail, and the Men were
furling the Mainſail, when the Lightning
ſhiver'd the Maſt, which was cut away
with the utmoſt Expedition. We lay
ſome time under a Mizzen-balaſt, but
were at laſt forc'd to put before the
Wind, and, for Four Days, we ſcudded
with the Gooſe-wings of our Foreſail, in
which

which Time we had not the leaft Glimpfe
of Sun or Stars, but by very fhort Intervals ; nor indeed did I feethem, till after
we ftruck, but by Slatches. The Fifth
Day, about Noon, our Foremaft came
by the board ; we broach'd to, and a Sea
fill'd us ; we were at our Dying Rowls,
and every Man gave himfelf for loft. But
in this Danger, which ought to have
awakened thofe unhappy Wretches, to
fome Care of their future Happinefs,
the Ship rang with Imprecations, and
not a Word was uttered, not back'd with
Oaths and Curfes. However, it pleafed
the Great Difpofer of Life and Death,
that the Ship cleared her felf of the Water, which had filled the Waift to the
Top of the Gunnel. They did all they
could to keep her Head to the Sea, and fetting up a fmall Jury-maft, to which they
clapp'd a Top-gallant-yard, we again fcud-
ded, altogether ignorant where we were ;
for a Sea which pooped us the fecond Day,
had carried away the Binnacle with the
Two Compaffes; and they either had
not, or knew not, where to find another.
We left our felves to the Mercy of the
Sea and Wind, for we had no other Party to take; and tho' the former run
Mountain-high, yet finding the Ship
made no Water, the Captain apprehended

hended no Danger, but that of being drove on some Coast.

I had not the least Compassion for any of the Pyrates, he alone excepted; for he was much more humane to us who would not take on with him, than could be expected from one of his Profession, which he told me, one Day, he had enter'd upon much against his Inclinations, and that he would gladly quit that detestable Life, were it possible for him: But as he had no Hopes of Pardon, having, on board a Man of War, killed a Boatswain, who abused him, he was obliged to continue his Villainies for his own Security. This Man alone shewed some Sense of a Deity. I never heard him in the Storm swear an Oath; but, on the contrary, I often heard him, as by stealth, say, *Lord have Mercy on me! Great God forgive me!* The Seventh Day, a Sea poop'd us, and wash'd away this unhappy Man, and the Two who were at the Wheel, whom we never more set Eyes on. Two others immediately stepp'd into their Places. The Loss of the Captain was an Addition to our Misfortune, which together with the violent Continuance of the Storm, took away all Hopes of Safety.

On

On the Tenth Day, about Nine in the Morning, we ftruck upon a Rock with that Violence, that thofe who were in their Hammocks were thrown out, and thofe who walk'd the Deck, were ftruck off their Legs. The Pumps were immediately try'd, and fome ran into the Hold, and found the Ship made a great deal of Water. They plied the Pumps, but in lefs than ten Minutes, fhe ftruck again, and a Sea coming over us, I faw no more either of the Ship or the Crew. I rofe by the Side of a large Timber, which I laid hold of, and got upon, heartily recommending my felf to my Creator, and fincerely endeavouring to reconcile myfelf to my God, by an unfeigned Repentance of the Follies of my paft Life, and by making a very folemn Refolution, that if his Mercy fhould preferve me from a Danger which none but his Omnipotence could draw me out of, to have, for the future, a ftrict Guard upon all my Thoughts, Words, and Actions, and to fhew my Gratitude, by the Purity and Uprightnefs of my future Life.

The Want of an Obfervation for fo many Days, and the Lofs of our Captain, the only Artift on board, with the Want of a Compafs, was the Reafon of our being altogether ignorant of the Coaft

on

on which our Veffel perifh'd. The Piece of the Wreck which I was upon, was, after being tofs'd fome Hours, thrown afhore, and I got fo far on Land, that the returning Surf did not reach me. What became of the reft of the Crew, I know not, but concluded they all pe-rifh'd, till fome Years after, I met in *England* one of the *Englifhmen* who would not take on with the Pyrates, and who told me, that, by a peculiar Providence, he and the other Seven, were, after four Days floating on broken Pieces of the Ship, taken up by fome *Indian* Canoes; that they were two Years among the *Indians*, who treated them very human-ly; and when they were one Day a-fifh-ing with them about three Leagues from the Shore, they fpied a Sail at a great Diftance, and fignifying their Defire to return to *Europe*, the *Indians* very cour-teoufly gave them a Canoe and Eight Paddles, with which they reach'd the Ship, it being becalm'd, and found her *French*. They were received on board in the Latitude of   Degrees North, and when they arrived at *Rochelle*, were kindly ufed, and fent to *England*.

As we naturally are fond of Life, I return'd Thanks to Providence for my Efcape, and thought myfelf extreamly happy,

happy, tho' thrown on an unknown
Coaft, and deftitute of every thing neceffary to fuftain me: But I trufted in
that Goodnefs which had preferved, and
which I hoped would provide for me.
To defpond, I thought, would be mif-
trufting the Bounty of our Creator, and
might be the ready way to plunge me
into the Miferies Men naturally apprehend in my Circumftances. I therefore
heartily recommended me to the Divine Protection, and enter'd the Woods
which lay along the Coaft.

The Storm, which feem'd rais'd for
the Deftruction of thofe Enemies of
Mankind, and Shame of human Nature,
ceas'd in few Hours after the Veffel pe-
rifh'd. I found in the Woods all forts
of *Indian* Fruits, as, Guavers, Cufhoes,
Sowrefops, Oranges, &c. with which I
appeafed my Hunger. I was defirous,
yet fearful of difcovering, whether I was
in a defolate or inhabited Country, and
whether I was on the Continent, or fome
Ifland.

I wandered in the Woods till Sun-fet,
and then apprehending Danger from
wild Beafts, I climb'd a tall Tree, where
I fat, tho' I could not fleep, till Morning. By the time it had been dark about
an Hour, I was cruelly terrified by hearing

ing human Voices in the Air; for tho'
I did not underftand, I plainly heard
thefe Words: *Sup gravimiaco caputafcọ
deumorian*; with others which I could not
retain.

Let any Man fuppofe himfelf in my
Circumftances, and he will much eafier
form an Idea, than I defcribe the Agony
I was in on this furprizing Accident. The
Sun was two Hours high before I durft
defcend; but feeing nothing to apprehend, I came down, profecuted my Journey, as I had begun, Eaftward. In three
Hours, or thereabout, I came to the Extremity of the Wood, which was bound-
ed by a large Meadow, enamell'd with
the moft beautiful-coloured Flowers, and
hedg'd on the three other Sides with
Limes, and with large Orange-Trees,
placed at equal Diftances in the Fence.
This, with the Profpect I had of Corn
Fields, made me conclude the Country
inhabited by a civiliz'd People.

I crofs'd the Meadow, highly delighted with the agreeable Profpect which lay
before me. To avoid trampling on, and
doing Damage to the Corn, I turn'd a little to the Northward, in hopes of falling
in with fome Village, or meeting with
fome or other of the Inhabitants. I
found here very rich Paftures, and large
Flocks

Flocks of Sheep, intermix'd with Deer ;
the Sheep were, as in *Jamaica,* cover'd
with ſhort Hair, like that of a Grey-
hound ; and the Deer, which I wonder'd
at, inſtead of flying from, came up to me,
and gazed, as if I was a Creature which
they were not accuſtomed to the Sight of.
The Sheep following their Example, I
was ſo hemm'd in, that, had I not made
my way with a Stick I broke out of a
Hedge, I don't know how I ſhould have
got clear of them.

What aſtoniſhed me, was to ſee ſuch a
Number of Corn-fields and Paſture-
grounds, in a flouriſhing Condition, and
well fenced, and yet not meet with the
leaſt Track or Path. However, I walk'd
on till about Three o' Clock, as I gueſs'd
by the Sun, which, tho' it was exceſſive
hot, was no way uneaſy to me, being
ſheltered by the Hedges. Being come
to the Banks of a large River, bordered
with Cedars, the talleſt I ever ſaw, and
being under no Apprehenſion of wild
Beaſts in a Country ſo well cultivated, I
laid me down under one of the largeſt,
and ſlept till the Sun was near ſetting ;
and doubtleſs, not having cloſed my Eyes
the Night before, I ſhould have continued my Nap, had I not been wakened
with the Sound of human Voices.

I ſtart-

I ſtarted up, and look'd round me, but could perceive nothing like a Man. I then holloo'd, and heard ſomebody ſay, *Quaw ſhoomaw*: I anſwered, *Quaw ſhoomaw*; upon which I heard Two ſpeak, and anſwer each other, as I thought, over my Head. I look'd up, but could, by reaſon of the Thickneſs and Height of the Tree, ſee nothing. I went ſome Paces from it, and looking up again, I heard a Voice, which utered theſe Words haſtily, *Quaw ſhoomaw? ſtarts* ; which is, having afterwards learned the Language, *Who art thou? ſtand.*

Hardly had theſe Words reached my Ears, when I ſaw a Cock and Hen fly down from the Tree, and light near me ; they were about Six Foot tall, and their Bodies ſomewhat larger than a good Weather. The Cock who was the larger the Two, coming pretty near me, tho' he diſcover'd in his Eyes both Fear and Aſtoniſhment, repeated the Words, *Quaw ſhoomaw.* The Hen, who kept a greater Diſtance, cried out, *Ednu ſinvi,* which I ſince learn'd, is, *Whence come you?*

I was as much ſurprized to hear Fowls ſpeak, as they were to ſee ſuch a Monſter as I appeared to be. I anſwer'd in her own Words, *Ednu ſinvi* ; upon which ſhe

fhe ask'd me, I fuppofe, a String of Queftions, with a Loquacity common to the
Sex, and then fell a cackling. Three or
four Chickens came running to her, and
at the Sight of me hid their Heads under
their Mother's Wing, as I fuppos'd her.
One of them, who was a Cock not above
Five Foot high, at laft took Courage to
peep out, and faid fomething to his Father; and, as I guefs, taking Courage
from what Anfwer he return'd, ventured
to approach me. He walk'd round me,
tho' he kept fome Diftance, and fpoke in
a threatning Tone. I anfwer'd in a melancholy one, and in my own Language;
That I was an unfortunate fhipwreck'd
Man. The Youngfter, I fuppofe, thinking me a harmlefs Animal, ventured to
ftrike at me, and if I had not avoided the
Stroke, I believe he had fplit my Skull,
for his Spurrs were about Eighteen Inches
long, near Five about, and as fharp as
Needles.

I faw his Father angry at this Pro-
ceeding, and he gave him a terrible Cuff
with his Wing, and fent him home.
Then fpeaking to me, he made Signs I
fhould follow him; I underftood, and
obey'd him. After we had pafs'd a fmall
Copfe of about a Quarter of a Mile, we
came into a fine Meadow, where we faw

D   *feveral*

several Hens milking Goats; they sat on their Rumps, and were as dextrous with their two Feet, as any of our Dairy-Maids with their Hands. They carried two Pails a-piece with a Yoke, like our Tub-women; and indeed there are not in *Europe* any who exceed this Nation in Mechanicks, as far as they are useful to them. I have seen a *Cacklogallinian* (for so they call themselves) hover with a Pair of Sheers in his two Feet, and cut Trees with all the Regularity imaginable; for, in a Walk of a League long, which is very common before the Houses of the Nobility, you won't see (not to say a Bough, but even) a Leaf grow beyond the rest. They are the best Weavers in the Universe, and make Cloath of stript Feathers, which they have the Art of spinning, and which is the Staple Commodity of the Kingdom; for no Feathers are comparable to these for this Manufacture. When I pass'd the Meadow, every one quitted her Employment to come and stare at me; they all spoke together so loud, and with such Volubility, that I almost fancied my self among a Score of Gammers at a Country Christening.

This Meadow led to a Farm House which belong'd to my Guide, or more properly,

properly, Mafter; for I foon was made fenfible, that they look'd upon me as an irrational Beaft, of a Species hitherto unknown to them. We were no fooner within Doors, than the Family flock'd round to admire me, asking Abundance of Queftions which I did not underftand. One of the Hens brought me a Bowl of Goats Milk, which I received very thankfully, and drank off.. They then offer'd me Corn, which I rejecting, one of them went out, and fetch'd me a Piece of boil'd Mutton ; for thefe *Cacklogallinians*, contrary to the Nature of *European* Cocks, live moftly on Flefh, except the poorer Sort, who feed on Grain. They do not go to Rooft, but lye on Feather-beds and Matrafs, with warm Coverings; for, at the fetting of the Sun, there falls fo great a Dew, that I was, in the Night, as fenfible of Cold, as ever I was in *Europe* in the Winter.

After I had eat my Piece of Meat, a Bed was made for me in my Mafter's Chamber, whither he conducted me. He made Signs, that I fhould lye down, and was not a little aftonifh'd, I perceived, to fee me open the Bedding, go into it, and cover my felf up. The pulling off my Cloaths he did not wonder at, for the Rich and Great among 'em wear

D 2 Mantles,

Mantles, and cover their Legs with fine Cloath.

I flept very heartily, and very much at my Eafe. My Mafter, who was a rich Farmer, went the next Day to *Ludbitallya*, the Metropolis of the Kingdom, about Forty Miles from his Home, to acquaint his Landlord, who was a Minifter of State, what a Rarity he had in Poffeffion. He fet out about Six in the Morning, and returned at Noon; for the *Cacklogallinians* will fly at the Rate of Twenty Miles an Hour. His Landlord came in lefs than that Space after in great State. He was preceded by Half a Dozen Servants, who carried large Battons in their right Feet, and made no Ceremony of knocking any on the Head who came in their Way. He was in a fort of Palanquin, covered with fine Cloth, and powdered with filver Stars in Circles, fupported by four *Cacklogallinians* adorn'd with filver Chains. As to his Perfon, he was about Nine Foot high when he ftood upright, and very corpulent; for, what is wonderful among thefe People (if I may be allow'd that Term) they grow in Bulk, and their Appetites increafe in Proportion to their Riches and Honour, of which I was an Eye-witnefs in the Perfons of my Mafter and

and his Male Children, for the Females are not perceivably affected with a Change of Fortune. This holds good in its Oppofite, for Adverfity will bring down the talleft to the Size of a Dwarf, that is, to Three Foot.

But to return to this Minifter, whofe Name was *Brufquallio.* He was cover'd with a rich loofe Garment embroider'd, and wore on his Neck a yellow, green and red Ribbon, from which hung a Gold Medal of a Cock trampling on a Lion, which is the Badge of the greateft Honour the Emperor of *Cacklogallinia* can beftow on a Subject. He had a great Number of Followers, who paid him a fort of Adoration. When he alighted, my Mafter met him on the Out-fide of the Door, threw himfelf on his Belly, and held his Beak to the Ground, till the other order'd him to rife; for I have fince learnt both their Cuftoms and Language. When he came in, I was brought to him.

My Mafter, as I have fince learnt, told his Lordfhip, that he fancied I had fome Glimmerings of Reafon, notwithftanding the hideous Make of my Perfon, and gave for an Inftance, my getting into my Bed as decently as a *Cacklogallinian*; and that thofe of my Species certainly had a Lan-

D 3   guage

guage among 'em, for he had heard me very diſtinctly utter ſome unintelligible Words, and even repeat ſome after him.

I threw my ſelf on my Knees, and in the moſt humble Poſture addreſs'd my ſelf to his Lordſhip, telling him in *Engliſh*, that I was a harmleſs unfortunate Man, who was caſt upon their Coaſt, was an Object of Compaſſion, and below their Anger; that as I never did, nor meant Harm to any, I hoped to experience his Lordſhip's Mercy.

He ſeem'd highly delighted to hear me ſpeak, and viewed me with a viſible Surprize. My Maſter coming to me, ſaid, *Ednu ſinvi?* which I repeated after him (as I perceiv'd he was deſirous I ſhould) to the great Satisfaction of the Miniſter, who, as I have ſince known, deſired to purchaſe, have me taught the *Cacklogallinian* and Court Language (for the Court did not ſpeak that of the Country, for a Reaſon hereafter to be mention'd) and preſent me to his Imperial Majeſty, as the greateſt Rarity in Nature. When he bid my Maſter ſet a Price, he anſwer'd, That his Lordſhip's doing him the Honour to accept ſuch a Trifle from his Slave, he eſteem'd beyond any Sum of Money, notwithſtanding his Poverty. *Well,* ſays
the

the Grandee, *bring him to me to-morrow,*
I accept the Prefent, and you fhall have
no Reafon to repent your trufting to me.

The Minifter got into his Palanquin,
and his four Bearers flew off with him
with that incredible Swiftnefs, his Attendance had much ado to keep up
with it.

The next Morning, my Mafter taking
me by the Sleeve with his Beak, led me
out of Doors, and then walk'd forward.
I ftood ftill, and he return'd, pull'd me
by the Coat, and walk'd on again ; by
which I guefs'd he would have me follow him, as I accordingly did, accompanied by one of his Servants, who kept by
my Side. He went too faft, for me to
keep him Company ; which he perceiving, fpoke to the Servant, and they took
Wing together, and each of them laying
hold on an Arm, lifted me about Thirty
Foot from the Ground, and in Four
Hours, alighted about a Quarter of a
Mile diftant from a very large Town.

I had forgot to acquaint the Reader,
that before I began this airy Journey,
my Mafter took a Mantle, which his Servant carried under his Wing, and cover'd
me, that I had only an Open to fee and
refpire : This was to prevent the Impertinence he might expect from the Mob

at

at the Sight of fuch a Novelty as I
was.

When we alighted, he made Signs to
me to lye down, fent his Servant to the
Town, and cover'd me all over. The
Servant foon return'd with a clofe Palanquin, which they made me Signs to
go into, and I was in an Inftant hurried
thro' the Air, and fet down in a Stable
Yard, and conducted from thence into
a little Houfe, to which this Yard afforded the only Paffage. Both the Avenue,
and the Smallnefs of the Houfe no way
anfwerable to the Charge and Titles of
the Minifter to whom it belong'd, were
Matter of Surprize to me; tho' I fince
learnt it was in him Policy, that he made
no greater Figure in Town than a private
Gentleman, not to encreafe the Number
of thofe who envied him; for tho' he was
now Nine Foot high, yet in a late Reign
he was dwindled from the Height peculiar to the Rank of his Family, of Six
Foot Nine Inches, to Three Foot Ten.
In the Country, I was told his Seat far
exceeded any of the Royal Palaces, tho'
as yet not finifh'd, and both his Furniture and Equipage were anfwerable; and
he never travelled without a great Number of Servants, who join'd him a Mile
or two without the Gates.

This

This great Perfon fhewed me to his Family, every one of which admired me as a moft monftrous Production of Nature. My Mafter was rewarded, by being made *Nofocomionarcha*, or Paymafter to the Invalids, had the Title of *Quityardo*, which anfwers to our *Squire*, conferred on him, and was ever after a Favourite of the Minifter. He fprung up immediately Nine Inches higher, grew confiderably more bulky, and would eat you Three or Four *Cacklogallinian* Chicks in a Day; for the Minifters, and thofe in Poft, feed on their own Species, and not one of the poorer Sort is in any Security of their Lives, in cafe a hungry Grandee fets his Eyes on, and has a Mind to him. Nay, the flavifh Spirit of the *Cacklogallinians* is fuch, that many of them, thro' Folly or Superftition, will come in Bodies to the Houfe of a Minifter, and beg as the greateft Favour and Honour, they and their Families may be ferved up to his Lordfhip's Table; and I have feen the Fools, who had thus offered themfelves, and been accepted, if there was not immediate Occafion for them, ftrut in the Streets with a Chain of Silver about their Necks, which they look'd upon as the greateft Honour; and when call'd for by his Lordfhip's Cook, run

exulting,

exulting, and offer their Throats to his Knife; tho' this Nation was, in Time paſt, the braveſt, and the moſt tenacious of their Liberty, of any of the feather'd Race. But I have digreſs'd too far.

My new Maſter, or, more properly, Lord, order'd an Apartment and a Table for me, with a Tutor to teach me the Languages, by whoſe Diligence, and my own *Avidity* of Learning, I began in Four Months to underſtand a great Part of what was ſaid to me; and my Lord was ſo very much pleaſed at my Progreſs, that he gave my Tutor a Poſt, which raiſed him about Four Inches. My Lord forbore aſking me any Queſtions concerning my ſelf, till I was perfectly Maſter of the Languages, which I was in about Eleven Months.

He one Day ſent for me into his Chamber, and accoſted me in the following Words: *Probuſomo* (which is, Monſter of Nature, the Name he gave me) *I have ſuſpended my Curioſity of enquiring whence, and how you came into this Kingdom, till we could perfectly underſtand each other, that I might not be troubled with an imperfect Relation: Now that you are Maſter of our Language, tell me of what Part of the World you are; whether you are of a ſavage, or a civiliz'd Nation? if of the latter,*

latter, what is your Policy, what are your Manners and Customs, and what Accident brought you hither? I threw my felf on my Face, and kifs'd his right golden Spur (for the Grandees faw off thofe which Nature has provided them, and fubftitute thefe in their Places) then rifing, I anfwer'd, That I was of *Europe,* a Country fo diftant from *Cacklogallinia,* that I was near Six Moons at Sea, before I was caft on its Coaft. *Why,* faid he, *is it poffible you can fwim fo long? for you being deftitute of Wings, can have no other Method of paffing fo vaft a Water.* I told him we pafs'd the Seas in Ships, and gave him a Defcription of them, but could not make him have the leaft Idea of what I meant, till the next Day, that I hollow'd, fhap'd, and rigg'd a Piece of Cork, made Sails of fine Linnen, and brought it to his Excellency in a Bafon of Water. I told him, we were a civiliz'd Nation, and govern'd by a King, who however did nothing without the Advice of his Great Council, which confifted of Grandees born to that Honour, and *Quityardo's* elected by the People to reprefent them. That, to thefe Reprefentatives the People had delegated the Power of acting for them, and entrufted their Liberty and Eftates to their Probity; con-

fequently

fequently nothing could be fuppofed to
be done by the Prince, but by the univerfal Confent of the Nation, and the
People could bear no Burthens, but what
they voluntarily took upon themfelves
for the common Good.

I have never, anfwer'd he, *read, that
any of your Species was feen in this Kingdom before you; but it is certain you muft
have copy'd your Policy from us. But,*
faid he, *are all thefe Reprefentatives publick-fpirited, zealous for the common Welfare, Proof againft Preferments, Titles,
and private Advantages? Have they always the Good of the Nation at Heart fo
far, as to prefer it to that of their Families? Do they follicite the People to chufe
them, or are they their free Choice? If the
latter, what Amends do the People make
to thefe Reprefentatives, who neglect their
private Affairs, to apply themfelves to thofe
of the Publick?*

I told his Excellency, that I did not
doubt their being fuch Men as he fpoke
them ; that I was very young when I
left my Country, and befide I was not
born in a Rank which, had I been of
riper Years, permitted me to meddle
with State Affairs: However, I had heard
from my Elders, that none were elected,
till the King fent his Mandates to the
feveral

feveral Provinces, ordering them to chufe
the wifeft among them to affift his Majefty with their Advice: And as the Intereft of each Province in particular, and
of the whole Nation in general, turn'd
upon the Probity and Judgment of the
Reprefentatives, to whom an unlimited
Power was delegated, it did not ftand to
Reafon, that they would make Choice
of any, whofe Love for his Country,
whofe Sagacity and Honour they had not
made Proof of; or at leaft, whofe Life did
not give them Hopes, that he would
prove a real Patriot.

That they were the free Choice of the
People, was plain, by the Backwardnefs
fhewn by thofe elected to undertake fo
weighty a Charge, which had no other
Recompence than the Applaufe of the
Publick, for the faithful Execution of their
Truft. Another Reafon which induced
me to believe the Choice fuch, was, that
the *Englifh*, (of which Nation I own'd
my felf) were any one rich enough to
bribe the Majority of a Province, and
ate too wife a People to entruft their
Liberty to fuch a Perfon; for it's natural to believe, whoever would buy their
Votes, would fell his own: But, that the
Majority of a Province was to be brib'd,
or that a free People would, on any account,

count, rifque their Liberty, by giving
their Reprefentatives a Power to enflave
'em, either by making the Prince abfolute, and furnifhing him with Standing
Armies, to maintain a defpotick Power,
or elfe by felling them to Foreigners,
could never enter into the Thoughts of
a reafonable Creature.

Has, faid he, (who fmiled all the while
I held this Difcourfe) *your Nation any
near Neighbours?* I anfwer'd, That, by
the means of our Shipping, we might
be faid near Neighbours to every Nation; but that our Ifland was feparated
but Seven Leagues from the Continent,
inhabited by a warlike and powerful People. *Have you any Commerce with the
Nations on the Continent?* We are, faid
I, the greateft Dealers in *Europe. Have
you any Religion among you?* We have,
in the main, I replied, but one, tho' it
is branch'd out into a great many Sects,
differing only in fome trifling Ceremonies, in Effentials we all agree. *Religion,*
anfwer'd my Lord, *is abfolutely neceffary
in a well-govern'd State*; but do your great
Men make any *Profeffion of Religion? or,
to ask a more proper Queftion, do they do
more than profefs it?* My Lord, faid I,
our great Men are the brighteft Examples of Piety. Their Veracity is fuch,
that

that they would not for an Empire falſi-
fy their Word once given. Their Juſtice
won't ſuffer a Creditor to go from their
Gate unſatisfied : Their Chaſtity makes
them look on Adultery and Furnication
as the moſt abominable Crimes ; and even
the naming of them will make their
Bloods run cold. They exhauſt their
Revenues in Acts of Charity, and every
great Man among us is a Husband and
Father to the Widow and Orphan. They
eſteem themſelves Stewards to the Poor,
and that in a future State they are ac-
countable for every Doit laviſh'd in Equipage or ſuperfluous Diſhes. Their Ta-
bles are not nicely, but plentifully ſerved,
and always open to the honeſt Needy.
At Court, as I have learn'd, there is
neither Envy nor Detraction, no one
undermines another, nor intercepts the
Prince's Bounty or Favour by ſlandrous
Reports ; and neither Intereſt, Riches,
nor Quality, but Merit only recommends
the Candidate to a Poſt : A Bribe was
never heard of there ; which, together
with the exact Juſtice practiſed, is the
Reaſon that a Miniſter, after Twelve or
Fourteen Years, ſhall die not a Doit
richer than he was at the Entrance upon his Office : Nay, I've been told, that
a Paymaſter General of the Army, after
he

he had paſt his Accounts before the
Grand Council of the Nation, with a
general Applauſe, found his Patrimony
ſo impoveriſh'd by his Charity to Soldiers Widows, he was oblig'd to turn Merchant for his Support; but being unfortunate, he petition'd for a ſmall Government. *As you ſay you have divers Sects
of Religion, you muſt have Prieſts among
you, pray what ſort of Men are they?* I
anſwer'd, their Lives and Doctrine were
of a-piece, their Example differing nothing from their Precepts: That Hypocriſy, Avarice, Ambition, litigious Suits,
Lying, Revenge, and Obſcenity, were
Vices known to 'em by Name only: That
they were a mortify'd Set of Men, who
look'd upon nothing tranſitory worth
their Concern; and having their Thoughts
always employ'd on Meditations of a future Happineſs, neglected every thing on
Earth but their Duty; and for this Reaſon, they often became a Prey to Knaves,
who ſlipp'd no Opportunity of ſpoiling
them, knowing their Lenity ſuch, that,
if detected, they ſhould not be proſecu-
ted. I have been aſſured, that a Prieſt
being told, ſuch a Farmer had ſtole away
a great many Tithe Sheafs, the good Divine anſwer'd, *If he's poor, it's no Theft;
what I have belongs to the Needy, and he*
takes

takes but his own. The Day after he
fent him all the Corn he was Mafter of,
and by this Act of Charity, wou'd have
ftarved before next Harveft, if a Minifter of State, in love with his Virtue,
had not provided for him. And 1 myfelf knew one, who hearing black Puddings were a Prefervative againft pefti-
lential Infections, and that the Plague
was within Two Thoufand Leagues of
our Ifland, laid out his whole Patrimony in Puddings, and fent 'em to every
Sea-port in the Kingdom.

Have you Phyficians among you? We
have, faid I, Men of extenfive Charity,
great Humility, profound Learning, without the leaft Tincture of Vanity. They
are fo very confcientious, that fhou'd
they prefcribe for a Patient, and he recover before he had taken all the Druggs
brought in, they will pay for thofe
which remain, out of their own Pockets.
They never take a Fee, but when they
prefcribe, tho' they vifit you frequently,
and never prefcribe, without they fee an
abfolute Neceffity. They are fo modeft,
that they attribute the Recovery of a Perfon to divine Providence, and are ready
to accufe themfelves of Ignorance or
Negligence fhould he die under their
Hands.

E   *Have*

Have you any Lawyers in your part of the World? Lawyers, faid I, we have, but not more than neceffary.

You have then, faid my Lord, *very few, or are a litigious People. What fort of Creatures are they?* They are, faid I, brought up many Years in the Study of the Laws, and pafs a ftrict Examination, not only as to their Knowledge, but their Morals, before they are admitted to the Bar; which is the Reafon, that we have no Tricks, no Delays, to weary and ruine the poor Client who has a Right, but no Money; they come directly to the Merits of the Caufe, and never endeavour by their Rhetorick to put a fair Face on a bad one; and not one, if his Client does not deceive him, will appear on the Side of Oppreffion or Injuftice; and if he is himfelf impos'd upon, when he perceives it, he will not defend the Wrong. This Care of examining into the Probity of the Students, and Candidates for the Bar, is the Reafon our Lawyers are very near in as great Reputation as our Priefts.

Do you know from what you have faid, Probufomo, *that I conclude your Statefmen Fools, and that you will foon fall a Prey to fome other Nation; or you either very ignorant of your National Affairs, or*

a very

*a very great Lyar ; or otherwife think me
eafily impos'd upon. I have been many Years
at the Head of the* Cacklogallinian *Affairs, under our Auguft Mafter,* Hippomina
Connuferento, *Darling of the Sun, Delight of the Moon, Terror of the Univerfe,
Gate of Happinefs, Source of Honour,
Difpofer of Kingdoms, and High Prieft of
the* Cacklogallinian *Church. I have, I
fay, long, in Obedience to this Moft Potent
Prince, acted as Prime Minifter, and to
tell me, that fuch a one will baulk his Mafter's, or his own Intereft, on the Score of
Religion ; nay, in his publick Capacity,
that he believes one Word of it, or has
Ears for Juftice or Compaffion. wou'd be
the fame thing as telling me, a Flatterer
in his Encomiums has a ftrict Eye to Truth,
or that a Poet who writes in Praife of
great Men, believes them really poffefs'd of
the Virtues he attributes to 'em, and has
no other View in his Epiftle than that of
edifying others, by fhewing the bright Example of his Patrons. My Bufinefs now
calls me to Court ; the Emperor, as yet,
has never heard of you : For whoever dares
acquaint him with any thing, without my
Permiffion, paffes his Time very ill. To
Morrow, I'll prefent you to His Majefty.*

He left the Room, and I retired to
my Apartment, where none cou'd come

at me, but who pass'd thro' my Lord's, which was Death to do, or even to fly within Twenty Yards of his House, without Permiffion. Nay, the proudeft among them, and thofe of the higheft Rank, alight at his Outer-gate, and walk into the Houfe.

The next Morning my Lord came into my Apartment : " Well, *Probufomo,*
" *faid he,* I intend this Day to prefent
" you to his Imperial Majefty; and tho'
" you are of a Species hitherto unknown
" in our Parts of the World, and are,
" for that Reafon, look'd upon as a kind
" of Monfter, as perhaps one of us fhould
" be, were we to appear in your Nati-
" on, yet I have obferv'd fome Points of
" Difcretion in your Behaviour, and I
" begin to have a Kindnefs for you, for
" which Reafon I intend to inftruct you
" how to demean your felf; and if you
" are wife enough to act and be guided
" by the Counfels I fhall prefcribe to
" you, while you are at Court, I can,
" in fpite of your awkard Form, get you
" naturalized, and then perhaps may
" prefer you to fome Charge in the Go-
" vernment, confiderable enough to en-
" able you to pafs the reft of your Days
" in Eafe and Plenty.

" You

" You that don't know what a Court
" is (*proceeded he*) fhould receive fome
" Idea of it before you enter there. You
" muft firft be informed, that Emperors
" do not always trouble themfelves with
" the Affairs of State; for they fome-
" times pafs their whole Lives in a con-
" tinued Round of indolent Pleafures,
" while their Favourites govern all. I
" don't doubt but you have already made
" your Obfervation upon the fervile
" Crowd who attend my Motions, who
" wait upon my Commands, with an
" Obfequioufnefs that perhaps is not
" praƐtifed in your Parts of the World,
" betwixt Creatures of the fame Species,
" yet many of them hate me, as I do
" them, —— perhaps you'll think this
" ftrange; but when the fecret Springs
" of this Attachment to my Intereft come
" to unfold themfelves to you, which will
" foon happen, by the Obfervations I fee
" you are capable of making, your Ad-
" miration will ceafe. However, I fhall
" be a little particular in explaining fome
" Matters to you, that you may there-
" by be the better qualified to ferve my
" Intereft.
" You muft then know, that all this
" affiduous Court is not paid to my Per-
" fon, but to my Place. They know,

that

" that I not only hold the Reins of the
" Government in my Hands, but keep
" the publick Treaſure under my own
" Eye, and that the Power of giving is
" only mine. It is not their Love, but
" their Avarice, that makes them thus
" obedient to my Nod; and the ſame
" Reſpect would be paid to the meaneſt
" of my Domeſticks, were ſuch a one
" put in my Place.

 " Their Hatred to me proceeds from
" various Cauſes. In ſome it is Envy,
" becauſe they think themſelves affront-
" ed and injur'd by my great Riſe, as
" knowing themſelves to be of greater
" Conſideration in their Country, and
" fancifying themſelves themſelves to be
" as well qualified by their Parts. Others
" again are out of Humour, becauſe I
" do not comply with all their unreaſon-
" able Demands, their Luxnry always
" keeping them neceſſitous. Some of
" theſe are ſuch as have Parts enough to
" be troubleſome; they are hard to be
" managed, and indeed are the moſt dan-
" gerous Creatures I have to deal with.
" There is a third Sort, who hate and
" oppoſe me, only becauſe they love
" their Country, but theſe I don't much
" fear, for their Party is very weak at
" preſent,

" And

" And fince I am upon this Subject,
" I can't forbear obferving to you, that
" were it not for the Luxury of fome,
" and the Folly of others, I could never
" have ftood my Ground fo long, and
" executed thofe Meafures which I have
" brought about ; and happy it is for a
" Perfon in my Station (if he has any odd
" Meafures in View) that many of the
" upper Rank fhould happen to be Fools;
" I have myfelf kept feveral Perfons
" dancing Attendance after me, Year af-
" ter Year, made them maintain in pub-
" lick Affemblies, that Nine was more
" than Fifteen; that Black was White,
" and a Hundred other things of equal
" Abfurdity, only by promifing to ftick
" a parti-colour'd Feather in their Tails;
" and when this was done, it only made
" them the Scorn and Jeft of every thing
" of good Senfe : Yet it anfwered my
" Purpofe, and did not hinder others of
" equal Folly from making Court for the
" fame thing.

" Thus I have accounted with you
" why thefe People are fubfervient to
" me, while they hate me ; but I have
" not given you the Reafons on my Side
" for keeping up this Correfpondence
" and Union with them, for whom I
" have as little Efteem as they can have

E 4   " for

" for me. Then, in a Word it is, I can't
" do without them. This you'll eafily
" comprehend when you underftand the
" Nature of our Government; for you'll
" know, that this Power here is lodged
" in the many, not in the few: It is
" they who can abolifh old Laws, and
" make new; the Power of Life and
" Death is in them, and from their De-
" crees there is no Appeal; and tho' I
" do all, and command all, nay, com-
" mand even them, yet the Right is
" theirs, and they might exert it all times,
" if they had Virtue enough to break off
" their Correfpondence with me.

" Things being in this Situation, no
" doubt, you'll think my Eftablifhment
" well fix'd; but I am not without my
" Fears and my Dangers, and there is
" no judging of the Power of one in my
" Station, by the Flattery that is paid
" him, for Flatterers take things fre-
" quently by outward Appearances; and
" notwithftanding my arbitrary manner
" of treating fome Perfons, my Safety is
" depending upon the Breath of others,
" and I am obliged to pay a more fervile
" Court to fome behind the Curtain,
" than is paid to me without.

" Thofe upon whom my Fate and
" Fortune depend, are the *Squabbaws*
" of

" of the Court" (the Reader is to underſtand, that this is a Name for certain Females, who are maintain'd for
the Emperor's Luxury and Pleaſure,
and always ſojourn at Court) " and it
" is to their Avarice that I owe my
" Grandeur, as well as its Continuance
" ſo long. There was a Time, when I
" fooliſhly miſtook my own Intereſt ſo
" far, as by my Conduct to give ſome
" Offence to theſe *Squabbaws*, for which
" I ſuffered a ſevere Diſgrace: I then
" endeavour'd to ſhelter my ſelf among
" thoſe who are ſtiled the Patriots, but
" they would neither receive me into
" their Counſels, nor put the leaſt Truſt
" in me. I had then Leiſure to reflect
" on the Folly of this Conduct, and had
" Time to compute how much I was a
" Loſer, by putting on the Mask of the
" Patriot; and, I confeſs, it had ſuch an
" Effect upon me, and gave me ſuch an
" Averſion to Patriotiſm, that I could
" never prevail upon myſelf to do any
" thing for the publick Good ever ſince.

" I then immediately apply'd all my
" Thoughts towards making my Peace,
" and there fell out a Chain of lucky In-
" cidents, which happily brought it
" about. One of theſe was the Death
" of ſeveral great Perſonages, who were
" too

" too mighty for me at that time in
" Rank and Dignity, and whose Parts
" eclipsed mine in the Opinion of the
" Publick, tho' I always thought other-
" wise.

" Their Deaths were so sudden, that
" the Emperor was puzzled whom to
" chuse in their Places, (it being necessa-
" ry they should soon be fill'd up) and
" he had but a very small Acquaintance
" among his People; so that he was un-
" der a kind of Necessity of throwing
" his Affairs into my Hands, I having the
" Reputation of being pretty well pra-
" ctised in certain Branches of his Re-
" venues.

" I had Reason to suspect, that this
" new Preferment was not intended as
" a Favour, and that I was to continue
" no longer in this Station, than till
" some other Person more agreeable
" could be fix'd upon; but in order to
" improve the Opportunity, I apply'd
" my self strenuously to the Avarice of
" the *Squabbaws*, and gave with Prodi-
" gality; for I bore in Mind my former
" Miscarriages. This had all its Effect;
" they had never met with a Person so
" fit for their Purpose, and by these Ar-
" guments they began to be convinc'd,
" that if another should be preferr'd to
" my

" my Place, they would be no Gainers
" by the Change.

" Since this good Underftanding be-
" twixt us, Matters have been fo mana-
" ged, that no Perfon has had Accefs to
" the Emperor, but thro' my Recom-
" mendation; fo that my Enemies can-
" not fill his Ears with Complaints of my
" Adminiftration; and whenever I ob-
" ferve any Perfon attempting to lay the
" State of Affairs before his Imperial
" Majefty, the *Squabbaws*, by my In-
" ftruƈtions, are to infinuate into the
" royal Ear fome Jealoufies and Fears of
" that Perfon, that the Emperor may
" forbid his Admittance; fo that he on-
" ly fees with my Eyes, and hears by
" my Report.

" As this in a great Meafure has ren-
" der'd me fafe againft the Attempts of
" my Enemies, yet I can't deny but that
" it has encreas'd their Number, and fur-
" nifh'd them with Matter to clamour
" againft me; and thefe Clamours have
" poffefs'd the Publick with a kind of an
" Averfion to my Conduƈt, tho' they
" have not reach'd the Throne.

" But as it is not poffible, but that
" the Officers of State belonging to a
" great Emperor, of which there muft
" be many in Number, muft fometimes
                                   " have

" have Opportunities of talking with
" him, I have taken Care to prevent any
" Danger from thence, by chufing for
" thofe Pofts Birds of the weakeft Capa-
" cities, altogether ignorant of the Af-
" fairs of the Empire; for one in a high
" Station, who makes the publick Intereft
" fubfervient to his own, will never be
" fafe, unlefs he takes Care, that no Crea-
" ture who acts with him, fhall have
" any Senfe except himfelf. I am not
" the firft who have laid this down as a
" Maxim; fome of my Predeceffors be-
" gan to practife it, as a neceffary Piece
" of Self-Defence. 'Tis true I have car-
" ried it a little further than they, and
" with greater Reafon, becaufe I have
" not forgot in how bad a Light I ftood
" when *Fowls* of Parts fway'd the pub-
" lick Counfels, with what Sagacity they
" faw thro' all my private Views and
" Defigns, and with what Facility they
" brought about my Difgrace; and
" therefore, when I have difcover'd in
" any of thofe concern'd with me in
" Bufinefs, a fine Difcernment, and a
" Genius for great Affairs, I have from
" that Minute look'd upon fuch as dan-
" gerous, and for that Reafon either
" procured their Difgrace, or under the
" Pretence of doing them Honour, pre-
" vail'd

" vail'd upon the Emperor to confer up-
" on them the Government of fome
" diftant Province, where they are re-
" moved too far from the Imperial Coun-
" fels, to be able to do me any Harm.

" But to come nearer to my prefent
" Purpofe ; my Defign of placing you at
" Court, is to ferve as a Spy for me upon
" the *Squabbaws*; for my Enemies, who
" have tried in vain all other Means to
" overturn me, may perhaps at laft at-
" tempt it that Way ; and the Avarice
" of thefe *Squabbaws*, which has hither-
" to been my Support, may one Time
" or other (if I am not very vigilant)
" prove my Ruine. For if my Enemies
" fhould bribe them, to be privately in-
" troduced to confer with the Emperor,
" there is an End of my Reign ; for I
" am not infenfible, that his Imperial
" Majefty has no Perfonal Affection for
" me, and it is his own Eafe and Indo-
" lence that hinders him from looking
" out for fome other Servant to fupply
" my Place ; for Alterations cannot be
" made without fome little Trouble.

" Be therefore vigilant for my Intereft,
" as you value your own : Be always
" quick in your Intelligence, watch eve-
" ry Step and Motion of the *Squabbaws*,
" and acquaint me with every thing
that

" that paſſes in their moſt ſecret Tranſ-
" actions.   Let me know who are their
" Adviſers, their Favourites, their Com-
" panions; but above all, be quick in
" informing me, if any Perſon ſhould be
" admitted to confer with the Empe-
" ror; and if poſſible, hear what is the
" Subject of their Diſcourſe.   Your gro-
" teſque Form may recommend you to
" the *Squabbaws*; for Animals ſometimes
" become Favourites amongſt us, only
" for the Oddneſs of their Figure.
" They will ſay or do any thing before
" you, becauſe they will never imagine
" you capable of making any Remarks;
" for the *Cacklogallinians* have ſuch a
" Notion, that no Creatures are endued
" with Reaſon like themſelves.

" But it will be neceſſary to inſtruct
" you in the Manner of making your
" Addreſs, when you enter the Court.
" You muſt remember then to pay your
" Compliments to the *Squabbaws*, be-
" fore you do to the Emperor; and of
" theſe the *Vultuaquilians* claim the Pre-
" cedence to thoſe of our own Nation,
" particularly the bulkieſt.   It is the
" Practice here to do ſo, for the Empe-
" ror, as to what regards himſelf, is no
" great Lover of Ceremony. The Form
" of addreſſing theſe *Squabbaws* has
                                " ſome-

" fomething in it very fingular; but the
" fervile Manners of the *Cacklogallinians*
" to thofe in any Power has made it ne-
" ceffary to be comply'd with, and is the
" Caufe that they now expect it. You
" muft make a low Obeifance to the
" Ground, at which time they will turn
" their Backfides upon you, and fpread-
" ing all the Feathers of their Tails, give
" you an Opportunity of faluting them
" behind. You will fee the *Cacklogalli-*
" *nians* of Figure and Rank preffing in,
" endeavouring who fhall be firft in kif-
" fing the Pofteriors of thefe *Squabbaws*;
" and thofe upon whom they are graci-
" oufly pleafed to turn their Backfides,
" and fpread their Tails, return highly
" fatisfied, as if fome extraordinary Ho-
" nour had been conferr'd upon them;
" nay, I my felf am obliged to do it in
" as obfequious a Manner as any other,
" every time I approach them.

When he had fpoke thefe Words, a
Servant came in to give him Notice, that
the Coach was ready. He ordered me
to put on my Mantle, and attend him:
I did fo, and he was pleafed to do me
the Honour to carry me with him in his
Coach. In the Way, he difcourfed me
upon feveral Subjects. Among other
things, it came into his Head to enquire
of

of me, whether, in the Parts of the
World from whence I came, there were
any fuch things as Poets. I gave him
to underftand, that we had feveral who
had been famous in my own Country.
He defired to know what kind of Perfons they were: I anfwered him, they
were the faithful Regifters of the glorious Actions of great Men, whofe Praifes
they fung, in order to ftir up others, by
their Examples, to the Practice of Vertue, and Love of their Country; and
that as it required a great Genius, and
fine Underftanding, to be a good Poet,
they were, for that Reafon, highly careffed by the Great, and their Works fo
well paid for, that it was as rare to fee a
Poet poor, as a Minifter of State grow
rich by his Employment. This I faid,
as well out of Regard to Truth, as for
the Honour of my Country. He appeared pretty much furpriz'd at this
Account of our Poets, and told me theirs
were of a different Character, and met
with a different Fate; for they were but
little regarded by any great Birds, except the Vain and the Silly, who wanted a little Flattery, for which they paid
fome fmall Gratuity, while they wou'd
not accept of them as Companions;
for it was not fafhionable for thofe of

Figure

Figure to converfe with any thing inferior to them in Wealth or Quality,
which was reputed to have Senfe : On
the contrary, when they receiv'd fuch
for Companions, it was upon the Account
of their being either *Buffoons* or *Pandars*; and this he was pleafed to fay was
the Fafhion.

He alfo confefs'd to me, that he himfelf
never had any great Regard for that
Sort of Perfons, which he own'd he fometimes had Reafon to repent; for he found
that by their Verfes and Difcourfes,
they influenced the Publick very much,
by whom they were look'd upon with
more Efteem, than by the Courtiers;
and that his Enemies had made a proper Advantage of his Contempt of them;
for they had taken the moft ingenious
amongft them into their Party, and ex-
afperated them againft him ; fo that
their Compofitions had kept up a Spirit againft him, and he had the Mortification of feeing the People always receive with Pleafure any thing that ex-
pofed and fatyriz'd his Conduct.   That
indeed, in his own Defence, he had im-
ploy'd fome others to chant his Praife;
but they were fuch wretched Poetafters,
and did it fo awkardly, that their Performances prov'd more bitter Invectives

F   than

than the Satyrs of the others; for whenever there happen'd the leaſt Flaw in his
Adminiſtration, he was ſure to receive
congratulatory Verſes immediately upon
it; and that was the Time they choſe
to proclaim the Happineſs the Subject
enjoy'd by his wiſe Management: And
they carried this Matter to ſuch a ridiculous Height, that there was not a Vice
or a Folly, that either he or any of his
Family were remarkable for, but they
were prais'd for the contrary Vertues
and Accompliſhments.

By this Time we arriv'd at the Gates
of the Palace; for the Coach being drawn
by Six Oſtriches, we were but a little
Time upon the Way; and mounting
the great Stair-caſe, without being any
way moleſted by the People's Curioſity
(for the Moment my Lord appear'd every Fowl of what Quality ſoever, clapp'd
his Beak to the Ground, and did not alter that Poſture till he was paſt) he bid
me ſtay in the Anti-chamber till ſent for,
and went himſelf into the Preſence. He
had not been there five Minutes, before
I heard that Door open, and a Jay with
a ſtrait-body'd Coat, which button'd on
his Breaſt, and thro' which his Wings
and Legs paſs'd, came hopping into
the Room where I was, ſurrounded by
the

the Courtiers, who view'd me with Surprize, but were fo well bred as to whifper their Sentiments of me. This impertinent Jay peck'd 'em by the Legs, or pull'd 'em by the Crown-feathers, without Diftinction: Nay, I faw fome *Cacklogallinians* of the great Order, whofe Heads he could not reach, ftoop to him, and beg he would do them the Honour to pull their Crowns. Every one fhew'd him Refpect, and made way for him to come up to me; he view'd me fome time, and then peck'd me by the Finger; for he did not reach higher than my Hand, when it hung down. I returned the Compliment with a Wherret of my Fift, which knock'd him over, and had coft me my Life, durft any have ftruck in the Palace. There was a terrible Uproar, and I was apprehenfive, that I fhould pay dear for my Refentment; but the Emperor to whom my Lord was then giving an Account of me, being inform'd, that the Impertinence of the Jay had caus'd the Difturbance, he order'd him to be carried to the Guard, that he fhould be lock'd up for three Days, and take two Purges and a Vomit (for Criminals not guilty of Capital Crimes, are punifh'd by a Number of Vomits or Purges, which are

more

more or lefs, according to the Vilenefs
of the Fact) I was called into the Pre-
fence-chamber, where I made my Compliment as inftructed, and then addrefs'd
my felf to the Ladies, giving the Prece-
dence always to the bulkieft, according
to my Inftructions. The firft *Squabbaw*
whom I addrefs'd my felf to, was about
Seven Foot round ; her Crop hung
within Six Inches of the Floor, which
I have fince learn'd is a particular Beauty ; the Effluvia of her Body were extreamly ftrong, and oblig'd his Imperial Majefty, when fhe fpread her Tail
to me, to fmell to an Aromatick Leaf.

This Prince, tho' of a very advanced
Age, has been reprefented, both by the
Reports of his Minifters, and others, as
a Perfon of great Incontinency, in which
I think he was injured ; for tho' he pafs'd
moft of his private Hours only in the
Company of the *Vultuaquilian Squabbaws*
(fo call'd from the Province where they
were born) he did it, partly becaufe of
his long Accquaintance with them, and
partly to hinder the too frequent Vifits
of the firft Minifter, who fcarce ever
came into his Prefence, but to importune
him, for new Grants and Promotions
for Himfelf and Family ; and as to the
Cacklogallinian Squabbaws, he fometimes
admit-

admitted them to pleafe their Husbands and Relations, who flatter themfelves with an imaginary Honour, to have their Wives and Daughters near him. I have good Grounds for what I advance; for I was Five Years in his Court, and frequently convers'd with his *Squabbaws*. This won't I hope, be thought a piece of Vanity in me, when the Reader reflects, that I was look'd upon as a Monkey is with our Ladies.

The Emperor was highly delighted with the Prefent his Minifter made him, and order'd all poffible Care to be taken of me. My Lord told him I might be as ufeful to his Majefty as my Make was curious, for he found me very intelligent, learning the Languages with great Facility, and that it was poffible I might be ferviceable in extending his Dominions, by bringing that Part of the World, which my Species inhabited, in Subjection to his Imperial Majefty.

Have they, faid the Emperor, *any Gold among them?* I took the Liberty of affuring his Majefty, that we were the richeft Nation in the Univerfe; that by our Trade, which never was fo flourifhing as at this Time, we brought in immenfe Quantities of that valuable Metal, and that we fuffer'd none to be

exported.

exported. *It may then,* replied his Majesty, *be worth our while, one Day to think of this.*

The Emperor order'd me to be conducted to an Apartment, and Leave was given to all the *Vultuaquilian* firſt, and *Cacklogallinian* Quality, to ſee me the next Day. I had every thing I could wiſh provided for me, and a Month after I had been at Court, I had the Liberty of the Palace, and the Emperor would often call me into his Cloſet (as he found I was not ignorant in Arithmetick) to help him weigh and count his Wedges of Gold, and ſet down the Number, Weight and Value of each Piece; for this was a Diverſion in which he amuſed himſelf.

This Prince was not very curious, for in the five Years I was in his Court, he ſcarce ever asked me one Queſtion concerning the *Europeans ;* nor was he in one Reſpect the Bubble of his Favourites, for I never ſaw him give one Piece of Gold to any of them, even the *Squabbaws.*

The Grandees, who perceived me grow in Favour ſo far, as that the Jay was turn'd out of Court for his Sawcineſs to me, which he redoubled after his having been confined, ſtrove who ſhou'd ſhew me the moſt Reſpect, and make

make me the greateſt Profeſſions of Friendſhip. They not only offer'd me their Purſes, but even their Wives and Daughters, whom they often left with me, and whoſe Immodeſty has often put me to the Bluſh. Nay, a *Boutofallalian*, a Title anſwering to our Duke, told me, if I continued this Shyneſs, and would not do him the Honour to paſs now and then an Hour with his Lady, he ſhou'd not take me for his Friend; and leaving her with me, he lock'd the Door.

Her Grace was as generous as her Spouſe; and when I urg'd the Difference of our Species, ſhe ſaid, ſhe was ſatisfied that wou'd be no Impediment, by what ſhe had ſeen, for I had indeed no other Covering than a Mantle, and both his Majeſty and his *Squabbaws* took a Pleaſure to teaze me, by pulling it off, and leaving me naked in a full Circle. In ſhort, I was forc'd to ſave my ſelf by the Window being on a Ground Floor, after all my Excuſes were to no Purpoſe: But fearing the Lady's Reſentment, I begg'd the Miniſter, exaggerating her Husband's Merits, to give him a Penſion, and I my ſelf carried and delivered the Grant to her Grace, which made my Peace with both.

F 4　　　　One

One Day, an old Colonel, who was very poor, accosted me in the Emperor's Garden. *My Lord,* said he, *I beg you will vouchsafe me an Audience of a Quarter of an Hour; I shall look upon it as the greatest Condescension in you, and as the greatest Honour done me.* I told him he mistook my Title, and gave me one I never did aspire to ; but that I was very ready to hear and serve him, for I had seen him often at Court offering Petitions, which were always rejected, and I had a Compassion for him. " Your Goodness, *said he,* can alone be " equalled by your Modesty ; give me " Leave then to tell you, I have served " long and faithfully in the late Wars " against the *Owls* and *Magpyes,* but " to my great Surprize, at my Return " home ; my Regiment, without any " Fault alledg'd, was taken from me, " and given to a *Valet de Chambre* who " had never seen an Enemy ; his Master " was a *Boutofallalian,* had a Mind to " reward his Pimp, and all that I cou'd " say, might as well have been let alone. " I had no Estate but what I sold, " and gave to a Courtier to get this " Regiment, after I had served many " Years as a Captain, without the least " Blemish in my Character. I have

" since

" since been in almost a starving Con-
" dition, and have wearied my self out
" with Petitions to no Purpose; for if
" any, as very few, were received,
" they were never answered, and perhaps
" never read. I have therefore no Hopes
" but what are founded on your Cha-
" rity: I see it vain to hope for Employ-
" ment, and shall change my Suit to
" that of being put into the Hospital
" of the *Meritorians* (*which in* English,
" *signifies disabled and superannuated*
" *Soldiers*) I beg your Compassion for
" a most unfortunate and perishing
" Man, who has served his Prince and
" Country with Fidelity, and on several
" Occasions has distinguish'd himself, as
" Your Honour will be satisfied, if you
" will take the Pains to examine these
" Certificates.

He put several into my Hands; one
mentioned his being the first who broke
Ranks, and put the right Wing of the
Enemy in Disorder, which was followed by a signal Victory over the *Magpyes* and *Owls*: Then another mentioned his taking the Royal Banner, in the
Battle of *Bellfugaro*: A third certify'd
his surprizing a great Convoy of Provisions, carrying to the Enemy's Camp,
the

the Lofs of which, made them break up the Siege of *Barbaquero*. In fhort, he had about Twenty, figned by the General and chief Officers, which fpoke him a Fool of fingular Gallantry. When I had return'd them, I afk'd, in what he thought I could ferve him? " I beg, " *faid he*, you wou'd recommend me to " the Minifter to be provided for as a " fuperannuated Officer; your Honour " cannot do an Act of greater Charity. " Sir, *faid I*, is it poffible you can be fo " great a Stranger to the Court, as to " imagine Merit carries any Weight with " it. Your Certificates prove you have " done your Duty like a gallant Officer; " but then you have done no more than " what was expected from you, and what " you were paid for. I acknowledge what " your Honour fays, *replied the Colonel*, " but I can name many, who have run " away, or been taken violently ill at the " time of a Battle, and who are not only " continued in Poft, but even advanced. I anfwer'd, it was very true; but that fuch Fowls were otherwife ferviceable in the Government, had handfome Wives or Daughters, or could procure fuch of their Acquaintance, or perhaps were elected into the Grand Council of the Nation, and had a Vote to difpofe of. *But, Sir,*

Sir, I will deal with you ingenuously, I can do you no Service at all in this Affair; *for the Minister has so many* Bable-Cypherians (in *English*, Members of the Great Council) *to oblige, and they have so many* Valet de Chambres, *Butlers, and Footmen to provide for in the Hospital, that it's more likely the Officers and Soldiers now there will be turn'd out to make Place for them, than any other will be admitted. If you have Interest to get a Number of these* Bable-Cypherians *to back your Petition, which you may get, if you can bribe and cajole the Attendants of their* Squabbaws, *or their own Valets, it's possible you may succeed in your Pretensions.* " I'll " sooner, *said he*, starve, than be guilty " of so great a Condescension, or more " properly, so mean an Action." This he said with some Warmth, and I replied as coolly, it was in his own Option. " I find then, *said the Colonel*, you won't " serve me. *I have*, said I, *given you Reasons which prove this Way I cannot: But if giving your Petition and Certificates to the Emperor will be of use, I'll venture to do it for you.* " The Emperor, *replied* " *he*, is a good Prince, but has little In- " terest with the Minister; and to hope " any thing, but thro' his Canal, is al- " toherget vain." Saying this, he took
" his

his Leave in a very courteous manner. The Minister was inform'd, that I had entertain'd a long Discourse with this Officer, and ask'd me the Subject of it. I told him what he desired, but that I declined troubling his Excellency with such Trifles. " These Fowls, *said he,* " who build on their own Merit, are " extremely impertinent. The Colonel " now in Question is one of your Fowls " who might by his Principles have made " a Fortune, had he lived Two or Three " Hundred Years ago; but they are now " obsolete, and he starves by tenaciously " practising his musty Morals. Why, he'll " have the Impudence to be always speak- " ing Truth; and tho' he has been thrust " out of the Palace for this Vice more " than once, he is not to be corrected. He " will tell a Fowl of Quality without Ce- " remony, that he's a Pimp, and was raised " by the Hens of his Family: He'll make " no Bones of telling another, if his Pru- " dence made him decline Danger, that " he's a Coward: A Third he'll impu- " dently remind of his former Livery, " tho' his good Fortune has raised him " to the Title of a Grandee. Nay, he " had the Face to tell me, upon my re- " fusing to take his Petition, That it was " great Pity, when I was imprisoned for
" Pecu-

" Peculation, that the Juſtice of the Na-
" tion did not firſt purge, and then hang
" me; that I was a publick Robber, and
" deſerv'd the Gallows more richly than
" a common Thief. His Poverty and
" Folly made me pity and pardon him,
" if leaving him to be laugh'd at and
" ſtarv'd, are to be eſteemed no Puniſh-
" ment. As I really pity'd the Fowl, I
" found where he lodged, and ſupplied
" him with ſufficient to keep him above
" Want, tho' I would never truſt him
" with the Knowledge of his Benefactor,
" nor would ever after be ſeen to give
" him the leaſt Countenance.

The Character of the Cacklogallinians *in general.*

THE *Cacklogallinians* were, in former Ages, a Wiſe and a Warlike
Nation, both fear'd and eſteem'd by their
Neighbours. Their Blood was pure,
without being mix'd with that of the
*Owls, Magpies, Eagles, Vulturs, Jays,
Partridges, Herns, Hawks,* or any other
Species; the Scum of which Nation, by
the Fertility of the Country, and the
want of Foreſight in the *Cacklogallinians,*
has

has been allured to, and permitted to settle in *Cacklogallinia*, and by their Intermarriages has caufed the great Degeneracy thofe Families, which have kept their Blood untainted, complain of.

The Hiftory of their Neighbours are ftanding Witneffes of the Worth of their Anceftors, and fhew the vaft Difference between the ancient and modern *Cacklogallinians.* The former, tho' tenacious of their Liberty, were remarkable for their Loyalty; and each thought it his peculiar Intereft zealoufly to promote that of the Publick. But not to be prolix in the Charaēter of the old *Cacklogallinians*, I fhall give it in few Words. They were what the *Englifh* now are, Wife, Modeft, Brave, Human, Loyal, Publick-fpirited, capable of governing their own, and conquering other Kingdoms; Hofpitable to Strangers: They encourag'd Merit, and abominated Flattery. A Pimp in thofe Days wou'd have ftarv'd, and even the Concubine of a Prince not been admitted among Hens of Virtue, tho' to make the Fortune of a Husband. There was no Upftarts among the Nobility, and if any were rais'd to Titles, it was by Force of a confpicuous Merit, which gave a Luftre to the Auguft Affembly in which he was enroll'd.

Juftice

Juſtice was impartially adminiſter'd, and the ſelling of the People to a Prince or Miniſter, was a Villainy unknown. None bribed the People to chuſe 'em for their Repreſentatives; Poſts in the Government were given to Fowls capable to ſerve it, without being burthened with this or that Family, nor were their Revenues loaded with Penſions to worthleſs and vicious Perſons, and given for Services which would be a Diſgrace to publiſh. Trade flouriſh'd, Money was plenty, none of their Neighbours durſt encroach on their Commerce; their Taxes were inconſiderable: In a Word, as I before ſaid, they were what our happy Nation now is, admired for the Prudence of their Adminiſtration at home, and the Terror of their Arms abroad. They are now directly the Reverſe of what they were, and even in my Time, they were ſinking in the Opinion of their Neighbours, who began to conſider them as a declining Nation, which Alteration, I muſt own (for I love to ſpeak the Truth) was not a little owing to the Adminiſtration of my Friend, the firſt Miniſter, who in taking upon him to manage the Intereſts of Nations, went out of his Depth, for Affairs of that Nature ſeemed to be above his Capacity. His Education,

cation, his Study, his Practice, were rather mercantile, than otherwife, and all
that Knowledge which his Partizans
boaft fo much in him, was confined to
the Bufinefs of the Taxes, a Road in
which he was (as it were) grown old,
and to Money-Projects, which was owing
to a ftrict Correfpondence he always
kept with certain projecting and mercantile People, and being ufed to carry
all Points at home by Gold, he knew no
other way of doing Bufinefs abroad; fo
that when their Neighbours ufed to differ among themfelves, about fome Points
of Intereft, and one Side or other ftood
in Need of the Affiftance of the *Cacklogallinians*, they fometimes pufh'd themfelves into the Quarrel, and perhaps paid
great Sums of Money for the Favour of
fending Armies to the Succour of one
Side or other; fo that they became the
Tools which other Nations work'd with.
They are naturally prone to Rebellion,
have let the *Cormorants* choufe them
out of feveral valuable Branches of
their Commerce; and yet the *Cormorants* are People with whom they have
kept the moft lafting Friendfhip of all
their Neighbours. They love War, and
rather than not fight, they will give Money to be let into the Quarrel (as has
been

been hinted before) they know before-
hand, however victorious they may prove,
nothing but Blows will fall to their Share.
If they are under a mild Government,
and grow rich, they are always finding
Fault with their Superiors, and ever
ready to revolt: But if they are oppress'd
and kept poor, like our Spaniels, they
fawn on their Masters, and seem in Love
with Tyranny ; which should any dare to
speak against, he is esteem'd an Enemy
to the Happiness of his Country. They
are very proud, yet very mean in some
Particulars, and will, for their Interest,
sacrifice the Honour of their Families.
They look upon nothing infamous but
Poverty, for which Reason, the most
scandalous Methods of procuring Riches,
such as Lying, Robbing the Publick,
Cheating Orphans, Pimping, Perjury, &c.
are not look'd upon with evil Eyes, provided they prove successful. This Maxim
holds with 'em, both in publick and
private Affairs. I knew One rais'd from
a Fowl of Three Foot Six Inches, to be
a *Makeseulsibi*, a Post which rais'd him
to Eight Foot Six, and is one of the
greatest in the Kingdom. He is to in-
struct the Grandees, when in Council,
in Points of Law, and is Guardian to all
Orphans. Complaint was made to the

G   Empe-

Emperor, that he converted their Eftates
to his own Ufe, and left them all to
ftarve ; he was therefore, by the Emperor's Confent, and to fatisfy the People,
brought to a Tryal. He anfwer'd, That
he did not deny the Charge ; but that
he wanted the Money to make a Figure
equal to his Poft : However, the Enquiry
difcover'd his vaft Acqufitions, and prov'd
him to be fo rich, that he was look'd upon with Refpect, and he lived and died
in as much Grandeur, and Tranquillity,
as if he had been a Patriot, and at his
Funeral, his great Service to his Country
was blazon'd out in Figures and Hiero-
glyphicks by the Heralds; which being a
thing I feem'd amaz'd at, and enquiring
of many, how it came to pafs, that a
Fowl fhould be treated with Honour,
who had been efteem'd an Oppreffor ? the
common Anfwer was, he died rich, and
that was enough for all Honours.

The *Religion* of the Cacklogallinians.

THIS Nation pretends to believe a
firft Being, and to worfhip one
God, tho' I confefs, when I was firft
amongft them, I thought otherwife ; for
I found

I found the People of the beft Rank amongft them always ridiculing Religion. They had formerly a Globe of pure Gold in their Temples, an Emblem of Eternity: It was infcribed with unintelligible Charaɛters, by which they figured the Infcrutability of his Decrees. This fome call'd fuperftitious, and were for having razed, and the Ball, which was, in their Opinion, too big, new melted, and caft into a different Form. Some were for a Square, to give an Emblem of Juftice; others would have it, an Oɛtogon, by which they would fhadow his Ubiquity. Another Party infifted upon its being caft again, but in no regular Form ; for all Forms and Regularity they look'd upon fuperftitious. Their Difputes on this Subjeɛt ran fo high, that they came to Blows, and each Party, as it was viɛtorious, modell'd the Globe to his own Humour or Caprice. But the Ball being fo often melted, and Part of the Gold being loft in each Fufion, it was at laft almoft imperceivable. Thefe Bickerings fhed a great deal of Blood, and being at length tired with worrying each other upon this Account, a new Globe was caft, but not exaɛtly round, to fatisfy tender Confciences. In procefs of Time, it was thought that a

brazen

brazen Globe might do as well as one of Gold, and and new Difputes beginning to arife, it was decreed, that this Globe fhould ftand in the Temple, but that every one in particular fhould have at home an Idol after his own Fafhion, provided they wou'd only bow to this, and the Revenues were continued to the Priefts to furnifh Sacrifices. The Heads of the Priefts at laft thinking thefe Sacrifices altogether needlefs, and a very great Expence, dropp'd 'em by Degrees: However, fome fay this was done by fome of the Grandees, as a Means to make the Priefts lefs refpeéted, and put the Money in their own Coffers, which has made them both rich and infolent. They were formerly a cunning Set, but they are not look'd upon as fuch now, for they take but little Care, either to cultivate the Intereft, or fupport the Credit and Dignity of their Order; and as fome of them are given to Luxury, which they have not taken due Care to conceal, the common Sort do not entertain the fame Refpeét for them they did in former Times.

However, the poor Clergy (for they are not all rich) Affairs of Religion being modell'd after thofe of the State, the Great devouring the Small) lead moral Lives,

Lives, and there is a Sect amongst them, which keeps up the golden Ball, continues the Sacrifices, and detests Perjury; but thefe are obliged to perform their Ceremonies by Stealth, and are profecuted as an obftinate ill-defigning People.

The Grandees have no Statues in their Houfes; they own indeed a Deity, fome of them at leaft, but don't think the worfhipping that Deity of any Confequence. The meaner People began to be as polite as the Courtiers, and to have as little Religion, before I left *Cacklogallinia.* This Irreligion I can attribute to nothing fo much as the Contempt of the Clergy, whom fome of the Nobility, efpecially of the Court, have endeavour'd to render hateful and ridiculous to the People, by reprefenting them as a lazy, ufelefs, Order of Birds, no better than the Drones. They alfo chufe out now and then, fome to place at their Head, who had diftinguifh'd themfelves for their Infidelity, and had declared themfelves Enemies to the Religion of the Country, by which means the whole Order loft their Sway with the People; befides which, the richer Sort amongft them were generally reputed to be much addicted to Gluttony.

Of the Policy and Government of the
Cacklogallinians.

THE *Cacklogallinians* boaſt mightily
of their being the only Nation in
the World which enjoys Liberty, and
therefore, upon all Occaſions, they talk
of, and treat the reſt of the World as
Slaves. They pretend to maintain, that
their Monarchy being elective, their Emperors are no more than their Servants,
and that they can exerciſe no longer
a Power, than they are pleas'd to give it
them, which is juſt as much as will ſerve
to put the Laws in Execution, and keep
the great Machine of Government in
good Order; and that whenever he attempts to tranſgreſs thoſe Bounds, they
make no Ceremony of turning him out,
and ſetting up another in his Room.
But, by what I could judge by my own
proper Obſervation, this appeared to
me, to be no more than an empty Boaſt
(for indeed the *Cacklogallinians* are apt
to run into an Extravagance of Vanity,
whenever they ſpeak of themſelves) for
in my Time my Friend and Patron the
firſt Miniſter acted as abſolutely, and in-
depen-

dependently of all Creatures (except of the *Squabbaws*) as the moft arbitrary Prince, who acknowledges no Law but his own Will and Pleafure.

It is, true there is a Council confifting of a great Number of Perfons, in whofe Name all great Affairs relating to the Civil Government are tranfacted, the Members of which Council are call'd *Bable-Cypherians ;* but it is no Secret, that the firft Minifter caufes whom he pleafes to fit in this Council, as well as turns out any Perfon he diflikes ; and while I was amongft them, there happen'd fome Inftances of what I maintain ; and he contrived to have feveral whom he fufpected of being Enemies to his Family, or to his Adminiftration, to be difgraced from the faid Council, and others appointed in their Places : Nay, I have often feen feveral worthlefs Birds paying their Court to the firft Minifter, and folliciting him to be admitted into the Great Council, in the fame manner that they begg'd for an Employment ; yet at the fame time, if you were to talk to a *Caeklogallinian,* he wou'd pretend to perfuade you, that no Fowl of any Rank or Quality whatfoever can ever fit in the faid Council, but by the Majority of free Voices of Perfons who

are

are his Equals. But as 1 oferv'd before, they are fo poffefs'd with a Spirit of boafting, that when they talk of themfelves, there is no Regard to be had to any thing they fay.

What is moft remarkable is, that Hens as well as Cocks frequently ftand Candidates to be Members of the faid Council, and efpecially thofe who are diftinguifh'd by the Name of *Squabbaws*; and tho' the important Affairs of managing their Amours takes up fo much of their Time, that they have but little Leifure to attend fuch publick Affairs, yet they very much influence what paffes there, efpecially the Court *Squabbaws*, whom I have frequently feen to receive Prefents from Perfons who had Matters to lay before the faid Council. When this happen'd, it was their Cuftom to fend for my Friend the firft Minifter, and inftruct him how they would have the thing done; upon which Occafions they defignedly abfented themfelves from the faid Council, that by their not appearing to favour or oppofe fuch things, the Bribery might not be fufpected; and it generally pafs'd as well without them, for my good Patron who carried it fo loftily to the reft of the World, was neverthelefs extreamly their Slave.

As

As to their Laws, which they pretend to be the beſt and wiſeſt of any in the World, they are, in Effect, a Source of continual Plague and Vexation to the Subject, which is owing to many Cauſes, but principally to this, that when a new Law is agreed to paſs, the great Council generally appoint ſuch amongſt them as are Lawyers by Profeſſion, to word it, or (as we ſay) to draw it up, who always, in Order to promote the Buſineſs of their own Profeſſion, contrive it in ambiguous Terms; ſo that there is a double Meaning runs thro' every Sentence. This furniſhes eternal Matter of Diſpute betwixt Party and Party, and at the ſame time gives the *Caja* (for ſo they call a Judge) a Power of putting what Conſtruction he pleaſes upon the Law. I have my ſelf been frequently preſent, when the *Caja* has been ſitting to hear and determine Cauſes, and have obſerv'd, that when the *Cacklogallinian* Advocates have been ſetting forth the Merit of their Cauſe, and one of them has produced a Precedent, to ſhew, that ſuch a *Caja*, in former Times, put ſuch a Conſtruction upon ſuch a Law, yet the *Caja* then preſiding has determined the thing quite otherwiſe, giving for a Reaſon, *That might be his Opinion, but this is ours.*

Upon

Upon the whole, the Property of private Birds, which they would make you believe was much safer amongst them, than under any other Government in the World, appear'd to me to stand upon a very precarious Foot, since it was always at the Mercy of the Law, and the most cunning and sagacious amongst them could never pretend to be sure what Law was: Nay, it was often found by Experience, that what was Law one Day amongst them, was not so another; so that I could not help thinking, that whenever Party and Party differr'd concerning Matters of Property, the least expensive, and most prudent Method would have been, to have referr'd the Decision of the Cause to some Game of Hazard.

This Ambiguity of the Law makes a corrupt *Caja* a terrible Plague to the Subject; and it is a Plague which they have often felt, as I found, by consulting their Annals; for frequently, under bad Ministers, Birds have been chosen out for *Caja's*, not for their Integrity or Knowledge, but for their Obsequiousness to the Commands of those who chose them; and my Patron, the first Minister, was censured for endeavouring to corrupt, and making them as bad as he could.

could. By which Means, and by retaining Spies in the Houfes of all Fowl
of great Intereft and Figure in their
Country, it was reported he awed them
from attempting any Meafures againft
his Intereft, or that of his Family, and
that he had threaten'd feveral with
Confifcation and Banifhment, when he
found them attempting to introduce better Schemes than his own, becaufe fuch
Proceedings might tend to overthrow
him.

But this I fpeak from common Report ; for I cannot give any Inftances of
Corruption in any of the *Caja's* from my
own perfonal Knowledge; for I conceiv-
ed fo dreadful a Notion of their Laws,
that I endeavour'd to avoid all Converfe
with any who belong'd to it.

How often have I reflected on the
Happinefs of my dear Country, in that
Liberty there enjoy'd, where none are
opprefs'd by Force, or allured by Bribes,
to give up their native Freedom ; where
a felf-interefted and defigning Minifter is
fure to anfwer for his Adminiftration to
a Parliament freely chofen, confifting of
Gentlemen of publick Spirits, Honour,
known Probity and Wifdom ; whofe
Fortunes put them above a fervile De-
pendence ; who have an Eye to nothing
but

but the publick Good, and exact from the
Minifters a juft Account of the *Publick
Treafure!* When I have feen the Fowl
of Honour thruft out to make Place for
a Sycophant, Court paid to Pandars and
lewd Hens, and no Pofts difpofed of, but
thro' the Intereft of Luft ; how often,
Britain, have I congratulated thy Happinefs, where Virtue is rewarded, Vice
difcountenanc'd and punifh'd ; where the
Man of Merit is provided for, and not
oblig'd to pay a Levee to the kept Miftrefs
of a Statefman ; and where the Ignorant,
Pufillanimous, and Vicious, however diftinguifh'd by Birth and Fortune, are held
in Contempt, and never admitted to
publick Employment!

When among the *Cacklogallinians* Taxes
are laid, the Money is brought into the
publick Treafury, of which the Minifter
keeps the Keys : He lets this Money out
upon Pawns, at an exorbitant Intereft.
If an inferior Agent is to pafs his Accounts, he muft fhare the Pillage with
the Minifter, and fome few Heads of the
Grand Council. I knew one paid him
Three Hundred Thoufand *Rackfantaffines,*
equal to a Hundred Thoufand Pounds
Sterling, which he computed was about
one Third of his Acquifition ; and Birds
of moft abandon'd Reputations are fometimes

times put into Places of Profit, which, like Spunges, ſuck all they can, and are eaſily ſqueezed again.

As to their Trade, they have, of late Years, loſt ſome of the moſt advantageous Parts of it to the *Cormorants*, which perhaps might be brought about by ſeveral that were *Cormorants* by Birth, who found Means of working themſelves into the Management of their publick Affairs. They ſeem to endeavour all they can, (for what Policy I know not) to encourage the young *Cacklogallinian* Nobility and Gentry, in a Contempt of Religion, and in all Debauchery, perhaps to render them ſupine and thoughtleſs; and bringing them up without Principle, they may be fit Tools to work the enſlaving their Country.

They are extremely ſevere in their military Diſcipline: A Soldier, for a trifling Fault, ſhall have all the Feathers ſtripp'd off his Back, and a corroding Plaiſter clapp'd on, which will eat to the Bones in a ſmall Space of Time. For a capital Crime, every one in the Regiment is ordered to peck him as he's ty'd to a Poſt, till he dies. I have ſeen one who was condemn'd to this Death have Part of his Entrails torn out of his Side in a few Pecks.

Who-

Whoever fpeaks againft the Miniftry, is purged or vomited fo feverely, that he fometimes dies. Even Want of Complaifance to any menial Servant of a Minifter, is efteem'd an Affront to his Mafter, and punifh'd by a Year's Imprifonment; but a Slight put on any of the *Squabbaws*, is fo heinous, that the Offender is punifh'd, as for the higheft Scandal. Sometimes it has happen'd, that Perfons Queftion'd and Convicted for Fraud, Bribery, or other Crimes, by fome Turn of Fortune having better'd their Circumftances, have afterwards been raifed to Pofts of Honour and Truft, and afterwards growing more wealthy, have been look'd upon with the fame Efteem as the moft worthy. I've known a Sharper, who could neither write nor read, made a *Battano*, in *Englifh*, a Judge Advocate; and what rais'd him was his Dexterity at *Geftaro*, which is like the Play our School-boys divert themfelves with, call'd *Hufsle-cap*.

Tho' they have a Standing Army, yet the *Cacklogallinians* are all inlifted, and obliged to ferve (in cafe of an Invafion) without Pay. They have no fortify'd Places, they being look'd upon as a Refuge for Malecontents, except only the imperial Palace. The Reader may wonder

der how any Place can be fortified againſt
thoſe who can fly over the higheſt Walls;
I muſt therefore inform him, that their
ſtrong Holds have all the open Places cover'd with Canvaſs ſtretch'd from Side to
Side; upon which is ſtrew'd an Herb ſo
venemous, that, in ſix Hours after it has
been expos'd to the Sun, it emits ſo peſti-
ferous a Stench, that no Fowl can approach it by many Yards, but what will
fall dead; and this Stench, by the Effluvia mounting, is no way offenſive to thoſe
below. This is the Reaſon their Sieges
are rather Blockades, and no fortify'd
Town was ever taken but by ſtarving:
For tho' I have ſaid, the *Cacklogallinians*
have no ſuch, yet their Neighbours have
this Canvaſs, and Plenty of the Herb in
and about moſt of their Towns, and can,
in Twenty four Hours, put them in a
Poſture of Defence.

Upon the Deceaſe of any Party, his
Eſtate goes to the eldeſt of his Children,
whether Male or Female; for the others,
the Cocks are put into the Army, or to
Trades; the Hens are married to the next
Relations, who are obliged to take them,
or allow them a Penſion for Life, according to their Quality. Polygamy is forbid,
tho' univerſally practiſed among the better Sort. There were publick Colleges
erected

erected for the Education and Provision of poor Chickens; but as there is a strong Party, which takes them to be of ill Consequence; they are discountenanc'd so much, that it is thought they must fall some time or other.

✿✿✿✿✿✿✿✿✿✿✿✿✿✿✿✿✿✿✿✿

The Cuſtoms, Manners, Dreſs, and Diverſions of the Cacklogallinians.

THE *Cacklogallinians* value themselves on being a polite Nation; and indeed thoſe amongſt them who have travell'd, are very complaiſant, full of their Profeſſions of Friendſhip, and Offers of Service, tho' it's the firſt time they ever ſet Eyes on the Party to whom they make them; but if he takes this for any more than the Effects of good Breeding, and reminds a Courtier of his Promiſe, he is look'd upon as one who wants Education, and treated as a Peaſant.

They are not at all ſociable, tho' they frequently viſit each other, which is with much Ceremony amongſt the better Sort; for he who makes the Viſit, ſends before him a Servant to give Notice,

that

that he intends to do himſelf the Honour to kiſs the Spur of the Maſter of the Houſe. If he is, or will be at home, Anſwer is made, that he returns Thanks for the Honour intended him, which he will expect with Impatience. When the Viſiter arrives, Notice is given to the Family by one of his Servants, who ſtrikes a braſs Pan (hung at the Doors of all Perſons of Diſtinction) ſo long, and with ſuch Violence, that were it in *England*, he'd be indicted for a common Diſturber. After this Peal, the Door is open'd, and the Viſiter received according to his Quality, either at the Street Door, Parlour Door, or in the Hall. He's led in, and ſeated on a Carpet, enquires after the Welfare of the Family, after which he takes Notice of the Weather, and then with great Ceremony takes his Leave, conducted as he was received.

None viſit the Miniſter of State, neither is there any thing like the *Engliſh* Hoſpitality ſeen in the Viſits of private Perſons; for they never preſent you any Refreſhment, not even that of cold Water, except at a formal Invitation, or a Wedding. At the latter they are very profuſe. When a young Couple is married, for a Week they are never ſeen aſunder; but after that, it is look'd upon

indecent to be feen with a Wife in any
publick Company; and one would think
they married to be reveng'd on each
other for fome former Injuries; for the
Wife takes Care to fhew her Contempt
of her Husband, and he his Averfion to
his Wife. They are great Admirers of
Puppet-fhews and other Spectacles, and
will let their Families at Home want
Neceffaries, rather than not be feen at
the Booth. What they moft delight in
is bloody Spectacles. There are poor
Cacklogallinians, who fight on Stages for
Money; if they cut one another to Pieces,
the Spectators go away highly fatisfied;
but if their Art prevents their fhedding
much Blood, the Combatants are poorly
rewarded, and look'd upon as a Couple
of Cheats or Cowards.

A Goat had (as Tradition fays) done
formerly great Damage to the Corn of
Danafalio, a Saint in great Veneration
amongft them, who lived about Twelve
Hundred Years ago; for which Reafon,
every Family, on a certain Day, di-
verts it felf by breaking the Legs and
Ribs of a Goat, and flaying it alive.

Their Burial of the Dead is fo ex-
penfive, that it often ruines the Heir.
When the Corpfe is carried out of the
Houfe, a Herald goes before, who pro-
claims

claims the Titles of the Deceas'd : If he
has none, he has Three Days Notice to
make a Genealogy for him. I faw the
Burial of a *quondam* Taylor, who was
nearly ally'd to a firft Minifter, and
heard the Herald's Oration, which was as
near as I remember, in thefe Words. *See,
Fellow-Citizens, the Vanity of all fublunary Things ! and lament your own hard Fate
in the Lofs of the Illuftrious* Evanofma-
dor. *If Virtue, if Art, if Nobility of
Blood, could any way have influenc'd the
Tyrant Death, who could boaft a greater
Soul! Who exceed him in the Myfteries
of his Art ! Or laftly, Whofe Veins were
fill'd with a more noble Blood!*

Here he repeated his Genealogy, which
fpoke him defcended from a Number of
Sovereign Princes, Grandees, *Caja's,* &c.

When the Corpfe arrives at the great
Market-place, where all the Dead are
burnt, a Prieft makes a Funeral Oration ; which done, a great Number of
Mourners, hired for that purpofe, begin
their Lamentations, which laft till the Body is entirely confum'd. The Fire is made
with Billets, on which the Arms of the
Deceafed are either carv'd or painted,
which cannot coft lefs than an *Englifh*
Crown each. Every one of the Company is prefented with two of thefe Billets;

lets; one he lays on the Pile, the other
he carries home, and hangs up in his
Houfe. After the Confumption of the
Corpfe, the Picture of the Deceas'd is
hung over the Door for the Space of
Twelve Moons. Their Ceremonies in
marfhalling the Company are tedious,
and therefore I fhall not mention them;
I fhall only take Notice, that the Dead
are drawn by Six, or Eight Oftriches,
cover'd with Cloath of Gold, upon an
open Chariot.

When any begins to ficken, a Phyfician is fent for, who, after having exa-
min'd the Patient, fends for a *Venenugall-
potior*, fomething like our Apothecary,
and gives him his Direction, takes his
Fee, which is extravagant enough, and
goes into his *Palanquin*; for a Phyfician,
let him be a Second *Hermes*, or *Galen*,
will never get Bread, if he does not
make a Figure. He's fure to repeat
his Vifits, Morning and Even, if the
Patient as often repeats his Fees; but
whenever he finds any Symptoms of a
weak Purfe, he fets a Mark on that
Houfe, and no Intreaties will prevail
with him to go under that Roof.

When the Relations of the Sick perceive him paft Hopes of Recovery, they
fall to plundering his Houfe, neglect him
entirely,

entirely, and very often fall together by
the Ears, begin with Blows, and end
with a Law-fuit, which feldom fails ruin-
ing both Plaintiff and Defendant; for
their Lawyers rarely bring a Suit to Iffue,
till their Clients are brought to Beggary;
and tho' they all know this to be the
Confequence of their Litigation, yet is
there no Nation fo fond of going to Law.

When any one falls into Poverty, he's
look'd upon as infected; for all his Acquaintance fhun him; nay, very often
his own Children will not own him, if
in happier Circumftances: And what will
feem wonderful to a *Briton*, who efteems
Merit in Rags, and contemns the Vicious,
tho' encompafs'd with a Crowd of Servants, and diftinguifh'd by the glaring
Titles of his Family; no fooner does a
Cacklogallinian grow rich, but all the
World courts him, tho' fprung from a
Dunghill: And even thofe who can never hope any thing from him, fhew him
a profound Refpect. Ask who fuch a one
is, and they never tell you, that he is fuch
a Fowl of Honour, or of fuch good Qua-
lities, but anfwer, he is worth fo much:
Nay, Riches give a Man fuch Superio-
rity, that a Merchant, the Son of a Butcher, prefum'd fo much upon the immenfe
Sums he poffefs'd, that he had the Bold-

H 3   nefs

nefs to tell the Emperor to his Face, if
he did not prohibit the Importation of
Corn (which was then very much wanted) he having a great Quantity by him,
would draw his Money out of the publick
Treafury, and then his Majefty might fee
who was able to fupply him. The Emperor was advifed to lay him by the Heels
for his Sawcinefs, but the good Prince
forgave him.

Their Drefs is a clofe Doublet, and a
a loofe Mantle, which is either rich or
plain, fine or coarfe, not according to
the Quality, but according to the Ability
of the Wearer; for very often you can't
diftinguifh, in refpect of Drefs, the Grandee from the Merchant, or the *Squabbaw*
from her Attendant; for the meaner Sort
lay all on their Backs. Their Necks are
adorned with Ribbons, Bells, Medals, &c.
and their Tail-feathers are beautify'd with
additional ones from the Peacock, or Figures painted with various Colours, which
muft be by the Emperor's Permiffion, as
has been before obferv'd.

Their Exercifes are pretty violent, and
they are great Lovers of a Play for which
I can find no Name in *Englifh*. They
begin with giving their next Neighbour
a great Bang with the Wing, which is
return'd by a Kick or Peck, or Stroke
with

with the Spur; you would imagine they were fo many engaged in a Battle, for they ftrike without Fear or Wit, and never mind on whom the Strokes light; for every one deals them about promif-cuoufly, and as thick as he can lay them on. They will continue this Diverfion, till they are not able to ftand, or till fome of the Company gets a Wing, a Leg, or a Head broke, or fome other Da-mage, which the Party hurt never takes ill. This Play is indeed practifed only among the younger, or the meaner Sort.

They are mighty fond of the *Cuckoo,* and will fit two Hours upon a Stretch to hear a Set of them exercife their natu-ral Talent, for which they are paid and carefs'd. I knew a Lady of Quality who gave a Penfion of Five Thoufand *Spafma's,* each *Spafma* worth Two Shillings Ster-ling, to one of thefe Birds to fing her to Sleep every Night. The Air of this Coun-try is too cold for thefe *Cuckoo's,* who come from a more fouthern Clime, which is the Reafon they ftay not above three Years before they wing their Flight home, where they build Palaces with the Profits of their Journey: But as thofe who re-turn fend others in their ftead, the *Cack-logallinians* are never long deprived of the Entertainment thefe Birds afford 'em.

Ano-

Another Diverſion they have, is the making the Oſtriches run Races: The Feeding, Training, and Betting upon theſe Birds, have ruined many of the nobleſt Families. They are alſo mightily addicted to Dice, and will ſet and loſe their Wives and Children, which they ſometimes ſee eaten by the Winner, if he is of Quality.

This ſmall Sketch of the *Cacklogallinians* I thought neceſſary, that the Reader might have ſome Idea of them. I happen'd to be caſt on their Coaſt, juſt after they had made a Peace with the *Magpyes*, a puiſſant and neighbouring Nation, after a long, ſanguine, and expenſive War, which had well nigh exhauſted the Forces and Treaſure of both Parties, occaſioned by the *Cacklogallinians* pretending they had a Right to nominate a Succeſſor to the Emperor *Chuctinio*, who was in an advanc'd Age, and without Iſſue; and the *Magpyes* pretended their King, as a Relation to that Emperor, had a Right to ſucceed to the Throne of the *Bubohibonians*, which is the Nation of *Owls*.

All the neighbouring States join'd the *Cacklogallinians*, in endeavouring to prevent this vaſt Increaſe of Power to the
Magpyes,

Magpyes, since it must neceffarily deftroy
the Balance of Power; and as their
Prince was both powerful and ambitious,
they apprehended he would aim at an
univerfal Monarchy: But then they would
not allow the *Cacklogallinians* had any
more Right than their Neighbours, to
name a Succeffor; and if that Monarchy
were to fall to the Share of any powerful Prince, it might be as dangerous to
the common Good, as if yielded to the
Magpyes; they therefore would have it
divided.

The Peacock, who pretends to be the
High-Prieft of all Nations, and exacts on
that Account Tributes from them, and
calls himfelf the Difpofer of Kingdoms,
had his Tributes ftopp'd by the *Magpyes,*
about the fame time; and complaining of
this Injury, he invited *Bigoteafy* to declare
War againft *Gripeallyominte,* King of the
Magpyes, which, on account of former
Friendfhip, he abfolutely refufed. This
fo enraged the good High Prieft, that he
raifed a Rebellion againft him; he was
dethron'd, taken Prifoner by his Subjects,
and died in Confinement, and his Kingdom given by the Peacock, and the un-
animous Confent of the People, to the
greateft Prince that Hiftory ever mention'd, either for Wifdom or Bravery.

Thefe

These Wars lasted Sixty and Seven Years, and the *Cacklogallinians* bore the greatest Share of the Expence; which had so far indebted them, that every Brain was at Work to project Methods for raising Money to pay the Interest.

These Schemes, which were every Day presented to the Minister, grew so numerous, that, had he applied himself to nothing else but their Examination, it would have taken up a great Part of his Time: And, indeed, I must own, that my Friend, the first Minister, gave himself but very little Trouble in things of this Nature, for all his Schemes, and all his Thoughts center'd in himself; and when I have gone to carry him Intelligence in a Morning, and all the great Fowl that came to pay their Levee, have been answer'd, that he was busy in his Closet upon Affairs of Importance to the State, and saw no Company, I have found him (for there were Orders for admitting me) either writing Directions concerning his Ostriches, or his Country Sports, or his Buildings, or examining his private Accounts; and tho' I often thought but meanly of my own Species, yet I began to think, from the Conduct of this great Minister, that a Cock was a far more selfish, and more worthless Animal than Man;

Man; infomuch, that I have fo defpifed them ever fince, as to think them good for nothing but the Spit.

The Schemes which he put in Practice were all the Invention of others, tho' he affum'd the Credit of them; and I will be bold to fay, that, before my Time, amongft Numbers that were offer'd to him, he generally chofe the worft.

I was therefore order'd, after I had been two Years at Court, to take this Bufinefs upon me, with the Title of *Caftleairiano*, or Project-Examiner, and a Salary of Thirty Thoufand *Spafma's*. The firft Project offer'd me, was the laying a Tax on Cloath, and all manner of Stuffs. This I rejected, becaufe it being the chief Manufacture of the Country, it would, by raifing the Price abroad, be a Hindrance to the Commerce of the Nation, and give the *Cormorants* who made it, tho' nothing fo fine as the *Cacklogallinians*, an Opportunity, by under-felling them, to become the chief Merchants in this Branch of Trade. But it would be tedious to mention the many Offers, with my Reafons for accepting or rejecting them, which I once a Week gave a Lift of to the Minifter, who was often fo good as to approve my Judgment.

There

There were Projects for taxing Soot, Corn, Ribbons, for coining all the Plate of the Nobility, for prohibiting the wearing of Gold or Silver. Some were for the Government's taking all the Torchtrees (which gave a Light, and are used like our Candles) and dispose of them, by which great Sums might be raised. Some were for laying a Tax on all who kept Coaches; others upon all who wore Silver or Gold Spurs: But these touching only the Rich, the Minister would not listen to. The Tax which he approved of most, was on the Light of the Sun, according to the Hours it was enjoy'd; so that the poor Peasant, who rose with it, paid for Twelve Hours Day-light, and the Nobility and Gentry, who kept their Beds till Noon, paid only for Six.

Another Tax was laid upon those who drank only Spring Water. This fell altogether on the Poor, for the better Sort drank the Juice of a certain Tree imported from the *Bubohibonians.*

Whoever had not an Estate in Land of an Hundred *Spafina's* was also tax'd Ten *Spafina's* a Year, to be paid out of their Day Labour. He who deliver'd a Project of fetching Gold from the Moon, was caress'd prodigiously, and his way

of

of reafoning approved; tho' I gave it in with a ♓ as rejected by me, yet he was rewarded, and Preparation order'd for the Journey, in which I was command- ed to accompany him : For, he infinua- ted to the Minifter, that it was poffible the Inhabitants might be of my Species; nay, that I myfelf might have dropp'd out of that World, which was more reafonable than to believe the Story I told, of having pafs'd fo great a Sea; and that I very likely had form'd this Story out of a Tendernefs to my Coun- try left his Imperial Majefty fhould at- tempt its Conqueft.

He had fo poffefs'd the Minifter with this Notion, that my arguing againft it was to no purpofe. He told me one Day, That all the Philofophers allow'd, nay, maintain'd, that both Animals, Ve- getables, and Minerals, were generated, grew, and were nourifhed, by the Spi- rit of the World : A Quinteffence partak- ing of all the Four Elements, tho' it was no One, might be called Air, and was not; Fire, and was not Fire, &c. That this Spirit was affifted by the Influ- ence of the Planets, and tended to the higheft Perfection of Purity. That all Metals were generated by the faid Spirit, and differ'd from one another, but accord-

ing

ing to the Purity or Impurity of the *Matri-ces* which receiv'd it. That as the Planets Influence was neceſſary, that of the Moon muſt, as the neareſt to the Earth, be the moſt efficacious: That as it was viſible to the Eye, the Moon was more depurated than the Earth; was ſurrounded by a thinner Air, in which the Spirit of the World is more abundant, and was nearer to the other Planets, he naturally concluded, that it muſt abound in Gold Mines; and this Concluſion was ſtrengthened by the Mountains diſcernible in the Moon; and Mountains being moſtly rocky, afforded the pureſt *Matrice* for the Univerſal Spirit; ſo that it ſeem'd to him impoſſible, that any other Metal, leſs pure, could be generated in that World. That ſuch Metals, for their Uſe, were often preferable to Gold, and that in denying my Deſcent from thence, I was in Faƈt, doing an Injury to thoſe I wiſh'd to ſerve, ſince by Intercourſe with thoſe Inhabitants, both Worlds might find their Advantage.

I anſwered his Excellency, That I wiſhed he might ever find his and his Country's Good, in all his Undertakings, ſince I had ſo great Obligations to both; but that what I had told him of my ſelf was every way conſonant to Truth;
that

that I was fo far from being an Inha-
bitant of the Moon, that I did not believe it habitable; and if it were, I did
not think a Voyage thither practicable,
for Reafons I wou'd give the Projector,
whenever his Excellency would conde-
fcend to hear my Objections and his Anfwers: That if he, after that, would perfift in the Undertaking, fhe fhould find
me ready to facrifice that Life in the Attempt, which I held from his Goodnefs.
Well, return'd he, *to morrow I will have
him at my Houfe, don't fail being there at
Dinner; I will be denied to every one elfe,
and hope his Reafons will convince you; for
I have, I own, a greater Opinion of your
Veracity, in what relates to this Affair,
than of your Judgment.*

The next Day I waited on his Excellency, where I found the Projector mention'd. He began the Difcourfe, addref-
fing himfelf to me, after the ufual Ceremonies. " I am forry, *faid he*, to find
" what I propos'd meet with any Objecti-
" on from one whofe Penetration makes
" me fear fome Obftacle confiderable,
" which has efcaped my Scrutiny. How-
" ever, if I have the Mortification to
" have my Views baffled, yet fhall I reap
" the Advantage of being inftructed in
" what I am ignorant of. His Excellency
" has

" has commanded me to lay before you,
" what my Reasons are, for supposing
" the Moon an inhabited Globe. I shall
" therefore, with all possible Brevity,
" obey his Excellency's Commands.   I
" shall not name the ancient Sages, both
" of this and the neighbouring Nations,
" who have been of the same Opinion,
" because I have already cited them in
" my Memorial; but shall first offer you
" some Principles on which I have, be-
" side the Authorities mention'd, found-
" ed my own.

   " First, I esteem the Moon an opaque
" solid Body, as is our Earth, and conse-
" quently adapted for the Entertainment
" and Nourishment of its Inhabitants.
" Now, that it is a solid Body, is evi-
" dent by the Repercussion of the Light
" which it receives from the Sun.

   " Sir, *said I,* you are here begging the
" Question; for it is possible, that the
" Moon of itself is a luminous Body; and
" I am apt to believe it such for this
" Reason: Its Light is seen in more
" than one Place at a time, whereas a
" Body which gives a Light by Refle-
" ction only, that Light is perceivable
" in that Point alone, where the Angle
" of Reflection is equal to that of In-
" cidence.

He

He anfwer'd, " My Objection did not
" hold good in regard to a Body whofe
" Surface is rugged and uneven, as is
" that of the Moon. That it is an
" opaque and folid Body, is vifible by
" the Eclipfes of the Sun ; for a pellucid
" Body could not deprive us of the Light
" of that glorious Planet. That the
" Moon does eclipfe the Sun in the
" fame manner as our Earth eclipfes
" the Moon (as all know it does) makes
" me conclude thefe two Bodies of a
" Nature, fince the like Interpofition
" produces the like Effect. When I fay
" they are of a Nature, I mean opaque,
" which to prove, I argue thus : If this
" Planet be of it felf luminous, it muft
" appear much brighter when eclips'd
" in its *Perigée*, or neareft Diftance
" from the Earth, and its Light muft
" be lefs confequently when in its *Apogée*,
" or greateft Diftance from it ; for the
" nearer a luminous Body approaches
" the Eye, the ftronger Impreffion it
" makes upon the Sight. Befide, the
" Shadow of the Earth, had the Moon
" any innate and peculiar Light, cou'd
" not obfcure it, but, on the contrary,
" would render it more confpicuous, as
" is evident to Reafon.

I   " Now

" Now Experience fhews us, that the
" Moon appears with the greater Light
" eclips'd in its *Apogée*, or greater Di-
" ftance, and more obfcure when in its
" *Perigée*, or nearer Diftance, confequent-
" has no peculiar Light of its own. That
" a Shadow could obfcure its inherent
" Light, had it any, would be making a
" Body of a Shadow, which is fo far
" from being corporeal, that it is no-
" thing but a Deprivation of the Light
" of the Sun, by the Interpofition of
" the opaque Body of the Earth.

" I could give many more Reafons,
" but to avoid Prolixity, I refer you to
" my Memorial, knowing how precious
" Time is to your Excellency.

" I fhall now fpeak of the principal and
" conftituent Parts of this Planet; to wit,
" the Sea, the firm Land; its Extrin-
" ficks, as Meteors, Seafons, and Inha-
" bitants.

" I find, *faid his Excellency*, you have
" forgot what you promifed, the being
" concife; you have already couch'd
" what you are going to repeat, in Wri-
" ting. I am fatisfied that you have in
" your Memorial demonftrated, that the
" Moon is like ours, a World, and this
" Earth, like that, a Planet; I would
" willingly hear if *Probufomo* can bring
" any

" any Objection of Weight to the un-
" dertaking the Journey; for I look up-
" on the Diftance which you have com-
" puted to be about 179712 *Lapidians*
" (anfwerable to fo many *Englifh* Miles)
" to be none at all, fince we have *Cack-*
" *logallinians,* who, with Provifions for
" a Week, will fly 480 *Lapidians* a
" Day, and hold it for many Days. But
" this Swiftnefs, as you have made ap-
" pear, is not requifite, fince you judge,
" that in afcending fome five *Lapidians,*
" you will have reach'd the Atmofphere,
" and the reft will be attended by no
" other Fatigue, than that of prevent-
" ing too fwift a Defcent. Propofe what
" you have to object, *Probufomo,* for I
" will provide you able Bearers, who
" fhall carry you, and with the Strength
" of theirs, fupply your Defect of Wings.

I anfwer'd, That fince his Excellency
commanded, I would give in thofe Objections which occurr'd: The firft was the
extream Coldnefs of the Air; the fecond
its great Subtlety, which to me made
this Undertaking impracticable; befides,
the Diftance is fuch, by the learned
Gentleman's Calculation, that could the
Cacklogallinians, without refting, fly at
the rate of 1500 *Lapidians* a Day, the
Journey could not be ended in lefs than

I 2   fix

fix Moons: That there were no Inns in the Way, nor Places to reft in; and fuppofing we could carry Provifions for that Length of Time, I could not perceive how they could be always on Wing, and fubfift without Sleep.

His Excellency feem'd to think the Difficulties I rais'd merited Confideration, and after fome Paufe, asked the Projector, if he could folve them.

" As to the firft Objection, my Lord,
" *faid he*, I anfwer, that altho' the fe-
" cond Region may be endow'd with
" Coldnefs proper for the Production of
" Meteors, yet may it not be unfuppor-
" table; neither can we fuppofe, that
" the Air above, which if not deftin'd to
" the fame End, is of the fame Nature,
" but on the contrary, we may rather
" fuppofe it exempt from all Extremes,
" confequently our Paffage thro' this
" cold Region being performed, which
" we have Reafon to conclude but fhort,
" for this condens'd Air which encom-
" paffes the Earth on every Part, weighs
" about 108 *Liparia's* on a Square Inch
" (*Liparia* is near a Sixth of our Pound)
" and we may very eafily compute from
" thence, what Space of this Air we
" have to pafs, by computing what is
" neceffary to fupport this Globe of
" Earth,

" Earth, we fhall find the Ætherial al-
" together temperate.

" As to the fecond Objeétion, I an-
" fwer, that the Subtlety of the Air
" I look upon no Obftacle; for the Air
" near the Earth, efpecially in dry Pla-
" ces, where there are no impure Ex-
" halations, by the intenfe Heat of the
" Sun, it is perhaps as thin, and as much
" rarified, as the Ætherial. This I fup-
" pofe from the Tenuity of the Air on
" the top of the Mountain *Tenera*, where
" 'tis faid none can inhabit on that ac-
" count. But I have my felf flown to
" the top of this Mountain, and carry'd
" with me a wet Spunge, thro' which
" I drew my Breath for fome time ; but
" by Degrees I became habituated to
" this Tenuity, and refpired with Eafe;
" nay, after ftaying there fome few Days,
" I found the denfer Air, on my Defcent,
" caus'd a Difficulty in my Refpiration:
" From whence I concluded, that, by
" Degrees, the thinneft Air may become
" Natural; and as I felt no Hunger
" while on the Mountain, I may fup-
" pofe the fame Air we breathe may al-
" fo nourifh us. And this is no vain
" Imagination, for the *Aker* (that is,
" Viper) we fee live by the Spirit in-
" cluded in the Air, which is the Prin-
I 3   " ciple

" ciple of Life in all; but in cafe I am
" out in this Conjecture, we may carry
" Provifions with us.

" As to the refting our felves, I affirm
" from the Principles of found Philofo-
" phy, that when once out of the Reach
" of the magnetick Power of the Earth,
" we fhall no longer gravitate, for what
" we call Gravity, is no other than At-
" traction, confequently we may repofe
" our felves in the Air, if there is Oc-
" cafion, which I believe there will not;
" for as we fhall then have no Weight
" to exhauft the Spirits, there can be
" no Need of refrefhing them either
" with Meat or Sleep.

The Minifter rofe up, and faid he was
fully fatisfied with his Anfwers; the only Thing gave him Uneafinefs, was the
Length of Time I faid was requifite to
make this Journey.

" My Lord, *replied the Projector*, I
" can't agree that fuch a Time is ne-
" ceffary; for being above the Attracti-
" on of the Earth, which is the only la-
" borious Part of our Paffage, we may
" go with an inconceivable Swiftnefs,
" efpecially when we come within the
" Attraction of the Moon, which will
" certainly be encreas'd by the Weight
" of Provifions, which we fhall by way
of

" of Precaution carry with us, and which
" will be no Burthen after we have
" pals'd the Atmofphere; fo that what
" Weight a Thoufand *Cacklogallinians*
" can hardly raife to that Heighth,
" one might fupport, the reft of the
" Journey.

His Excellency perceiv'd by my Countenance I was not fatisfied, and therefore bid me take Heart, he wou'd fend
a Number of *Palanquins* with us, and
if we found the fecond Region impervi-
ous by Reafon of the Cold, we fhou'd
have the Liberty to return.

The only Talk now in Town was our
defigned Journey to the Moon, for which
a great many of the fwifteft Flyers were
inlifted with Promifes of great Reward.
Palanquins were made fharp at each
End, to cut the Air; the warmeft Mantles and Hoods were made for the Bearers, and the Projeftor's and my *Palanquin* were clofe, and lined with Down.

A Company was erefted, Shares fold
of the Teafure we were to bring back;
and happy was he who could firft fubfcribe. Thefe Subfcriptions were fold at
2000 *per Cent.* Advantage, and in lefs
than two Months, the Time fpent in
preparing for our Journey, I faw at leaft
Five Hundred Lacqueys, who had fallen

into

into the Trade of buying and felling thefe Subfcriptions in their gilt *Palanquins*, and Train of Servants after them. The *Squabbaws*, the *Vultuaquilians*, the Minifter, and fome of the Grand Council, fhared amongft them Fifty Millions of *Spafma's*, ready Money, for what they fold of this chimerical Treafure.

This open'd my Eyes, and I found I had been very fhort-fighted, in condemning the Minifter for giving Ear to a Projeƈt fo contrary to Reafon : But when I faw the noblett Families, and fuch whofe Ruine was neceffary to his own Support, fell their Eftates to buy Shares, I look'd upon him as the wifeft Minifter in the known World; and was loft in Wonder, when I confider'd the Depth of his Defigns.

I took the Liberty, once to mention my Aftonifhment to him, with all the Deference due to his exalted Quality, and with the Praifes he juftly deferved. He anfwer'd me, that he fear'd I faw farther than was either convenient, or fafe for me, if my Taciturnity did not equal my Penetration. This he fpoke in a Tone which gave me Apprehenfion of Danger; I threw my felf at his Feet, and begg'd he would rather kill me, than fufpeƈt my Zeal for his Service; that what
I had

I had taken the Liberty of faying to his Excellency, I had never the Imprudence to mention to any other; and that I hop'd the Experience he had of me would affure him of my Secrecy. *Learn*, faid he, *that Minifters work like Moles, and it's as dangerous to fhew them you can en- ter into their Views, as to attempt their Lives: I have a Confidence in you; but had any other held me the fame Difcourfe, I would have put it out of his Power to have repeated it to a third Perfon.*

The

The Author begins his Journey to the
M O O N.

ALL things neceffary being provided, and the *Palanquins* of Provifions being fent before to join us at the Mountain *Tenera*, I had an Audience of Leave of his Imperial Majefty and his *Squabbaws*; after which, I went to receive my laft Inftrudions from his Excellency. He gave me a Paper, with Orders not to open it, till I was arrived at the Mountain, which was about a Thoufand Miles from the City. He having wifh'd me a good Journey, faid he had given Orders to fix lufty *Cacklogallinians* to obey thofe I fhould give them; that he depended on my Fidelity and Prudence, and therefore, as I would find, had repofed a great Truft in me. I made him a fuitable Anfwer, and retired to my Apartment in the Palace, where I found the Projedor, who told me we were to fet out the next Morning before Day. I

asked

asked him, in Cafe we fucceeded in our
Journey, and found the Riches we coveted,
how we fhould bring away any Quantity?
" If, *faid he*, that happens, we fhall, in a
" fecond Journey, be provided with Vehi-
" cles, if there is Occafion ; but I propofe
" to extract fuch a Quantity of the Soul of
" Gold, which I can infufe into Lead at
" our Return, that we may be rich enough
" to pave the Streets with that valuable
" Metal ; for a Grain will, infufed into
" Lead, make an Ounce of pure Gold.
" Now, if a Penny-weight of the Soul
" will make Twenty four Ounces, or
" Two Pound of Gold, confider what
" immenfe Treafure we may bring back
" with us, fince the *Palanquineers* can
" fly with Five Hundred Weight in a
" *Palanquin.*

The next Morning we fet forward at
about Three o' Clock, and reach'd the
Mountain in about Forty fix Hours. We
firft refrefh'd our felves, and when I was
alone, I open'd my Inftructions, which
ran thus :

*A*S *Experience proves you are not to
be led by chimerical Notions, and
that your Capacity and Fidelity render you
fit to undertake the moft difficult and fecret
Affairs, his Imperial Majefty thought none*

fo fit as yourfelf to be entrufted in the Ma-
nagement of the prefent Scheme; which
that you may do to his Majefty's Satisfa-
ction, and your own Intereft and Credit, you
are to obferve the following Inftructions.

" YOU are to order *Volatilio*, the firft
" Propofer of the Journey now
" undertaken, to go to the Top of the
" Hill a Day before you, and from thence
" to acquaint you with the Nature of the
" Air; and if you find it practicable, you
" are to follow him. If you gain the
" Summit, and that the Air is too thin
" for Refpiration, you are to defcend
" again, difpatch an Exprefs to his Ma-
" jefty, and clap *Volatilio* in Irons, then
" difpatch away one of the fix Meffen-
" gers whom I ordered to attend you:
" They, *Volatilio*, and the whole Cara-
" van, are to obey you, till you have
" pafs'd the Atmofphere, when you and
" they are to follow the Directions of
" *Volatilio*, in what regards the Way
" only; but, in Cafe that you can refpire
" on the Top of the Mountain, order
" *Volatilio* to precede you a Day's Afcent,
" return the next, and immediately dif-
" patch a fecond Meffenger with the Ac-
" count he gives, and continue on the
" Mountain for farther Inftructions, be-
" fore

" fore you proceed, fhould it prove pra-
" &icable. I need not tell you the Pub-
" lick muft be amufed with Hopes of
" Succefs, tho' you have Reafon to de-
" fpair of it; nor need I even hint to you
" what Method you ought to take. I
" wifh you Health, and that your Con-
" duƐ may anfwer my ExpeƐations.

I aƐed purfuant to thefe InftruƐions,
and fent *Volatilio* forward, who reach'd
the Top of the Hill; but finding the Air
too thin to continue there, without the
Help of humeƐed Spunges, he therefore fent thofe back he carried with him
to the mid Space of the Mountain, and
an Exprefs to me, by which he informed
me what he had done; that he refolved
to continue there a natural Day, and then
join me where he had fent his Followers,
to which Place he defired I would afcend,
and defer the difpatching any Exprefs to
his Majefty, till he faw me again.

I afcended to the Mid-fpace, and found
a vaft Alteration in the Air, which even
here was very fenfibly rarified.

My ProjeƐor came to me at his appointed Time, and told me he did not
queftion the Succefs of our Enterprize,
fince he imagined the Air above the fecond Region rather denfer than that near
the Earth, and hoped the Cold was not
more

more intenfe than on the Mountain's Top ;
and that if this prov'd fo, we cou'd breathe
and fupport the Cold with little Difficulty. I anfwer'd, that it was natural to
conclude the Air next the Earth more
denfe than that above it, as the weighti-
eft always defcends the firft. " That
" Reafon, *faid he*, is not conclufive, for
" the Air immediately encompaffing the
" Earth, is more fenfible of its attractive
" Power, than that at a greater Diftance,
" as you may be fatisfied, in placing two
" Pieces of Iron, one near, and the other
" at a Diftance from the Loadftone ; the
" neareft Piece will be ftrongly attracted,
" while that at a greater Diftance is but
" weakly affected. Now fuppofing the
" Air only of an equal Denfity thro'out
" when we have left the Earth, (which,
" by the Reflection of Heat from the
" Mountains, rarifies the circumambient
" Air, and renders it more fubtle than
" that above it) we may refpire with-
" out Pain ; for in lefs than Six Hours
" I, by Degrees, withdrew my Spunge.
I difpatch'd an Exprefs with the Account I had received, and fet forward,
refolving to wait for further Inftructions
on the top of the Mountain. I was at
a good Diftance from the Summit, when
I was obliged, by the Thinnefs of the
Air,

Air, to have Recourfe to my wet Spunge,
and was Four and Twenty Hours before
I could intirely remove it. The *Cacklo-*
gallinians found lefs Difficulty than I in
their Refpiration, but more in fupporting
the rigid Cold, efpecially at Night, when
the Damps fell. We ftaid here Eight
Days, that the Subtlety of the Air might
become habitual to us.

On the feventh Day, the Meffenger
return'd with Credentials for *Volatilio*
and my felf, to the Potentate in whofe
Dominions we might happen, and Orders
to proceed on our Journey. This Meffenger told me, that on the Contents of my
Letter being publifh'd, the Town was
illuminated throughout, and fuch a Number of Coaches and *Palanquins* befpoke,
that he believed, at our Return, we
fhould find none out of them but the
Oftriches. Our Credentials ran thus.

" HIPPOMENE-CONNUFERENTO,
" Emperor and abfolute Monarch
" of the greateft Empire in the Terre-
" ftrial Globe, Difpofer of Kingdoms,
" Judge of Kings, Difpenfer of Juftice,
" Light of the World, Joy of the Sun,
" Darling of Mortals, Scourge of Ty-
" rants, and Refuge of the Diftrefs'd, to
" the Puiffant Monarch of that Kingdom
" in

" in the Moon, to which our Ambaſſa-
" dors ſhall arrive : Or, To the Mighty
" and Sole Lord of that beautiful Planet,
" ſends Greeting.

  " Dearly Beloved Brother, and moſt
" Mighty Prince, as it has been long
" doubted by our Anceſtors, as well as
" by thoſe of our Time, whether the
" Moon were, or were not inhabited;
" We, who have ever encouraged thoſe
" who ſeek the univerſal Good of Mor-
" tals, ſuppoſing it poſſible, if that Planet
" were poſſeſs'd by ſuch, that an Inter-
" courſe between the two Worlds might
" be of mutual Advantage to both, have
" ſent our two Ambaſſadors, *Volatilio* and
" *Probuſomo*, to attempt a Paſſage to your
" World, and to aſſure you, if they ſuc-
" ceed, of the great Deſire we have of
" entertaining with you a reciprocal
" Friendſhip, of giving all poſſible De-
" monſtrations of our Affection, and to
" invite you to ſend to our World your
" Ambaſſadors, with whom we may
" conſult our common Intereſt. So re-
" commending ours to your Protection,
" we heartily bid you farewell.

       Given at our Court, *&c.*

According to the Orders we receiv'd,
Volatilio took his Flight in an oblique
                Aſcent;

Afcent, without a *Palanquin;* but wrapt up as warm as poffible, accompanied by two Servants. He parted with great Alacrity, and we foon loft Sight of him. Some Half a Score, in Complaifance, took a Flight of three Hours to fee him part of his Way towards his Difcovery.

He went off at break of Day, to avoid thofe Vapours which the Heat of the Sun exhales, and which by Night would have rendered his Paffage, he thought, impoffible ; for he hoped, in a fmall Space to gain beyond the Heighth they rife to. At the Return of thofe who con-voy'd him, I fent away an Exprefs, to acquaint the Emperor with their Report, which was; That they found no fenfi-ble Alteration as to the Rarefaction of the Air, and that the Cold was rather lefs intenfe. This News at Court made every one run mad after Shares, which the Proprietors fold at what Rate they pleas'd.

The next Day in the Even, we faw *Volatilio* on his Return : His firft Salu-tation was, *Courage my Friend, I have pafs'd the Atmofphere, and, by Experience, have found my Conjecture true ; for be-ing out of the magnetick Power of the Earth, we refted in the Air, as on the folid Earth, and in an Air extreamly*

K *tempe-*

temperate, and less subtle than what we breathe.

I sent again this Account to Court, but the Courtiers having no more Shares to sell, gave out, that *Volatilio* did not return as he promis'd, and it was expected, that I despair'd of the Undertaking, and believ'd him loft.

This was such a Damp to the Town, that Shares fell to Half Value, and none of the Courtiers would buy, sell they cou'd not, having (I mean those let into the Secret) already dispos'd of all by their Agents, tho' they pretended the contrary.

The Express return'd, with private Orders for me to confirm this Report, which I was oblig'd to do, and stay eight Days longer, as the publick Instructions to us both commanded.

This was a great Mortification to *Volatilio*, and, I own, the Report he made had rais'd my Curiosity so much, that I was uneasy at this Delay; but we were to obey, and not to enquire into the Reasons of it.

The Messenger returning, told me, that my last Letter had fallen the Shares to five *per Cent.* under *Par*, nothing but Lamentations eccho'd thro' the Streets, and it was impossible to give an Idea of
the

the Change it had occafion'd. The Letter the Minifter fent me order'd me to write him Word, that *Volatilio* was returned, had found no Obftacles, and that I was preparing to depart. That the Court had bought up a vaft Number of Shares, and that he took Care of my Intereft in particular; that I need ftay for no farther Inftructions, but make the beft of my Way.

I gave Notice to the Caravan, that we would fet forward the next Morning, which we accordingly did, and as near as I could compute, we flew that Day, 180 Miles. What furpriz'd me was, that in lefs than an Hour and half's Afcent, *Volatilio*, who would not go in his *Palanquin*, folded his Wings, and came to me on Foot, and told me I might get out and ftretch my Limbs. My *Palanquineers* ftood ftill, and confirm'd what he faid; and more, that they had not for a Quarter of an Hour paft been fenfible of my Weight, which had leffen'd by Degrees, fo as not to be felt at all.

I left my *Palanquin*, and found what *Volatilio* had conjectur'd, and his Report verified; for I could with as much Eafe lift a *Palanquin* of Provifions, which did not on Earth weigh lefs than 500 Weight, as I could on our Globe raife a Feather. The Cold was very much abated, and I found my Spirits rais'd.

I would here have fent back half the *Palanquin*-Bearers, but *Volatilio* was of Opinion we fhould keep them a Day longer; for, perhaps, faid he, we may fend them all (except thofe which carry you) away; for if the Univerfal Spirit included in the Air fhould fuffice for our Nourifhment, we have no Bufinefs with Provifions.

I approv'd his Reafon, and we proceeded on, fure of falling firft into the Attraction of the Moon, it being the neareft Planet to us.

I fhall not detain the Reader with my Obfervations in this aerial Journey; *Gallileus*, who by his Writings gives me room to believe he had, before me, vifited this Planet, whatever were his Reafons for not owning it, having left nothing, which is not mentioned in his *Syftema Mundi*.

I obferv'd only, which I take Notice of for thofe who have not read him, that when the Moon has but a fmall Part of his Body enlighten'd, that the Earth, the other Moon, has a proportionable Part of its Hemifphere vifibly darken'd; I mean a Part in proportion to that of the Moon which is enlighten'd; and that

both

both thefe Moons, of which ours is much
the larger, mutually participate the fame
Light of the Sun, and the fame Obfcurity
of the Eclipfes, and mutually affift each
other : For when the Moon is in Conjun-
&ion with the Sun, and its *pars fuperior*
receives all the Light, then its inferior
Hemifphere is enlighten'd by the Earth's
refle&ting the Rays of the Sun, otherwife it would be intirely dark; and
when thofe two Planets are in Oppofition, then that Part of the Earth which
is deprived of the Rays of the Sun, is
enlighten'd by a full Moon.

The next Day *Volatilio* was for fending back the Provifions, but I judg'd it
proper not to go forward, but to ftay
the Space of a natural Day, in the fame
Situation, becaufe in that time, or in no
other in the Journey, we fhould require
Suftenance, and alfo becaufe their Return
would be eafier, than if we carried them
ftill forward.

This was agreed to, and none of us
finding any Appetite, Weaknefs, or Sink-
ing of our Spirits, difmifs'd all but thofe
who carried my *Palanquin,* and proceeded forward with an incredible Swiftnefs.

We were about a Month before we
came into the Attra&ion of the Moon,
in all which time none of us had the

leaft

leaſt Inclination to Sleep or Meat, or
found our ſelves any way fatigued, nor,
till we reach'd that Planet, did we cloſe
our Eyes ; the Attraction was ſo great,
that it was all the Bearers and *Volatilio*
could do to prevent our being daſh'd to
Pieces on a Mountain ; we deſcended
with that inconceivable Swiftneſs, that
I apprehended it impoſſible, in our Return, to avoid that Misfortune in the
World we left ; ſince the Attraction, if
its Virtue was augmented in proportion
to its Magnitude, muſt be much ſtronger.

This Thought made me very uneaſy for
thoſe who return'd. I ſpoke of it to *Volati-*
lio, who bid me apprehend nothing ; for,
ſaid he, the Magnetick Virtue of the
Load-ſtone is ſo far from being in Proportion to its Size, that the very large
ones have leſs attractive Power than
thoſe which are middling.

When I had recover'd from the Fright,
which the Rapidity of our Deſcent had
put me into, I view'd the circumjacent
Country with equal Wonder and Delight ; Nature ſeem'd here to have laviſh'd all her Favours ; on whatſoever
Side I turn'd my Eye, the moſt raviſh-
ing Proſpect was offer'd to my Sight.
The Mountain yielded a gradual Deſcent to moſt beautiful Meadows, enamell'd

mell'd with Cowflips, Rofes, Lilies, Jef-
famines, Carnations, and other fragrant
Flowers, unknown to the Inhabitants of
our Globe, which were as grateful to the
Smell, as entertaining to the Eye. The
chryftal Rivulets which fmoothly glided
thro' thefe inchanting Meads, feem'd fo
many Mirrors reflecting the various Beauties of thofe odoriferous Flowers which
adorn'd their Banks. The Mountain,
which was of confiderable Height, afforded us a great Variety in our Profpect,
and the Woods, Paftures, Meads, and
fmall Arms of the Sea, were intermin-
gled with that furprizing Beauty and
Order, that they feem'd rather difpos'd
by Art, than the Product of Nature;
the Earth it felf yielded a grateful and
enlivening Scent, and is fo pure, that it
does not fully the Hands. The Cedars,
which cloath'd the middle Part of the
Summit, were ftreight, tall, and fo large,
that feven Men would hardly fathom
the Bowl of one; round thefe twin'd
the grateful Honey-fuckle, and encir-
cling Vine, whofe purple Grapes appearing frequent from among the Leaves of
the wide extended Branches, gave an inconceivable Pleafure to the Beholder.
The Lily of the Valley, Violet, Tube-
rofe, Pink, Julip and Jonquil, cloath'd

K 4   their

their spacious Roots, and the verdant Soil afforded every salutiferous Herb and Plant, whose Vertues diffus'd thro' the ambient Air (without the invenom'd and the griping Fift of the *Cacklogallinian* Empiricks) Preservatives to the blessed Inhabitants of the Lunar World.

The Heavens here were ever serene; no Thunder-bearing Cloud obscur'd the Sky; the whispering Zephyrs wanton'd in the Leaves, and gently bore along the enchanting Musick of the feather'd Choir: The Sea here knew no Storms, nor threatning Wave, with Mountain swell, menaced the Ships, which safely plough'd the peaceful Bosom of the Deep. *Æolus* and all his boisterous Sons were banish'd from these happy Seats, and only kindly Breezes fann'd the fragrant Air. In short, all was ravishing, and Nature seem'd here to have given her last Perfection to her Works, and to rejoice in her finish'd Labours.

I found my Spirits so invigorated by the refreshing Odours, of this Paradice, so elated with the Serenity of the Heavens, and the Beauties which every where entertained and rejoiced my Sight, that in Extasy I broke out into this grateful Soliloquy. *O Source of Wisdom, Eternal Light of the Universe! what Adora-*

*Adorations can exprefs the grateful Acknow-
ledgments of thy diffufive Bounty! Who
can contemplate the Beauty of thy Works,
the Product of thy fingle* Fiat, *and not acknowledge thy Omnipotence, Omnifcience,
and extenfive Goodnefs! What Tongue can
refrain from finging thy Praife! What
Heart fo hard, but mufl be melted into
Love! Oh Eternal Creator, pity my Weaknefs, and fince I cannot fpeak a Gratitude
adequate to thy Mercies, accept the Ful-
nefs of my Heart, too redundant for Ex-
preffion.*

As I fpoke this, in the *Cacklogallinian*
Tongue, *Volatilio* came up to me, and
faid, " Alas! *Probufomo,* how can a
" finite Being return Praifes adequate to
" infinite Mercies! Let us return fuch as
" we are capable of; let the Probity of
" our Lives fpeak our Gratitude; by our
" Charity for each other endeavour to
" imitate the Divine Goodnefs, and
" fpeak our Love to him, by that we
" fhew to Mortals, the Work of his Di-
" vine Will, however they may differ
" from us, and from one another, in
" their Species. I am glad I am not
" deceived in my Opinion of you. I be-
" lieved from the Obfervation I made
" of your Life in a corrupt and diffo-
" lute Court, that you fear'd the firft

Being

" Being of Beings, and for that Reason
" chose you Companion of this hither-
" to unattempted Journey; for I expect-
" ed a Bleſſing would attend my Un-
" dertaking, while ſuch a one was em-
" bark'd with me: For to the Shame of
" our Nation, we own a Deity in
" Words, but deny him in our Actions:
" We acknowledge this Divine Being
" muſt be pure and juſt, and that our
" Lives (as he muſt abominate all Im-
" purity and Injuſtice) ought to be con-
" formable to his Attributes, wou'd we
" hope his Favour and Protection, not-
" withſtanding we act diametrically op-
" poſite, as the moſt ready Method to
" procure our Happineſs.

Finding our ſelves preſs'd by Hunger,
we deſcended the Mountain, at the Foot
of which we found a Plantation of Olive
Trees, and abundance of Pear, ſtanding
Apricock, Nectarn, Peach, Orange, and
Lemon Trees, interſpers'd. We ſatisfied our craving Appetites with the Fruit
we gather'd, and then getting into my
Palanquin, Volatilio leading the Way,
we went in Search of the Inhabitants.
Our Flight was little better than a Soar,
that we might with more Advantage
view the Country,

After

After a couple of Hours, he faw a Houfe, but of fo great a Height, and fo very large, I who was fhort-fighted in Comparifon of the *Cacklogallinians*, took it for a great Hill; I told him my Opinion, but he affured me I was miftaken. We therefore urg'd forward, and I alighted not far from this Palace, for I could term it no other, from the Largenefs and Beauty of its Structure. We had been difcover'd, as I had reafon to believe, fome Time, and a Number of People about Thirty, at our alighting, immediately encompafs'd me. The gigantick Make of thefe Inhabitants ftruck me with a panick Fear, which I alfo difcover'd in the Eyes of the *Cacklogallinians*.

They were of different Statures, from Thirty to an Hundred and Fifty Foot high, as near as I cou'd guefs; fome of them were near as thick as long, fome proportionable, and others fhap'd like a Pine, being no thicker than my felf, tho' tall of an Hundred Foot.

I refolv'd however to conceal, if poffible, the Terror I was in, and coming out of my *Palanquin*, I went to falute the Company, when I obferv'd they retired from me in proportion as I advanced, and like a Vapour, or an *Ignis fatuus*,

fatuus, the Air being mov'd by my Motion, drove thofe which were directly oppofite ftill before me.

I ftood ftill, they did the fame; if I was aftonifh'd at their Make, and at what other things I had obferv'd, I was more fo, when I faw one of the talleft, dwindle in the Twinkling of an Eye, to a Pigmy, fly into the Air without Wings, and carry off a Giant in each Hand by the Hair of the Head.

They were all differently drefs'd at their firft Appearance; fome like Generals in Armour, fome were in Ecclefiaftical, and fome in Gowns not unlike our Barrifters at Law. Some were drefs'd as fine as Imagination could make 'em, but with the quicknefs of Thought, thefe Dreffes were all changed, who was cover'd with Rags one Moment, the next was in Purple, with a Crown on his Head; the Beau in Rags; the Prieft affum'd the Air and Drefs of a Bully, and the General was turn'd into a demure Figure refembling a *Quaker.*

I was ftruck dumb with Amazement, and while I was confidering with my felf what this fhould mean, I obferv'd a Man riding up to us, mounted on a Lion; when he came to the others, I found him of the common Size with the Inhabitants

bitants of our Globe; he had on his
Head a Crown of Bays, which in an
Inftant chang'd to a Fool's Cap, and his
Lion to an Afs. He drew from his
Breaft a Rowl like a Quire of Written
Paper, which ufing as a Sword, he fet upon the others, and difpers'd them. Some
ran over the Sea, as on dry Ground;
others flew into the Air, and fome funk
into the Earth. Then alighting from
his Afs, he opened the Jaws of the Animal, went down his Throat, and they
both vanifh'd.

After I had recover'd my Fright, I
told *Volatilio*, that I fear'd this Planet
was inhabited by evil Spirits. He anfwered, that what we had feen, was
fufficient to induce us to believe fo.
We look'd for the Houfe, which we
faw rife into the Air, and vanifh in Flame
and Smoke, which ftrengthen'd our Opinion. However, we refolv'd to go forward, when one of the *Palanquineers*
faid he faw a Houfe on the left, and People of my Size and Species making towards us.

We determin'd therefore to wait their
Arrival, which was in lefs than a Quarter
of an Hour. They accofted me very
courteoufly, as I could gather from their
Geftures, tho' they feem'd furprized at
the

the Size of the *Cacklogallinians*. I was not lefs amaz'd at the Beauty of their Perfons, and the Becomingnefs of their Drefs, either of which I can give no juft Idea of. Let it fuffice, that I feem'd both in my own, and in the Eyes of the *Cacklogallinians*, fomething of the fame Species, but frightfully ugly.

Thefe People are neither a corporeal, nor an aerial Subftance, but (I know not how otherwife to exprefs my felf) between both. They fpoke to me in a Language I did not underftand, but the Tone of their Voices, and the Smoothnefs of their Syllables, were divinely harmonious. I bow'd my Body to the Ground three times, and offer'd my Credentials, which one of them took, but by the fhaking of his Head, I found underftood nothing of the Contents. *Volatilio* then addrefs'd himfelf to them, which made them look on one another, as People who hardly believed their Senfes. As I had addrefs'd thefe *Selenites* in the *Cacklogallinian* Language, I had a Mind to try, if fpeaking in thofe of the *Europeans* (for I underftood, befide my own, the *French* and *Spanifh*) I fhould have any better Succefs. I therefore fpoke in *Englifh*, and, to my great Joy, one of the Company anfwer'd me. He ask'd me, Whether

ther I came from the World? if fo, how
I durft undertake fo perilous a Journey?
I told him, I would fatisfy his Curiofity
in anfwering all his Queftions, but defired
he would give me fome Time; for I had
been fo terrified by Phantoms, fince my
Arrival, that I was hardly capable of Re-
collection.

While I was fpeaking, a Man on Horfe-
back ran full fpeed upon me with a drawn
Sabre, to cleave me down; but the *Sele-*
nite waving his Hand, he foon vanifh'd.
" You need, *faid he,* apprehend nothing
" from thefe Shades; they are the Souls
" of the Inhabitants of your World,
" which being loos'd from the Body by
" Sleep, refort here, and for the fhort
" Space allotted them, indulge the Paffi-
" ons which predominate, or undergo the
" Misfortunes they fear while they are
" in your Globe. Look ye, *faid he,* yon-
" der is a Wretch going to the Gallows,
" and his Soul feels the fame Agony, as
" if it was a real Sentence to be executed
" on him. Our Charity obliges us, when
" we fee thofe imaginary Ills, to drive
" the Soul back to its Body, which we
" do, by waving our Hand in the Air,
" and the agonizing Dreamer wakes.
" We do alfo retain them by a Virtue
" peculiar to the *Selenites,* and as they
　　　　　　　　　　　　　　" fome-

" fometimes adminifter a great deal of
" Diverfion, we do it for our Entertain-
" ment, which is the Reafon of thofe
" long Naps of two or three Days, nay, of
" as many Weeks, which caufe the Won-
" der of your World. The Souls of your
" impure Dreamers never reach beyond
" the middle Region. But we delay too
" long inviting you to our. Habitations,
" where you fhall have all poffible Care
" taken of you. But by what Art have
" you taught Fowls articulate Sounds?
" and where could you poffibly find
" them of that Size?

I told him they were rational Beings,
but that the Story was now too long
to tell him; he prefented me to the
reft of the Company; and, at my Re-
queft, the *Cacklogallinians* were human-
ly treated, whom otherwife they had
look'd upon as overgrown dunghill Fowls.
Volatilio did not appear much furpriz'd
at this, who had once efteem'd me a
Prodigy of Nature. As we walk'd to
the Houfe, one of the *Selenites* addrefs'd
me in the *Spanifh* Language, with the
known Affiability and Gravity of that
Nation.

" Sir, *faid he,* I cannot confider you
" as other, than the braveft and wifeft
" of all Mortals, who could find the
" Way

" Way to reach our World, and had
" the Courage to undertake the Jour-
" ney; for it's certain, none cloath'd in
" Flefh ever (before you) made fo bold
" an Attempt, or at leaft fucceeded in
" it: Tho' I have read the Chimera's
" of *Dominick Gonzales.* While you
" ftay amongft us, you may depend up-
" on our treating you with all the Re-
" fpect anfwerable to fo great Merit,
" and in every thing endeavour, as far
" as the Power we have will permit,
" that the Defign of your Journey may
" not be fruftrated, which I am apt to
" believe, is no other than to extend your
" Knowledge.

I return'd him many Thanks for his
Humanity, but told him I durft not attribute to my felf the Character he gave
me; that I was a Lover of Truth, and
would not, on any Account, difguife the
real Motive which fent me on an Undertaking I look'd upon impoffible to go
thro' with, and which I very unwilling-
ly embark'd in: But fince, contrary to
my Expectations, Providence has guided
me to this Terreftrial Paradice, I fhould
efteem my felf extreamly happy, if I
might be permitted to ask fuch Queftions as my Curiofity might prompt me
to.

L   He

He anfwer'd, that nothing I defir'd to know fhould be kept from me. We foon reach'd the Houfe, which was regular, neat, and convenient. We all fat down in an inner Hall, and he who fpoke *Englifh*, defired I would give an Account, both of the Motives, the Manner, and Accidents of my Journey, which I did as fuccinctly as poffible, interpreting the Credentials, when I gave them.

He was aftonifh'd at the Account I gave him of the *Cacklogallinians*, and faid, if my Account was not back'd with ocular Demonftration, he fhould take their Story for the Ravings of a diftemper'd Brain.

" I find, *faid he*, you begin to
" be drowzy; I would therefore have
" you and your rational Fowls (as you
" call them) repofe your felves, while
" I in the *Vernacular* Language, repeat
" to my Companions the Wonders I
" have heard from you.

We were indeed very fleepy, and I was heartily glad of the Propofal, as were alfo the *Cacklogallinians*, when I mention'd it to them. They, as well as my felf, were provided each of them with a Bed, in very handfome and commodious Rooms. Thefe Beds were fo very foft, that I feem'd to lye on a
Couch

Couch of Air. When we awak'd, the *Selenites* came into my Chamber, and told me it was time to take fome Nourifhment; that they had provided Corn for my Companions, and defir'd I would fit down to Supper with them, it being their ufual time. " Why, Sir, *faid I,* " to our *Englifh* Interpreter, do you fup " by Day-light? You miftake, *faid he,* " it is now Night; your World to the " Inhabitants of this Hemifphere (which " is always turn'd to it, this Planet " moving in an Epicycle) reflects fo " ftrong the Sun's Light, that your Er- " ror is excufable. What then, *faid I,* " do thofe of the other Hemifphere " for Light? They have it, *faid he,* from " the Planets.

" I went with them into a Parlour, " where, after a Hymn was fung, we " fat down to a Table cover'd with Sal- " lets and all forts of Fruits.

" You muft, *faid the Selenite,* content " your felf with what we can offer you, " which is nothing but the fpontaneous " Products of the Earth: We cannot in- " vite you to other, fince the eating " any thing that has had Life, is look'd " upon with Abhorrence, and never " known in this World: But I am fa- " tisfied you will eafily accommodate

L 2   " your

" your felf to our Diet, fince the **Tafte**
" of our Fruits is much more exquifite
" than yours, fince they fully fatisfy,
" and never cloy :" Which I found true
by Experience, and I was fo far from
hankering after Flefh, that even the
Thoughts of it were fhocking and naufeous to me.

We drank the moft delicious Wine,
which they prefs'd from the Grape into
their Cups, and which was no way in-
toxicating. After Supper, the *Selenite*
addrefs'd himfelf to me in Words to this
Effect.

" I have acquainted my Friends here
" prefent, who are come to pafs fome
" Days with me, both with the Contents
" of the *Cacklogallinian* Emperor's Letter,
" and the Reafons which mov'd this
" Prince to defire an Intercourfe between
" the two Worlds, and we will all of us
" wait on you to our Prince's Court, tho'
" ftrictly fpeaking, we neither have, nor
" need a Governour; and we pay the
" diftant Refpect due to your Princes to
" the eldeft among us, as he is the near-
" eft to eternal Happinefs. But that I
" may give you fome Idea, both of this
" World, and its Inhabitants, you muft
" learn, that Men in yours are endued
" with a Soul and an Underftanding;
" the

" the Soul is a material Subftance, and
" cloathes the Underftanding, as the Bo-
" dy does the Soul; at the Separation of
" thefe two, the Body is again refolved
" into Earth, and the Soul of the Vir-
" tuous is placed in this Planet, till the
" Underftanding being freed from it by a
" Separation we may call Death, tho' not
" attended with Fear or Agony, it is re-
" folved into our Earth, and its Principle
" of Life, the Underftanding, returns to
" the Great Creator; for till we have
" here purg'd off what of Humanity re-
" mains attach'd to the Soul, we can ne-
" ver hope to appear before the pure
" Eyes of the Deity.

 " We are here, *faid he,* in a State of
" Eafe and Happinefs, tho' no way com-
" parable to that we expect at our Diffo-
" lution, which we as earneftly long for,
" as you Mortals carefully avoid it. We
" forget nothing that pafs'd while we were
" cloath'd in Flefh, and Inhabitants of
" your Globe, and have no other Un-
" eafinefs, than what the Reflection of
" our Ingratitude to the Eternal Good-
" nefs, while in Life, creates in us,
" which the Eternal leffens in proportion
" to our Repentance, which is here very
" fincere. This will ceafe your Wonder
" at hearing the Sublunary Languages.
   L 3   " We

" We have here no Paffions to grati-
" fy, no Wants to fupply, the Roots of
" Vice, which under no Denominati-
" on is known among us; confequent-
" ly no Laws, nor Governours to exe-
" cute them, are here neceffary.

" Had the *Cacklogallinian* Prince
" known thus much, he would have
" been fenfible how vain were his Ex-
" pectations of getting from us the Gold
" he thirfts after: For were we to meet
" with the pureft Veins of that Metal, by
" removing only one Turf, not a *Selenite*
" would think it worth his while.

" This is a Place of Peace and Tran-
" quillity, and this World is exactly ad-
" apted to the Temper of its Inhabitants;
" Nature here is in an Eternal Calm;
" we enjoy an everlafting Spring; the
" Soil yields nothing noxious, and we can
" never want the Neceffaries of Life,
" fince every Herb affords a falubrious
" Repaft to the *Selenites.*

" We pafs our Days without Labour,
" without other Anxiety, than what I
" mention'd, and the longing Defire we
" have for our Diffolution, makes every
" coming Day encreafe our Happinefs.

" We have not here, as in your World,
" Diftinction of Sexes; for know, all
" Souls are mafculine (if I may be allow'd
" that

" that Term, after what I've faid) how-
" ever diftinguifh'd in the Body; and
" tho' of late Years the Number of thofe
" which change your World for this
" (efpecially of the *Europ̈ean* Quarter) is
" very fmall ; yet we do not apprehend
" our World will be left unpeopled.

" You fay, *replied I,* that none but
" the virtuous Soul reaches thefe blifs-
" ful Seats; what then becomes of the
" Vicious ? and how comes it, that the
" Soul, when loofed by Sleep, I fuppofe
" without Diftinction, retires hither ?

" The Decrees, *faid he,* of the Almigh-
" ty are infcrutable, and you ask me
" Queftions are not in my Power to re-
" folve you.

" Have not, *faid I,* the *Cacklogallini-*
" *ans* Souls, think you, fince they're en-
" dued with Reafon? If they have, *faid*
" *he,* they never are fent hither.

" I repeated this Difcourfe to the
" *Cacklogallinians,* which made *Volatilio*
" extreamly melancholly. *Happy Men !*
faid he, *to whofe Species the divine Good-*
nefs has been fo indulgent ! Miferable Cacklogallinians *! if deftin'd, after bearing the*
Ills of Life, to Annihilation. Let us,
Probúfomo, *never think of returning, but*
beg we may be allow'd to end our Days
with thefe Favourites of Heaven.

I in-

I interpreted this to the *Selenite*, who shook his Head, and said it was, he believ'd, impossible. That he did not doubt but Providence would reward the Virtuous of his Species; that his Mercy and Justice were without Bound, which ought to keep him from desponding.

The next Day a great Number of *Selenites* came to see me, and entertain'd me with abundance of Candour. I seeing no Difference in Dress, nor any Deference paid to any, as distinguish'd by a superior Rank, I took Liberty to ask my *English Selenite*, if all the Inhabitants were upon a Level, and if they had no Servants nor Artificers?

" We have, *said he*, no Distinctions
" among us; who in your World begg'd
" Alms, with us, has the same Respect
" as he who govern'd a Province: Tho',
" to say Truth, we have but few of
" your sublunary Quality among us.
" We have no Occasion for Servants;
" we are all Artificers, and none where
" Help is necessary, but offers his with
" Alacrity. For Example, would I build
" a House, every one here, and as many
" more as were wanting, would take a
" Pleasure to assist me. He told me, that
" the next Day they intended to present
" me to *Abrahijo*, the oldest *Selenite*.

Accord-

'Accordingly, we fet out at Sun-rifing, and entered a Bark about a League from the Houfe, and having pafs'd about four Leagues on a River which ran thro' a Valley beautiful beyond Defcription, we went afhore within an Hundred Yards of *Abrahijo's* Place of Abode.

When we came in, the venerable old Man, whofe compos'd and chearful Countenance fpoke the Heaven of his Mind, rofe from his Chair, and came to meet us; he was of a great Age, but free from the Infirmities which attend it in our World.

The *Englifh Selenite* prefented me to him with few Words, and he received me with Tendernefs.

After he was inform'd of my Story, he fpoke to me by our Interpreter, to this Effect.

" My Son, I hope you will reap a fo-
" lid Advantage from the perilous Jour-
" ney you have made, tho' your Expecta-
" tion of finding Riches among us is
" fruftrated. All that I have to give you,
" is my Advice to return to your World,
" place your Happinefs in nothing tran-
" fitory; nor imagine that any Riches,
" but thofe which are Eternal, which
" neither *Thief can carry away, nor Ruft*
" *corrupt,* are worthy of your Purfuit.
" Keep

" Keep continually in your Eye the Joys
" prepared for thofe who employ the
" Talents they are entrufted with, as they
" ought: Refleᵭ upon the little Content
" your World can afford you: Confider
" how fhort is Life, and that you have
" but little Time to fpare for Trifles,
" when the grand Bufinefs, the fecuring
" your eternal Reft, ought to employ
" your Mind. You are there in a State
" of Probation, and you muft there chufe
" whether you will be happy or mifera-
" ble; you will not be put to a fecond
" Trial; you fign at once your own Sen-
" tence, and it will ftand irrevocable,
" either for or againft you. Weigh well
" the Difference between a momentary
" and imperfeᵭ, and an eternal and fo-
" lid Happinefs, to which the Divine
" Goodnefs invites you; nay, by that
" Calmnefs, that Peace of Mind, which
" attends a virtuous Life, bribes you to
" make Choice of, if you defire to be
" among us, be your own Friend, and
" you will be fure to have thofe Defires
" gratify'd. But you muft now return,
" fince it was never known, that grofs
" Flefh and Blood ever before breath'd
" this Air, and that your Stay may be
" fatal to you, and difturb the Tranquil-
" lity of the *Selenites.* This I prophefy,
" and

" and my Compaffion obliges me to warn
" you of it.

I made him a profound Reverence,
thank'd him for his charitable Admonition, and told him I hoped nothing fhould
win me from the Performance of a Duty
which carry'd with it fuch ineffable Rewards. That if no greater were promis'd,
than thofe indulg'd to the *Selenites*, I
would refufe no Mifery attending the
moft abje& Life, to be enroll'd in the
Number of the Inhabitants of that happy Region.

" I wifh, *replied he,* the falfe Glare of
" the World does not hinder the Execu-
" tion of thefe juft Refolutions : But that
" I may give you what Affiftance is in our
" Power, in hopes of having you among
" us, we will fhew the World unmask'd;
" that is, we will detain fome time the
" Souls of Sleepers, that you may fee
" what Man is, how falfe, how vain, in
" all he a&s or wifhes. Know, that the
" Soul loos'd by Sleep, has the Power to
" call about it all the Images which it
" would employ, can raife imaginary
" Stru&ures, form Seas, Lands, Fowls,
" Beafts, or whatever the rational Fa-
" culty is intent upon. You fhall now
" take fome Refrefhment, and after that
" we will both divert and inftru& you.

The

The Table was fpread by himfelf and
the other *Selenites*, the *Cacklogallinians*
and my felf invited, and I obferv'd it differ'd nothing, either in Quality or Quantity, from that of my *Englifh* Hoft.

After a folemn Adoration of the ineffable Creator, each took his Place; having finifh'd our Meal, at which a ftrict
Silence was obferved, *Abrahijo* took me
by the Hand, and led me into a neighbouring Field, the Beauty of which far
excell'd that of the moft labour'd and ar-
tificial Garden among us.

" Here, *faid he*, obferve yon Shade :
" I fhall not detain it, that you may fee
" the Care and Uneafinefs attending
" Riches.

The Shade reprefented an old wither'd
ftarv'd Carcafs, brooding over Chefts of
Money. Immediately appear'd three ill-
look'd Fellows; Want, Defpair, and Murder, were lively-pictur'd in their Faces;
they were taking out the Iron Bars of the
old Man's Window, when all vanifh'd of
a fudden. I ask'd the Meaning of it; he
told me, the Terror the Dream of Thieves
put him into, had awaken'd him; and
the Minute he flept again, I fhould fee
again his Shade. Hardly had *Abrahijo*
done fpeaking, when I again faw the old
Man, with a young well-drefs'd Spark
ftanding

ſtanding by him, who paid him great Reſpect. I heard him ſay very diſtinct-ly, " Sir, do you think I am made of
" Money, or can you imagine the Trea-
" ſure of a Nation will ſupply your Ex-
" travagance? The Value I have for you
" on Account of your Father, who was
" my good Friend, has made me tire all
" my Acquaintance, by borrowing of
" them to furniſh your Pockets: How-
" ever, I'll try, if I cannot borrow One
" Thouſand more for you, tho' I wiſh
" your Eſtate will bear it, and that I
" don't out of my Love to you, raſhly
" bring myſelf into Trouble. You know
" I am engaged for all; and if the Mort-
" gage you have given ſhould not be va-
" lid, I am an undone Man. I can't, I
" proteſt, raiſe this Money under Fifteen
" *per Cent*, and it's cheap, very cheap,
" conſidering how ſcarce a Commodity
" it is grown. It's a Pity ſo generous a
" young Gentleman ſhould be ſtraiten'd.
" I don't queſtion a Pair of Gloves for
" the Trouble I have. I know you too
" well to infiſt on't: I am old and crazy,
" Coach-hire is very dear, I can't walk,
" God help me, and my Circumſtances
" won't afford a Coach. A Couple of
" Guineas is a Trifle with you: I'll get
" you the Thouſand Pound, if I can, at
Fifteen

" Fifteen *per Cent.* but if my Friend fhould
" infift on Twenty (for Money is very
" hard to be got with the beft Securi-
" ty) muft I refufe it? Yes; I can't fuf-
" fer you to pay fuch an exorbitant Pre-
" mium; it is too much, too much in
" Confcience; I can't advife you to it.

The young Gentleman anfwer'd, he
was fenfible of his Friendfhip, and left
all to him. " Well, well, *faid the Mifer,*
" come again two Hours hence, I'll fee
" what's to be done.

He went away, t'other barr'd the Door
after him, and falls to rummaging his
Bags, and telling out the Sum to be lent
to the young Gentleman: When, on a
fudden, his Doors flew open, and a Couple of Rogues bound him in his Bed, and
went off laden with Baggs. Soon after,
a meagre Servant comes in, and unbinds
him; he tears his Hair, raves, ftamps,
and has all the Geftures of a Madman;
he fends the Servant out, takes a Halter,
throws it over a Beam, and going to
hang himfelf, vanifhes.

Soon after, he appear'd again with
Officers, who hurry the young Gentleman to Goal. He follows him, gets his
Eftate made over to him, and then fets
his Prifoner at Liberty: The Scene of
the Goal vanifhes, and he's in a noble

Man-

Manfion-Seat with the young Gentleman
in Rags, who gives him Poffeffion, and
receives a Trifle from him for that Confideration. He turns away all the Servants, and in a Palace he is alone roaft-
ing an Egg over a Handful of Fire for his
Dinner. His Son comes in, as he is by
himfelf, goes to murder him, and he vanifhes again. He returns to our Sight,
digging in his Garden, and hiding Money, for Soldiers appear in the neighbouring Village: He has fcarce buried it, when
they rifle his Houfe; this makes us lofe
him again for a little Space. His Coachman comes to him, tells him his Son is
kill'd; he anfwers, " No matter, he
" was a great Expence, I fhall fave at
" leaft Forty Pounds a Year by his Death,
" it's a good Legacy, *Tom.*

He tells him a Lord offer'd him Five
Hundred Pounds to carry off his young
Lady, but that he refufed it, and thought
himfelf obliged to acquaint him with his
Lordfhip's Defign. " You are a Fool,
replies the old Man; take the Money, I'll
" confent, we'll fnack it — Quit of ano-
" ther. My Lord fhan't have a Groat
" with her. What a Charge are Chil-
" dren! This Lord is the beft Friend. I
" have, to take her off my Hands. To
" be fure bring the Money, carry her to
my

" my Lord, and bring the Money; go
" take Time by the Fore-lock, he may
" recant, then fo much Money's loft. Go,
" run to my Lord, tell him you'll do it.
Here he thruft the Fellow out, and appear'd with a fmiling Countenance. A
Man comes in, and tells him the Exchequer is fhut up, Stocks are fallen, a War
declar'd, and a new Tax laid on Land;
he beats his Breaft, groans aloud, and
vanifhes.

" By this Wretch, *faid Abrahijo,* you
" fee the Care and Anxiety wait on the
" Miferable. The Love of Gold in him
" has extinguifh'd Nature; nay, it pre-
" dominates over Self-love; for he haftens
" his End, by not allowing his Body ei-
" ther Reft, or fufficient Nourifhment,
" only that he may encreafe the Num-
" ber of his Coffers.

Another Shade appear'd with a great
Crowd of People, huzzaing, a *Venditor,*
a *Venditor*; he goes before them, fteps
into every Shop, enquires after the Health
of each Family, kiffes the Wives, and
out of his thrufts Gold into their Mouths.
Here he bows to a Tinker, there embraces a Cobler, fhakes a Scavinger by the
Hand, ftands bare-headed, and compliments an Ale-Wife, invites a Score of
Shoemakers, Taylors, Pedlars, Weavers,
and

and Hoftlers, to do him the Honour of their Company to Dinner.

The Scene changes ; he's at Court, the Minifters repay him his fervile Cringes by theirs ; one comes up to him, and fays, he hopes, when the Bill comes into the Houfe, he will favour him with his Vote for its paffing : He anfwers, he fhall difcharge the Truft repofed in him, like a Man of Honour, in forwarding what is for the Good of his Country, and oppofing the contrary, tho' the Confequence were his own Ruin : That he begg'd his Lordfhip's Pardon, if he diffented from him in Opinion, and did not think what he required warrantable in a Man of Honour.

" You are not well inform'd, *replied*
" *the Nobleman,* but we'll talk of that
" another Day, when I hope I fhall con-
" vince you, that you did not well un-
" derftand me; my prefent Bufinefs is to
" wifh you Joy, *Courvite*'s Reigment is
" vacant, and tho' you have never ferv'd,
" your perfonal Bravery and good Con-
" duct in the Senate have fpoke fo much
" in your behalf, that you will to mor-
" row have the Commiffion fent you.
" My Lord, *replied the Patriot,* this is an
" unexpected Favour, and I am fatisfied I
" owe it to your Lordfhip's Goodnefs.

M　" I hope

" I hope an Opportunity to fpeak my
" Gratitude, will prefent it felf; in the
" mean while count upon me, in what-
" ever I can ferve your Intereft." At
thefe Words, with a vifible Joy in his
Looks, he vanifh'd.

Three dirty Mechanicks appeared in a
Shoemaker's Shop, who was a Dreamer.
He was declaiming to his Companions
over a Pot of Beer, after the following
Manner. " Look ye, Neighbours, there's
" an old Proverb fays, *It is not the Hood*
" *which makes the Monk*; the being born
" a Gentleman does not make a Man of
" Senfe; and the being bred a Tradef-
" man, does not deprive us of it; for
" how many great Men have leap'd from
" the Shop-board, fprung up from the
" Stall, and have, by patching and heel-
" piecing Religion and the State, made
" their Names famous to After-Ages? I
" can name many, but I fhall mention
" only *John* of *Leyden*. Now, I fee no
" Reafon, why Meannefs of Birth fhould
" be an Obftacle to Merit, and I am
" refolved, as I find a great many Things
" which ought to be redrefs'd both in
" Church and State, if you my Friends
" will ftand by me, to aim at the fet-
" ting both upright : For you muft own,
" they are bafely trod awry. Trade is
dead,

" dead, Money is fcarce, the Parfons are
" proud, rich and lazy; War is neceffa-
" ry for the Circulation of Money; and
" an honeft Man may ftarve in thefe
" Times of Peace and Beggary.

" There are a great many Myfteries
" in Religion, which, as we don't know
" what to make of them, are altoge-
" ther unneceffary, and ought to be
" laid afide, as well as a great many
" Ceremonies, which ought to be lopp'd
" off for being chargeable.

The reft gave their affenting Nod,
and feem'd to wonder at, and applaud
his Eloquency. In a Moment, I faw him
preaching to a Mobb againft the Luxury of the Age, and telling them it fhew'd
a Meannefs of Spirit to want Neceffaries,
while the Gentry, by force of long Ufur-
pations on their Rights, rioted in all
manner of Excefs. That Providence
brought none into the World that he
might ftarve; but that all on Earth
had a Right to what was neceffary to
their Support, which they ought to fieze,
fince the Rich refus'd to fhare with them.
From a Preacher I faw him a Captain
of a Rabble, plundering the Houfes of
the Nobility, was terrible to all; and tho'
he declared for levelling, would be ferv'd
with the Pomp and Delicacy of a Prince;

marries

marries his Daughters to Lords, hoards
an immense Treasure, and wakes from
his golden Dream.

Another Shade I saw suborning Wit-
nesses, giving them Instructions what to
swear, packing Juries, banishing, hang-
ing and beheading all his Enemies, send-
ing immense Sums to foreign Courts, to
support his Power at Home, bribing Se-
nates, and carrying all before him without Controul, when he vanish'd. My
English Friend told me, that Soul belong'd
to the Body of a Money-Scrivener, who
almost crack'd his Brain with Politicks,
and thought of nothing less than being
a prime Minister. I knew him while I
was in the World; his whole Discourse
always ran on Liberty, Trade, Free Ele-
ctions, &c. and constantly inveigh'd against
all corrupt and self-interested Practices.
I saw Persons descended from the ancient
Nobility fawning on Valets who were arrived to great Preferment for Pimping;
I beheld others contriving Schemes, to
bring their Wives and Daughters into
the Company of Persons in Power, and
aiming to gain Preferment for themselves,
at the Expence of the Vertue of their
Families; nor was there a Vice, a Folly
or a Baseness, practised in this World
below, tho' ever so secret, which I did
not

not fee there reprefented, the Particu-
lars of which being too long for this Place,
I muft beg Leave to refer them to the
Second Volume of my Voyages.

In the mean time I was allow'd a Week
to fatisfy my Curiofity, and make my
Obfervations on all the ftrange things
which were there to be feen, which I
may juftly reckon the moft agreeable Part
of my whole Life; and alfo a further
Time to refrefh my felf: Which being
done, we prepared for our Journey, being provided with all things neceffary for
that Purpofe.

As I found in my felf that longing Defire (which is natural to all Men, who
have been long abfent from Home) of
returning to fee my own Country; and
being befides unwilling to go back to
Cacklogallinia, the Actions and Defigns of
the firft Minifter, to which I was privy,
having made fuch Impreffions upon me,
that I was prejudic'd againft their whole
Nation; nor was that Prejudice remov'd,
by being acquainted with their Laws,
Cuftoms and Manners, fome of which
appear'd to me unreafonable, and others
barbarous.

I fay, upon the aforefaid Confiderations, I apply'd my felf to fome of the
Selenites, whofe Courtefy I had already
expe-

experienced, asking them, whether they could direct me to find out some Part of the Terrestrial World, known and frequented to by *Europeans*: They were so good to give me full and plain Instructions what Course to steer thro' the Air for that Purpose, which I was very well able to follow, having a Pocket Compass about me, which I brought from *England*, it having long been my Custom never to stir any where without one.

It being necessary to bring *Volatilio* into the Design, I went to him and told him, that as we were so unfortunate not to succeed in finding out the Country of Gold, it would be adviseable to return home some other Way, in hopes of better Success in going back; otherwise we might, in all Probability, meet with a disagreeable Welcome from the Emperor and the whole Court. *Volatilio* hearken'd to these Reasons, and besides having the true Spirit of a Projector in him, which is, not to be discouraged at Disappointments, he consented to my Proposal.

Accordingly we set out, and after some Days travelling, we meeting with little or nothing in our Journey differing from our former, we lighted safely upon the *Blue Mountain* in *Jamaica*. Here I was within

within my own Knowledge; for having formerly made feveral Voyages to *Jamaica,* I was no Stranger to the Place.

Now therefore I thought it time to acquaint the *Cacklogallinians* with the innocent Fraud I had put upon them; they feem'd frighted and furprized, as not knowing how to get home to their own Country: For *Volatilio* apear'd to be quite out of his Element. However, I directed them which Way to fteer, which was directly Southward; and having refted for fome time, they took their Leave of me, and *Volatilio,* with his *Palanquineers,* began their Flight, as I had directed them, and I never faw them more.

As for my Part, I made the beft of my Way to *Kingfton,* where coming acquainted with one Captain *Madden,* Commander of the *London Frigate,* he was fo kind, upon hearing my Story, to offer to give me my Paffage *gratis,* with whom having embark'd at *Port Royal,* I reach'd my native Country, after a Paffage of Nine Weeks.

F I N I S.